Winter
in the Air

SYLVIA TOWNSEND WARNER

Winter in the Air

& Other Stories

faber

First published in 1938

This paperback edition first published in 2022
by Faber & Faber Limited
Bloomsbury House, 74–77 Great Russell Street
London WC1B 3DA

First published in the USA in 2023

Typeset by Typo•glyphix, Burton-on-Trent DE14 3HE
Printed and bound in the UK by CPI Group Ltd, Croydon CR0 4YY

The following stories appeared originally in the *New Yorker*: 'Hee-Haw!',
'The Children's Grandmother', 'Evan', 'Shadwell', 'A Kitchen Knife',
'Uncle Blair', 'Emil', 'A Second Visit', 'Idenborough', 'A Passing Weakness'
(under the title 'There but for the Grace of God …'), 'A Priestess of Delphi'
(under the title 'Wherefore, Unlaurell'd Boy'), 'Winter in the Air'
(under the title 'Farewell, My Love') and 'The Reredos'
(under the title 'Matthew, Mark, Luke and John').

*This is a collection of stories published from 1938 onwards.
The language in these pages is a reflection of the historical period
in which the book was originally written.*

A CIP record for this book
is available from the British Library

ISBN 978–0–571–37546–2

MIX
Paper from
responsible sources
FSC® C171272

2 4 6 8 10 9 7 5 3 1

Contents

Winter in the Air

The furniture, assembled once more under the high ceiling of a London room, seemed to be wearing a look of quiet satisfaction, as though, slightly shrugging their polished shoulders, the desk had remarked to the bookcase, the Regency armchair to the Chippendale mirror, 'Well, here we are again.' And then, after a creak or two, silence had fallen on the dustless room.

It was morbidly dustless, morbidly unlittered. Rolling up her apron, Mrs Darbyshire, the charwoman, said, 'I think that is all I can do for you to-day,' in tones of professional self-righteousness. Indeed, Barbara thought, there was nothing more to ask; everything, from the slight dampness on the floor of the kitchenette to the embonpoint of the cushions on the sofa, was as it should be. She had not seen such neatness for years.

The thought of someone like Mrs Darbyshire had confirmed her decision to live in London again. A London charwoman does her work, takes her money and goes away, sterile as the wind of the desert. She does not spongily, greedily, absorb your concerns, study your nose to see if you have been crying again, count the greying hairs of your head, proffer sympathetic sighs and vacuum pauses and then hurry off to wring herself out, spongily, all over the village, with news of what's going on between those two at Pond

House. Not to mention the fact that a London charwoman is immeasurably better at charing.

Except that Mrs Darbyshire went away in trousers, her exit in 1950 was just as the exits of Mrs Shelley had been in the mid-thirties—the same healing order left behind, the same tonic appearance of everything wound up for a fresh start, with a filled kettle sitting on the hot-plate ready to be heated. And the flat of now, Barbara thought, in which she was again a single lady, was not very different from the flat of then; it was smaller, and the window glass, replacing glass that had been blown out in an air-raid, was of inferior quality, and the rent was a great deal higher, but the sitting-room and bedroom of the new flat were of the same sober, Victorian proportions, and, considering the housing shortage, she was lucky to get it, above all at such short notice—only two months. Two months and eight days, to be precise, for it was on the seventeenth of August that Willie broke the news, coming slowly across the sunburned lawn to where she stood repainting the front door of Pond House, little thinking how soon she would go out by it and Annelies come in.

'But why?' she had asked. 'Why must she come and *live* with you? I thought it was all over, months ago.'

'So did I.'

'But Annelies doesn't. Is that it?'

'She is so wretched,' he had said. 'So desperately, incompetently wretched. I can't let her go on suffering like this.'

While they spoke, she continued spreading the blue

paint, brushing it into the knots and cajoling it round the door-knocker. Dreamily, under the shock of these tidings, there had persisted a small, steady dissatisfaction because the paint was not the right shade of blue.

The flat of now seemed lighter than the flat of then. This was partly because her pieces of rosewood furniture were now so much paler in tone; twelve years in a country house, with windows open and sun shining in and not enough furniture polish, had bleached the rosewood to a tint of *feuille-morte*. Outside there was a difference, too—more air, more light, welling like fountains from the bombed sites. The room was full of light, as full of light as it was full of silence. In the centre stood the rosewood table, and as she bent over it, it reflected her with the whole length of its uncluttered surface, darkened here and there with old ink-stains like sea-leopard skin.

'I shall leave you the rosewood table,' she had said to Willie. 'It's the only one that is the right height for you, and large enough to hold all your traps.'

'No, don't,' he had said. 'I shall take over the big kitchen table. It's the same height. I've measured it.'

'Very well. But you'll keep the wardrobe?'

'I'd rather not.'

'Nonsense! You must have something to keep your clothes in. Or to keep the moths in, for I suppose you'll never remember to shut the doors.'

'That's all right. Annelies has one of these compactum things. It belonged to her husband.'

'I see. How convenient.'

3

'My God, how I hate these practical conversations! Why must we have them? They always end like this.'

Planning ahead, Barbara had resolved that the furniture should not be arranged in the flat of now as in the flat of then. But London rooms impose a formula. Now, as then, the desk stood in the recess on the left side of the fireplace, and the bookcase in the recess on the right; the sofa had its back to the window; and, on the wall opposite the fireplace, the Chippendale mirror hung above the bureau. Later on, she thought, readjusting the sofa cushions (for Mrs Darbyshire, like Mrs Shelley, had a passion for putting square objects cornerwise)—later on, people too will regroup themselves in this room. Mary Mackenzie's hand will dangle from the arm of the Regency chair as though its rings were too many and too heavy for it, and Julian will project his long legs obliquely from the stool, and Clive Thompson will stand with his back to the room, puffing at the bookcase. They will not have kept their outlines as unyieldingly as the furniture has, but their voices will be the same, and after the first constraint we shall find a great deal to talk about. It will be best, her thoughts went on, planning, foreseeing and planning as they had done during the breathless, interminable weeks before her departure from Pond House—it will be best to get them all here together one evening, when any awkwardness can be tided over by making them a trifle drunk. But that could be later on. It was still only her third day in the flat of now, and one must have a small decency-bit of time in which to lick one's wounds and wring the sea-water of shipwreck out of one's hair. *Such privilege belongs to women* . . . One of the advantages of a solitary life is that it allows one time to verify quotations instead of trailing them about all day, hanging them on gooseberry bushes, leaving them, like rings, above the sink. *Such privilege* . . . Hermione, in *The Winter's Tale,* said it.

Shakespeare was in the bedroom, to countervail against her dislike of it. It was a dislikable room, mutilated by the remodelling, which had shorn it for a bathroom. The tree beyond the bedroom window, she thought, coming back into the sitting-room with the book in her hand—even the tree, in itself a pleasant thing, must be contemplated as a sparrow-rack, where, from the first light onward, sparrows would congregate and clatter, making sleep impossible.

She found *The Winter's Tale,* and turned to the trial scene. Here it was:

> . . . *with immodest hatred,*
> *The child-bed privilege denied, which 'longs*
> *To women of all fashion. Lastly, hurried*
> *Here, to this place, i' the open air, before*
> *I have got strength of limit.*

Verifying quotations would indeed be an interesting pursuit if they all turned out to be as wide of the mark as this one. If Willie had shown a spark of even modest hate, she might have known a spark of hope.

She laid Shakespeare on the sofa and presently sat down beside him. To do so was a deliberate act, for she still retained, as a vestige of the last few weeks, an inability to sit down. One says 'a glutton for work', and during her

5

last month at Pond House she had exemplified that odious phrase, rushing gluttonously from one useful deed to another, cleaning, dispatching, repairing, turning out and destroying.

'All this revengeful housecleaning!' Willie had lamented.

'It's only fair to Annelies to get my smell out of the house,' she had replied.

In the first onset of grief, when grief was still pure enough to be magnanimous, the explanation might have been almost true, but not by the time she gave it. By then, she had no more magnanimity than a criminal on the run. There must be nothing left behind by which she could be tracked. A visual recollection of something overlooked and unscotched would strike her, as she lay sleepless—strike her violently, as though the object itself had been catapulted against her face. With her heart hammering and the blood pounding in her ears, she would begin to interrogate herself as to where, in their magpie's nest of a house, she had last set eyes on the red flannel heart embroidered with forget-me-nots, or the mug with 'William' on it that she had bought at Aberdovey. And all the while the most damning piece of evidence had slipped her memory, and only came to light by chance.

Invalided after Dunkirk, Willie had retained from his equipment one of those metal slides that isolate the military button for polishing. Thinking that this would serve the same purpose for the brass knobs on the spice cupboard, she began to search for it in the collector's cabinet, where Willie's father had kept his birds' eggs, where Willie hoarded his oddments. In the third drawer down, she came on the letters, her sight stumbling from Annelies's crisp blue sheets to her own letters, written from the flat of then to the Willie of then. She had looked at them no longer than to think how surprisingly and for the worse her handwriting had altered during the twelve years of happy married illiteracy, when she heard Willie saying, 'I know nothing about it. Do please go away,' to the children at the back door who had come to fetch the things for the jumble sale. Slamming the drawer to, she ran downstairs to recall the children. When she went back to the cabinet, the drawer was locked. Embarrassment tied her tongue.

Three days later, looking like a good dog, Willie laid her letters on the dressing-table.

'I don't approve of what I am doing,' he said. 'But then I don't approve of anything I am doing.' After a pause, he added, 'I think I wish I were dead.'

'Not really,' she answered. 'Not really, my dear.'

They looked at each other in the mirror, then. In the mirror she watched him lay his head on her shoulder— deposit it there, as though it were a sick animal.

But it was from that hour—as though by the restitution of her letters a ghost had been laid or a cork drawn—that Willie began to recover, to ascend from being a mournful cipher in her preparations to becoming their animating spirit. The last joint days at Pond House were spent in a kind of battered exhilaration, with Willie circumventing inquiring droppers-in, beating carpets and sewing on buttons. It was not just speeding the parting guest. He had, somehow or other, to dispose of the mounting excitement with which he awaited Annelies, and to be the life and soul of Barbara's departure was at once a safety valve and a tribute to conjugality.

'Write to me, won't you?' he had said, tying on the last luggage label.

'We said we wouldn't write, except on business,' she had replied. 'It would hurt Annelies. You know how sensitive she is, how the least thing makes her suffer agonies.' (She could not deny herself this shaft, and anyhow it did not penetrate.)

'You owe me a letter, Barbara. I gave you back the others. I didn't want to, but I did. I have never been so unhappy as I was that morning.' It was true, as true as that he was now much less unhappy. 'At least write and tell me that you are settled in, that you are all right, that the roof doesn't leak, that there aren't black beetles. It might be called a letter of business, really—though it isn't.'

'I will write,' she had said.

Now she took up Shakespeare, in whose orisons all our sins are comprehended, and patted him. 'Dear Swan!' she said aloud, her voice, in the unexplored depths of the lofty London room, sounding like the voice of a stranger. She could feel her body furtively relaxing while she sat on the sofa, and beginning to enjoy itself. It sighed, and stretched its legs, and burrowed deeper into the cushions, and her nostrils quickened to the smell of furniture polish, as though there were promise in it. She had been happy in her former solitude; presently she would be solitarily happy again. Like the furniture, she would settle down in the old arrangement, and the silence of the room would not intimidate her long; it was no more than a pin-point of silence in the wide noise of London. The kettle was on the hot-plate, filled and ready to be heated. The room sat around her, attentive, ready for her to begin. But first she must write to Willie.

Crossing the room, she seemed to herself to wade through silence, as though she were wading out to sea against a mounting tide. Silence embraced her thighs and almost overthrew her. She sat down at the desk and took a sheet of paper from a pigeon-hole. The light from the window fell on the desk over her left shoulder, just as it had done in the flat of then. And, just as she had done in the flat of then, she wrote the date—the date of now—and the words 'My Dear.'

'I am keeping my promise,' she wrote. 'The flat is very comfortable. There are no black beetles, and the person overhead plays Bach by hand, which seems very old-fashioned and soothing. I have found a nice charwoman. She is called Mrs Darbyshire. She wears trousers. I hope—' The pen stopped. What did she hope?

After birthdays and Christmases there came the hour when one was set down to write the letters of thanks. 'Thank you so much for the gorgeous chocolates,' one wrote, or, 'It was very kind of you to give me that nice bottle of scent.' The chocolates had been eaten, the scent had been spilled—but still they had to be thanked for. One's handwriting sagged down the page as if from weariness, the words 'nice' or 'jolly' dogged one from sentence to sentence, and with every recommencement of gratitude the presents and the festivities became more irrevocably over and done with. One stared at the unfinished sentence and wondered what false thing to say next. Yet what she wanted to say to Willie was clear enough in her mind, clear as the printed words on India paper which had levelled themselves at her heart from that speech in *The Winter's Tale*:

> *To me can life be no commodity;*
> *The crown and comfort of my life, your favour*
> *I do give lost, for I do feel it gone,*
> *Yet know not how it went . . .*

But in real life one cannot write so plainly the plain truth; it would look theatrical. She must think of something she could legitimately hope. A hope about Mrs Darbyshire would do nicely. She wrote, 'I hope she will like me enough to look on me as a permanency.'

Oh, poor Willie! That sentence would not do at all. She tore up the unfinished letter and threw it into the grate, which Mrs Darbyshire had left neatly laid with crumpled paper and sticks and a few well-chosen lumps of coal, in case the lady should wish to light a fire in the evening; for a newly-moved-into place always strikes chilly at first, and though the autumn weather was keeping up wonderfully, almost as mild as spring, one could feel winter in the air.

Hee-Haw!

A mile or so on the hither side of the village of St Prew, Mrs Vincent stopped the taxi she had engaged at the railway station, telling the driver that she had an attack of cramp and must walk about a little. She could not give the excuse that she wanted to look at the view—the admired view of the cliffs, crested like bulls with shaggy moor and standing sullenly at bay against the Atlantic—for the forgotten, familiar sea fog obscured all but the immediate landscape of rough turf laid thinly over rocky ground, outcrops of granite, an unmortared stone wall laced with brambles and tufted with fern, and the telegraph poles. She walked forward along the road, seeming to carry this landscape with her through the surrounding mist, and looking about for something she could identify. Thirty years ago, every yard of this road had been as familiar to her as her own hand. She had walked it in all moods, in all weathers, and the last time she had come this way, but in the counter direction, she had seemed almost to fly along it, so great was the force of her anger, her frenzy to escape and never, never set foot on it again.

A stone gatepost came suddenly out of the fog. She thought she remembered that. Laying her bare hand on it, she felt its cold moisture drench into her flesh. A moment later, the sound of the foghorn from the lightship thumped on her hearing. *Hee-haw! Hee-haw!*——a descent from the minor seventh to the tonic. She remembered that, too. She waited for the loud, listless, booming syllables to recur. One counted ten. Subconsciously, she had begun to count, and at ten, *Hee-haw! Hee-haw!* struck in. It was as though she had never been out of earshot, as though the thirty years since her departure had been no more than another way of counting ten.

The sea fog, looking so light as it billowed past, so light and so oddly dry, as though it were smoke, had already begun to penetrate her. Her hand on the gatepost shone with moisture; minute drops bloomed her sleeve. *Eight, nine*—she could not go on!—*ten*. It was not to be endured. *Hee-haw! Hee-haw!* This time, there was no reason to endure it. She turned and walked briskly toward the waiting car, determined to tell the driver that she had changed her mind and would return to the station. But he said to her, 'How's the cramp? Better?' And in the moment of answering him she lost her purpose, got into the car, and let herself be driven on.

The ground began to waver downhill. From here, if it were not for the fog, she would see the rooftops of the village, the little bay, the scrolling iron-coloured cliffs beyond. There it would be. The post office, the bakery, the sheds where the nets were mended and the ground where they were hung to dry, the stone church-tower and the red-brick chapel, and the chemist's shop, no wider than a passage, where she used to buy oil of cloves for her toothache. On the outskirts of the village, lying in wait for her, was the bungalow where she had lived for three years with Ludovick. It had been built for a holiday house, flimsy and summerlike—too flimsy even for summer, in this sad seaward climate, so its owner had been glad to close with Ludovick's offer of twenty pounds a year and a new coat of paint. They had not unpacked before he began laying on his blue paint, dropping paint everywhere and getting painter's colic; a couple of months later, the blue paint was blotching, curling, scaling and flaking off, for he had used a cheap kind and it could not withstand the heavy charge of salt in the air. But by that time he did not mind. He had begun his first canvas of the series of sea anemones. And on the heels of that, having scorched himself raw with sunbathing, he went down with blood poisoning.

The car slid round a corner and changed gear. She started, and looked out of the window. They were passing the bungalow; she caught a flash of it, perched on its hillock behind the tamarisk hedge. There was a line of washing, so someone was living in it. The fuchsia was gone, and there was a flight of cement-block steps in place of the steep path.

In a whisk, in a glancing blow of recognition, she had seen it again, the place where she had lived for three years—in turmoil, in rapture, in drudgery, in fury, in the bitter patience of disillusionment; there, at the close of those three years, she had her last quarrel with Ludovick and walked for the last time down the steep path. Closing the gate, she had heard a sudden gay clatter of crockery. Ludovick, left to himself, was washing up. He'll soon tire of that, she had thought. He stayed on for another six months;

then he took himself abroad, and it was from Corsica that he sent her the evidence for their divorce.

The taxi drew up before The Good Hope. Standing on the pavement, she knew a moment of wincing panic. Because she recognized the narrow street, and the porch of The Good Hope, straddling out across the pavement on its short, clumsy pillars, and even the momentary amplification it gave to the voices of the two women who passed under it, deep in village conversation, she felt herself closed in on by recognitions. 'Proper foolish, I call it,' one of the women said. The words seemed to be spoken of her.

Saying to herself, 'But I am old, I am well dressed, my eyebrows are plucked, I am called Mrs Vincent, I have nothing to fear,' she entered The Good Hope and was conducted to the bedroom she had booked.

The interior of The Good Hope was considerably changed. It was so spruced, so glistening with white paint, chromium ashtrays, brass warming-pans and pink eiderdowns, that, looking down from her bedroom window into the street, she had the impression that she was in a box at the theatre, looking down a stage set. The stage set included a cinema and several newly antiqued teashops, and the stage crowd contained a new social element—people like herself, only younger, walking with a town gait and precision among the fishermen and the slow-footed women. Looking farther along the street, she noticed a hanging sign that wagged in the perpetual wind and bore the words 'Artist's Colours and Materials. Crafts.' Ludovick, the artlessly gratified, the childishly sanguine and childishly downcast, wagging like a

spaniel at any pat of recognition——what would he make of
this commemoration of his Cornish period, this tribute of
pink eiderdowns and warming-pans? 'Hee-haw! Hee-haw!'
she said, mimicking the foghorn. It was still blaring away,
but now, competing with the wireless downstairs and the
traffic outside, it was no longer portentous and obsessive,
as it had been on the cliff road. It sounded foolishly perse-
vering, like an obstinate donkey tethered on a common.
The mood of her journey evaporated. Hungry from the sea
air, ready to be dispassionately entertained, she went down
to the lounge and ordered tea.

Above her table there was a reproduction of the second
Sea Anemones, signed and dated with his painstakingly neat
'L. Dodge. July, 1921.' How cross everyone had been
about it when it was exhibited, and his friendly critics
crossest of all, because it had none of the qualities for
which they had previously commended him. 'A regret-
table, if wholly successful, attempt to reproduce the
wallpaper in the bedroom of some indulged Edwardian
kitchenmaid,' Boddick had written, and someone else
had referred to it as 'this jellied Venus rising from pink
froth'. Now the reproduction, in a most respectful frame,
hung on the wall where formerly old Mr Tregurtha's head
had left its greasy halo, and no one gave it a glance. With
every sup of China tea, with every bite of the solicitously
Cornish food——saffron buns and vinegar loaf cake——it
became easier to sterilize the past by the present. The
weather had changed, too. The fog had lifted; the sun was
shining. After tea, she would go for a walk.

It was surprisingly creditable (she was sufficiently conscious of the creditability to be surprised) that she could walk about in St Prew with no other emotion than a Londoner's response to an April evening in country air. She went down to the harbour, where the boats were gently waggling at their moorings. Their shadows plunged into the water that the reflected sunset had strewn with petals of tea-rose pink, and a gull was perched on every mast. She walked on the drying-ground, snuffing up the tar and the brine of the nets. She saw again the bust of Queen Victoria gazing seaward from the bayed front of The Fisherman's Friend, and it was still painted heliotrope. Fighting resolutely for breath, she climbed the flight of steps that was the short-cut to Prospect Terrace, where a half-circle of cottages, turning their backs to the sea, had concentrated the regard of their front windows, their lace curtains and geraniums, on the public urinal. But now the urinal had been replaced by a telephone kiosk, and the cottages had become self-consciously simple, with windows wide open and mugs of daffodils. From here, past pigsties and orchards, a lane had run, joining the main road just short of the bungalow where she and Ludovick had lived. It had a metalled surface now, and a perspective of trim little holiday cottages. She looked at the rise of moorland beyond and turned away. Why should she go walking on for another look at the bungalow? It was still there, for what it was worth. It was still there, and she wasn't. Let that be enough!

So the walk round St Prew did not take quite so long as

Mrs Vincent had intended, and to fill up the gap of time before dinner she ordered a glass of sherry to be brought to her in the lounge. Automatically, she sat down at the same table where she had had tea. *L. Dodge,* she read. *July,* 1921. That hot summer—the historically hot summer of 1921. How strange the colours of the parched landscape had been, at once violent and pale, and how strongly everything had smelled: the mown field where they had taken their supper one evening, and everything they ate tasted of warm stewed figs because of the intense, figlike sweetness of the cut clover, cooked all day in the blazing heat; the gorse along the cliffs, smelling as though a mad baker had been taking coconut bread out of the fiery oven's mouth; the drains in St Prew; and in the bungalow, oil paints and paraffin and fennel and the sea.

L. Dodge. July, 1921.

'Everyone is struck by that picture,' the waiter said, calling her attention to the glass of sherry he had set down. 'It was painted here, in St Prew. Sea Anemones, by Ludovick Dodge. Of course, this is only a copy. The original is in a London gallery, I believe. Bought for the nation.'

'Yes. I have seen it,' she said.

'Have you, now? Well, it was painted down here, in St Prew. He lived here for several years. Put St Prew on the map, you might say. People have been coming to see the place ever since. Of course, it was all a long time ago. Nineteen twenty-one.'

'Before you can remember,' she said.

'Well, in a manner of speaking, yes. But there's plenty

that do. There's old Mr Caunter—he can tell you any amount about the artist. He's got quite a name for it among our visitors, He's in the bar at this moment.'

She made a movement of dissent, but it was too late.

'He's a dear old soul, too,' continued the waiter. 'A real character. I'll tell you what, I'll ask him to step into the lounge. There's nothing he likes better than telling our visitors about Ludovick Dodge. Another sherry, Madam?'

'Please.'

'Yes, Madam. And I'll bring along Mr Caunter. He— well, he usually takes rum.'

'Then bring a rum with my sherry. Make it a double.'

Caunter, she said to herself. Caunter. Who was called Caunter? But a taproom bore by any other name would recognize her as easily. She had been a fool.

The huge old man, coming into the room like a ship, and piloted by the waiter, did not appear to recognize her, nor did she recognize him. He bowed portentously and sat down, and raised his glass.

'Good health to 'ee, my dear,' he said. 'And welcome to St Prew. I understand from Marky, here, that you come from London.' She nodded. 'Yes. And, what's more, that you've seen this picture, here—only it was the real one, and not a printed-off affair—in London. So've I seen it. Not in London, though. No, here in St Prew. Spit-new it was then—oh, and a wonder! 'Twasn't everyone liked it from the first. But I did.'

Were you the man who came to mend the roof? she thought.

'Because I liked the painter, d'you see? Mr Dodge. Young man, he was then. In his twenties, I reckon. Remarkable. Re-markable. There wasn't anything that young man couldn't do. Why, I've seen him go down over Shark Head as easy as a rabbit. Ah!—but he's dead, you know.'

'He died a few years ago, didn't he?'

'Eighteen of March, nineteen forty-nine. In a motoring accident. Near Amalfi. In Italy. Fishing-port, like St Prew, so I understand. I got it all, cut out of the newspaper. A pity, my dear! A wonderful pity! I've never seen a young man so full of life, nor so enjoying. I've seen him down in Bat Cove, when a swarm of jellyfish was coming in. "Look at them," he said to me. "Look at them, you old Caunter, you! I could go and bathe in them.""Don't 'ee go for to do that, sir," said I. And he burst out laughing, and walked up and down the beach with his arm round my neck, carrying on about those jellyfish and saying they made him as happy as a king. Happy and glorious, that's what he was. So was she—his young lady. You never saw such a pair of creatures as those two.'

Stop, stop, she said to herself. What does it matter? It's all over long ago. We're all dead. What the hell does it matter who Ludovick took up with?

'His young lady?' she asked.

Mr Caunter looked at her as one old crony might look at another, and smiled.

'Well—as to whether they were married or no, that I won't say. These artists don't think so much of matrimony as other folk do, seemingly.'

'No. Sometimes they don't think of it at all.'

'But, married or t'other thing,' said Mr Caunter, his shiplike bulk putting on a sudden majesty of full sail, 'I can say this. They were happy. Happy as the day is long. And loving each other. Head over ears in love. Fit to tear each other. Ah! One doesn't see the like of that more than once in a lifetime—and maybe not then. But there they were. I saw them. And I shan't forget it.'

He drank solemnly, and was silent, looking at her as though she were the same woman at whose table he had sat down five minutes before, as though, out of the neatly raked ashes, jealousy had not exploded and hurled her back from the security of being married to Charles Vincent to the agony of being married to Ludovick Dodge. It must have begun the moment her back was turned. Who was she? Where had he got her—this bitch with whom he had been so happy and glorious?

'What was she like, this young lady?' she asked conversationally, and, noticing the fires shaken from the diamonds on her fingers, she hid her twitching hands under the table.

'Well, now, that's a question I can't rightly answer. You know a lark by the song, and not by the feathers. And when you see a young lady so blazingly in love, you don't stop to notice what colour her eyes are. She was young, you know. Dressed herself in nice bright colours; never wore a hat. And nimble. Wonderfully light on her feet, she was. Many's the time I've seen her run up the steps from the harbour to Prospect Terrace, as though it were no more to her than the bedchamber stairs. Carrying a great parcel of fish, and the Lord knows what else.'

So you had to do that too, she thought. Hope you liked it.

'I never saw her sick or sorrowful but once,' said Mr Caunter. 'And that was when he was ill. He'd set his heart on a red mullet, and she came after it. I'd have dived into the sea and brought one out in my mouth for that young man. But there wasn't a red mullet in the catch that day. When I told her so, she stood there and cursed and damned me, with the tears raining down over her cheeks. But he soon picked up, and they were ramping and tearing over the moor, happy as ever.'

Different woman, but the same Ludovick, she thought.

'Not that they didn't have their little differences. Wouldn't have been like lovers not to.' A slow grin rocked his whiskers. 'One day, I happened to be going past their gate and I heard them disputing withindoors. He gave a yell and came running down the path, and she raced after him and clapped a pot of blue paint over his head. And what did he do? Knocked her clean into the hedge, and came walking on with his casel and all the rest of his gear. And the blue paint streaming down all over him.'

He's got it mixed, she said to herself desperately, reasonably. He's got it mixed. I was the paint, and the love and the happiness was the other one.

'Yes, my dear. That's what it is to be a genius, d'you see? He went on down to the cove, and put his feet in a pool, and sat drawing those little emonies. There was a young man you couldn't but help loving. Love him I did. And do to this day.'

'And when was this?' she asked, after a pause.

'Thirty years ago,' he said. 'Yes, that's when it was. Can't be less, for in nineteen twenty-two the fishing trade got so bad that soon after midsummer I packed up and went to work for a fishmonger in Birmingham. Funny ways they've got with fish in those parts.'

I suppose I shall remember that ridiculous sentence to my dying day, she thought.

'And when I came back to St Prew, he was gone,' the old man said.

Still silent, she laid her hands on the table and looked at them. They were not shaking now. Presently, she became aware that the other guests were beginning to bestir themselves and go into the dining-room, and that Mr Caunter was getting to his feet.

'Time I was going home,' he said. 'The fog is blowing in again. It will be another thick night. We'll be hearing the foghorn again in a minute or two. Ah. Well, it's been a pleasure. I could tell about him by the hour. But best not. The fog gets into my tubes, d'you see? And then I cough.'

It was as though the fog were billowing past, dry as smoke, between her and the old man with his stumbling attempts at the courtesies of farewell. Absorbed in her bitter melancholy, she did not notice when he went away.

The Children's Grandmother

Looking westward under the dusky winter skies, which had a russet tinge, as though the colour of the moor were reflected in the low-hanging clouds, one saw along the horizon a band of pale light, and that was the sky above the Atlantic.

'You say Roses is five miles from the sea?' my sister Anne had commented. 'Why, the children will grow up little sea monsters. You can whisk them into it in a moment, before the old lady has time to say no.' In fact, it was not so easy. The children's grandmother could not imagine the car—a large, old Daimler, a car for carrying dowagers to court rather than children to the sea—being driven by anyone but Job. Job understood it. We lived at Roses for nearly three years before I was allowed to drive the Daimler to the sea, and even then Job came too. Job also understood the tides; and as my children's Aunt Madeleine had been drowned off the beach where they paddled, I could not contest the importance of Job's understanding the tides. By then, I had become so much a piece of life at Roses that I was not sorry to have Job in the back of the car, representing, for he was an immensely impressive and solemn old man, the rightful dowager. Graciously rising and sinking, bowing to a non-existent populace at every jolt in the narrow lane, Job accompanied us to the sea, sat down on the flat rock that was called Job's Rock, as other rocks were called the Castle, the Maiden, and the Churn, and took out his knitting. He sat on his rock and watched the sea, and his needles clicked and flicked, gathering the wool into socks and scarves and jerseys for the children, and at some mysteriously indicated moment he would cry out in his foghorn bellow that the current was flowing round the Churn, that swimmers and paddlers must return to the beach. We obeyed him, knowing that he was our friend. We must have known it by intuition, for he hardly ever spoke, his face was as expressionless as the moon, and his eyes were like two large iron nails driven deep into it and fastened by rust.

There was another cove within much the same distance from Roses, but we were forbidden to go to it. To get there, one had to pass through a village called St Keul, where, so the children's grandmother said, there was always fever. At first, this prohibition was merely a mercy to me, and St Keul a place where I need not be paraded in my widow's dress, or repeat the story of the car accident in which my husband had been fatally injured and I scarcely injured at all, to listeners whose code of manners spared me no questions and whose loyalty to the old family inscribed very clearly on their severe countenances a loyally unspoken opinion that the wrong one had survived. Their sympathy, naturally enough, went to my husband's mother, who would oversee these conversations almost as a mother oversees her child's performance at the dancing-class, sternly attentive that I should not omit a single pirouette in the elaborate ritual of courtesy between high and low. As time went on, and I became better trained in these formalities, and saw her skilled and scrupulous observance of them, I found that I could not reconcile the ban on St Keul with the reason she gave for it. Any outbreak of sickness, any sickbed, childbed, deathbed, among our poor neighbours became her affair—not, I think, that she liked doing good but simply because she could not conceive herself not doing it. No danger or loathsomeness could turn her aside from a purpose. The Daimler swayed and sidled down chaseways and field tracks to carry her and her chest of homoeopathic medicines anywhere and everywhere—except to St Keul. Whatever the reason for her ban, it could not be fever—unless (the surmise darted upon me and darkened into belief) it was from St Keul that the infection had reached out to Guy and Everard, the twin sons who had died, one at midnight, the other before day, as though they had died in a ballad. No doubt I could have known the truth for the asking, but I could not bring myself to ask. There was something so hysterically ludicrous in the story of this doomed nursery that I dreaded to hear it consecutively told. Such narratives are more tolerable in the city, where, indeed, they can be a social asset, and people dine out on them: 'Max, Max, tell us that appalling story, that Seven Little N—— story of the family at Roses!' But at Roses one was a long way from any city.

My husband, the last of my mother-in-law's children, and born at a long interval after the others, was the only one who lived to grow up, his childhood intimidated by the absence, which was also a presence, of Madeleine, Guy, Everard, Lucas, Alice and Noel. He grew up an only child, in the middle of this shadowy band of brothers and sisters whom his father and the servants assured him were angels in heaven, whom his mother told him were dead. Unable to reconcile a discrepancy, he yet felt himself confronted with a choice between becoming another angel or another dead child at the feet of the white marble angel that showed up so embarrassingly among the wooden and small iron crosses in the village graveyard. Meanwhile, he lived among their vestiges—riding Guy's bicycle, filling the blank pages in Lucas's scrapbook, or giving tea parties under the weeping ash to the dolls of Madeleine, Alice and Noel. Twice a year, he stood to be measured against the nursery door, where their heights were recorded in his mother's handwriting, creeping up among and through them like a shoot of this year making its way through last year's thicket, until at last he surmounted them all and still remained alive. Their initials and his—a C for Charles—were still legible when I came to Roses with his four fatherless children and the measuring began again, the children's grandmother writing the new initials and the dates of the twentieth century in the same calm, cursive hand. Age for age, the new measurements all fell below the old. She never remarked on it, but I supposed that to herself she commented on the stocky inelegant stature inherited from a mother born of the sturdy middle class. She never remarked on my children's sturdy middle-class health, either. Beyond a few prohibitions—St Keul, venturing into the current that drowned

Madeleine, eating chocolates after teeth had been brushed for bedtime—she had no trace of grandmotherly fuss or grandmotherly fondness.

During our first years at Roses, while I was still capable of town-bred speculation and analysis, I used to wonder if her detachment sprang from a contained and despairing diffidence—if, having failed so pitiably to rear her own children, she had made some violent vow not to meddle with mine. Later, seeing her detachment persisting, quite unchanged, under her grandchildren's affection, I came to suppose her dislike of her son's marriage perpetuated in a stoical disapproval of the fruits of it—for she was completely a Stoic; in all the years I lived under her roof, I never heard her utter a regret or an aspiration. And at other times I had the simple and sentimental thought: She has lost all her children; she dares not love again. In spite of this detachment—or perhaps because of it—her relationship with her grandchildren was as easy as the relationship of sea and seaweed. We think of children as being our dependants; at best this is only a half-truth. The child is a social tyrant, imposing on its elders an obligation to conform, and as a rule the elderly, being on the outermost and most provincial rim of the child's society, transform themselves the most slavishly, and climb downward, so to speak, in a headlong flurry to be accepted. The children's grandmother was as equalitarian among my children as though she were another child. She spoke to them, even to the youngest, without a change of voice or manner, and bargained with them in such matters as winding her wool or stripping the gooseberry bushes as sternly as though they were horse-dealers. They, in turn, bargained with her and, by measuring their wits against hers, came to know her as confidently as Job understood the Daimler and the tides. In spite of her threescore years and ten, she was as active as a hound. It was an extraordinary sight to see them playing hide-and-seek in the orchard—the tall old woman running with her grey head stooped under the lichened boughs, or folded away in some narrow hiding-place, her eyes blazing with excitement. After a while, with a fickleness that matched the fickleness of a child, she would say curtly, 'That's all,' and walk out of the game without a trace of fatigue, for she played to please herself, not them. Even in that most grandmotherly role of storyteller, she retained an egoism of artistry. It was she who chose the stories; it was to her own ear they were addressed, or perhaps to the ghost of her unsurmisable childish self seated among my children, who listened with critical ease to her narratives, as a cultured audience listens to a first-rate performer. 'Nothing too much.' It is, I believe, a Stoic maxim; at any rate, it is a canon of classical performance, and she unfailingly observed it. I never heard her carried away into overdramatization or false emphasis. Her ghosts appeared without those preliminary warnings, lowered tones that say 'Here comes the ghost,' as stentorianly as the major-domo announces 'His Grace the Duke of So-and-So'; the squeals of the little pigs were related, not mimicked; her bears growled as a matter of course. Listening one evening to the dignified inflections of the Wolf Grandmother replying to the inquiries of Little Red Riding Hood, I realized that this was, in fact, the lot of my children: they had a Wolf Grandmother, a being who treated them with detached benignity, who played with them and dismissed them and enjoyed them without scruple, and would, at a pinch, defend them with uncontaminated fury. Her eyes were large the better to watch them with, her ears long the better to hear them, her claws sharp the better to tear—by an accident of kinship—not them but the village of St Keul, the malevolence of the sea, the Jesuitry of the bedtime chocolate.

They loved her with an unjaded love—as they love her memory to this day. They throve in her as they throve in the climate of moor and sea. What she felt for them I could not determine. Unless there be a kind of love that can exist without a breath of tenderness, it was not love. It was too passionate for affection. It had nothing in common with the wistful doting of old age. It had a quality, at once abstract and practical, that made it seem like some deeply felt bargain, as though, perhaps, she accepted them as the remission of her own tragedy, an indulgence of a maternal feeling that in her own maternity had been deformed by constant blasts of fate, as the thorn trees on the moor were warped by the wind from the sea. But she never made any move to take them from me or set them against me. Circumstances—my loneliness, my poverty, my husband's perplexing injunction that his children should grow up at Roses—all made it easy for her to avenge herself on me for a marriage she had disapproved; but, having brought herself to swallow me, she had, it appeared, no further wish than to make a good digestion of me.

Once only did I see her exhibit an unequivocal force of feeling, and the exhibition left me baffled as ever as to the nature of the feeling itself. There were vipers on the moor, and Job had taught the children how to handle them safely, since it was too much to expect that they would not handle them at all. The length of a viper lashing below the small brown fist that held it firmly just beneath the head, the smell of the viaticum chloroform on the wad of cotton-wool, and, later, the stink of a dissection, had become familiar to me, and not even very alarming. But on this occasion Paul's hand was still greasy from helping to lubricate the Daimler. The viper writhed out of his grasp, fell at Caroline's bare feet, and bit her in the toe. For several days she was danger-ously ill. During that time I had a horrible leisure in which to observe my mother-in-law. Under her reserve I saw a wild-cat fury at this misadventure, a rage so intense that I was afraid to leave Paul in the same room with her, for it seemed possible that in some self-contained trance of resentment she would turn and rend him to pieces. Her anxiety appeared to have carried her beyond the fact of a child in danger of dying; it was harsh and abstracted, akin to the anxiety of the speculator who has staked everything, future as well as fortune, on a coup and sees the market wavering against him; and when the doctor pronounced Caroline out of danger, she gave vent to a shuddering, astonished 'Whew-w!' as though it were she herself who had escaped a mortal peril.

While he was still congratulating us, she quitted him to unlock the wine cellar, bringing out bottle after bottle of burgundy, rum and sauterne. Standing in the kitchen like some descended Juno, she brewed a vast bowl of punch, from which we must all drink to celebrate Caroline's recovery, and the kitchenmaid was sent pelting off to summon the outlying people of the estate: the bailiff, the shepherds, the furze cutters. It was a cold evening, for though the month was August, a sea fog was coming in. Fetched out of the chilly dusk into the blazing kitchen and given mugfuls of punch, the celebrants became very drunk. It was alarming to see the familiar and sombre faces of everyday acquaintance smeared with looks of vinous beatitude, and though the congratulations they gave me were sincere, I felt as though I were hemmed in by a throng of sheepish satyrs. Perhaps I was a little drunk myself, though I had managed to spill out half my tumblerful. As soon as I could, I got my tipsy children away. I went to sit by Caroline's bed, hearing the shouts and songs of the retiring guests and the hubbub of the household folk still at it in the kitchen. Till this evening, I had never seen the children's grandmother anything but abstemious. Now I had watched her drinking glass after glass, drinking enough to put any man under the table. I was worried about her, concerned for her credit, and for her health. The noise died out at last, but still she did not come to bed. I had nerved myself to go in search of her, when I heard her foot on the stair, the firm, unhurried tread exactly as usual. She paused at the door, and I thought she would enter. Seized by an unaccountable sense of danger, I stood myself in front of the child's bed, as if to protect her. But the door did not open, and presently I

heard a calm, fragile sound: concluding some train of satisfied thought, the old lady had clicked her tongue against the
roof of her mouth; and then the footsteps went evenly on.

Apparently my children had inherited her knack for
hard drinking. On the morrow, they were none the worse
for having gone drunk to bed, and clamoured for another
occasion for punch. On her eightieth birthday, she said,
and with Wolf Grandmother dexterity boxed back their
endeavours to ascertain the happy date. The possibility
that she might die before then occurred to none of us. She
proceeded through old age as infallibly, as vitally, as my
children grew from childhood to youth.

In our small world, where she and they moved through
time like mowers through a field, scything down the years
and leaving them prone behind them, I alone seemed
unable to grow older. My middle-aged body showed few
changes; my circumstances even enforced on me a sort
of retrogression into girlishness. I had my four children,
and the wedding-ring on my finger, yet when the young
chauffeur who came after Job's death persisted in calling
me 'Miss', the error was felt to be natural, and even
fitting; a newcomer, he rightly discerned and proclaimed
the accomplishment of a process that the others had for a
long while been inattentively forwarding. Interpolated as
a daughter-in-law, I was now a daughter of the house, the
faithful, negligible daughter who has never left home.

Such daughters are usually scorned by their mothers. Soon
after my reclassification by Martin (the new chauffeur was
called Martin), the children's grandmother broke her severe

procedure and was rude to me. We were bound on one of her errands of mercy, and Martin, who piqued himself on already knowing his way everywhere, was settling us in the car. 'High Grange,' he said confidently. 'That's through St Keul, and then left?'

'No,' I answered. 'You turn left at the crossroads, and then—'

Her voice cut through mine. 'Idiot!' she exclaimed. 'Woolgathering as usual! Martin is perfectly right. Drive through St Keul, Martin.'

There is a moment when, still conscious under the anaesthetic, one crosses a frontier between a known and an incalculable world. That is how I felt when the car held on over the crossroads and I saw a landscape typically familiar but in fact strange, unassimilated, and raw; and because St Keul did not immediately start up before us, like some conjurer's castle, I had the impression that we were end-lessly going nowhere, or perhaps were dead. Martin, his ears still scarlet with embarrassment, was driving faster than she approved, but she made no move to check him. She sat upright and silent in an Egyptian gravity, clad in her smooth, dark tweed as though in basalt, her hands laid in rigid composure along her thighs. Only an occasional flick of her fingers, disquieting as the undulation that brings the heather root to life as a snake, escaped her self-control.

She had gratuitously insulted me, I had failed to defend myself, and now I was falling back on the private retaliation of pity—pitying her for being so old, and for the barren stubbornness that was forcing her to flout a superstition of

33

so many years' observance. The watery sunlight lit up some slate roofs clotted about a narrow church with a slated belfry. I saw her hands relax. Very softly, she began to whistle. It was a jiggling little tune of a few notes, the sort of tune one learns in the nursery; and Victor, my younger son, would whistle in just the same manner on the way back from the dentist. Absorbed in the whistling soliloquy, she was driven through St Keul. The infection of her odd merriment gained on me, and I began to feel meaninglessly merry myself.

'There!' she exclaimed as we left it behind us. 'So much for St Keul!'

Recklessly, dancing to the tune of her whistling, I asked, 'But what was the fever at St Keul? What kind of fever?'

'Only young children died of it,' she replied. 'I don't give a rap for it now. Yours have outgrown the danger. You really need not fuss about it any longer.'

I did not say that it was she, not I, who had laid the ban on St Keul. I was thinking of a different peril. It seemed to me that the passage of our unmistakable Daimler had roused unfavourable attention in the slighted village, and that on our return we should very probably be stoned. But at High Grange she learned that two sons of a fisherman's family had been drowned, and after visiting the bereaved household we went home by a different route.

It was on this return journey that Martin ran into a cow—a contributory reason for his dismissal a few weeks later. He did not understand the Daimler. But he understood my true status at Roses, and stayed long enough to see me established in it.

I suppose there is an inherent servility in my nature. The barter of an unspoken for an outspoken contempt did not seem to me too high a price to pay for the relief of being on easier terms with the children's grandmother, of having some claim on her affection, if only as her drudge. It was as though she would at last allow me to live again, after the long years during which I had been compelled to exist merely as a cipher. I took up my new life, and with the departure of my children to their boarding-schools I became the unmarried daughter. Living at her beck and call, submerged in busy economies that were to pay for the children's education, assenting to her opinions and listening to her stories (told with as much spirit as ever, and for her own entertainment), I had no time for the speculations and ruminations of my cipher days. St Keul, that Dark Tower, was now the place where we bought sardines, and the problem of the reserve and detachment qualifying her love for the children—the problem, even, as to whether she loved them at all—was not even a problem. At first, she had disliked us, and gradually they had overcome her dislike—that, and no more, was the explanation.

It was not the explanation. I did not arrive at the truth until the day she lay dying, whirled away like a dandelion clock by a brief pleurisy. She had lain for some hours without speaking, and only from time to time stirring her impatient hand. I sat beside her, grieving perhaps, or perhaps grieving that I could not grieve more, and straining my ears for the noise of the car that should bring Paul home from college in time to do his part as the elder male of the family. Becoming aware that I was being looked at, I turned and saw her glance dwelling on me. Her eyes gleamed in their sockets; her lips were forming painfully into a smile of contempt. She struggled to raise herself, and writhed across the bed toward me.

'Heh! You poor creature!' she said, taking hold of my chin in a violent, shaking grasp. 'Heh! You poor, luckless creature! You have not lost one of your children, not one!'

I thought she was raving, but her tone steadied, and there was the force of years of rational consideration in her voice as she continued, 'So when you are old, you will not have a single child left you. Nothing but strangers!'

Those were the last words she spoke. Then, it was the disclosure of her hoarded malice that appalled me. Now I am appalled for a different reason. I am beginning to think that her words are coming true.

Evan

His stepfather, in torments as usual at anything resembling a public appearance (and the platform of a country railway station is extremely public if it is the station of where you live), was in consequence talking too loud and too heartily. 'Well, that's all right. Your trunk is in the van, I've just seen it put in. You've got your suitcase, haven't you?'

'Yes.'

'Good! Don't forget it when you change at Market Beaton. And your sandwiches?'

'They are in the suitcase.'

'Hope they're good ones. Think I heard your mother mention ham. Lucky dog! She doesn't give *me* ham. Well, see you again at Easter. Hope you'll have a good term, and all that. And don't go catching mumps and measles if you can help it. But I suppose you're bound to.' Loyal to the English public-school system, Major Burroughs held as an article of faith the tenet that epidemics are peculiar to the Lent term.

'I've had measles. I had it last summer.'

'Yes, yes. Of course. So you did. Well, I'm sorry the holidays are over. Wish we'd had better weather, and you could have got out more. Dull work, hanging about indoors, reading, and amusing two small sisters. Very nice of you, to be so kind to Rhoda and Jenny. They appreciate it. So do I.'

'I think the train's starting.'

'Good Lord, so it is! Well, there we are. Goodbye, Evan, old chap. Sure you've got your ticket? Good, good! So long! See you soon.'

Dry-eyed and exhausted after this agonizing farewell, Evan pulled up the window, and then stumbled over the feet of the lady who was the only other traveller in that compartment. 'I beg your pardon,' he said.

'You didn't hurt me.'

He was startled. Though she was plainly not the type of lady who would say 'Granted,' he had expected a 'That's all right,' or something of that kind, in keeping with the impersonality of people in railway carriages. It was dis quieting to be reminded that the feet he had stumbled over were sentient objects, attached to a being to whom he could cause pain. Her voice was not impersonal, either. It was warm and low-pitched, and seemed directly addressed to reassuring him. So he himself snatched up the conventional phrase, saying, 'That's all right.' Spoken, it declared itself the wrong thing to have said—a pawn, when he should have moved out a knight. Becoming aware of a further threat in that the lady had no illustrated papers, and that he had none either, he began to look out of the window.

The lady at her leisure observed his long eyelashes. Long eyelashes being a beauty she herself regretfully lacked, this was always the first thing she looked for in man or woman. The shade in the eye sockets embellished them as art would have done, but was natural—he was a boy of sixteen, or perhaps seventeen, who had outgrown his strength. Other things to admire were his small ears, and the well-shaped hands that grew like brown lilies out of his long narrow wrists. If due care had been expended on him, he would have been handsome. But care had not been expended, and whoever sent him to that haircutter should have been shot.

Meanwhile, the view from the train had shaken off the brief suburbs of the town and displayed a landscape of small steep hills and hanging woods. A brook ran counter to the train's course. It was in flood, and a hackle of foam rode on it. Evan had fished it during the summer holidays, and during the summer holidays before that, and before that. There was not an alder bush along its course that his line had not tangled in. He was tired to death of it, and of the woods where his family took picnics, and of the fields where they looked for mushrooms. If it had not been for the absence of illustrated papers on the lap opposite, he would have opened his suitcase, taken out the volume of Thomas Hardy's poems, and read himself into detachment. But to do so under her observation would appear uncivil, so he continued to look out of the window, and the lady continued to admire his eyelashes.

She saw them flick suddenly, and remain poised apart. Instead of just looking, he was now staring with all his eyes. His attention was so obviously arrested that she glanced out, too. She could see nothing to account for such rapt interest. The railway track had turned eastward into a landscape of shaggy, muddied pastures, hitched to the contours of chalk downs. On the horizon a roofless barn stood out against the

39

sky. Beech trees had been planted round it as a windbreak; their boughs streamed in the wind like the skeleton of a wave. It was the image of desolation, so probably it was this that had caught his fancy. The young love desolation. Positively, he had flushed with pleasure, gazing at his gaunt and draughty Dulcinea.

But as Evan saw this same scene, the trees were heavy with foliage, and nothing stirred them but the occasional flight of a wood-pigeon, tumbling from one bough to another. At their feet were inlets of green moss, hot velvet in the sun, cold as ermine in the shade. Between the tree-trunks, as from a pillared portico, he looked out on the vast composure of a September day: the shorn fields, the ricks in the rickyards like loaves of bread on the baker's counter, the cattle grazing in the green aftermath meadows. He was alone there, with a day of flawless solitude before him, and he had never been there before, or known of it. The place was entirely his. Roofless to the blue sky, the barn was solemn as a cathedral, and so thickly carpeted with leaf mould that young trees were springing up within it. Stepping on a floor of thirty autumns, he had walked round—reading the epitaphs, as one does in a cathedral, but beset by no harrying verger or trailing sightseers; and the epitaphs had not a brag of virtue or regret or achievement among them, but were only names, or initials, or dates, with sometimes a heart, sometimes a phallus and sometimes a Union Jack scored in the chalk blocks of which the barn was built. His feet scuffed up the smell of leaf mould, and from a near-by field came the smell of a newly cut clover crop, steadfast, caressing and sweet as the sea is salt. He had spent the whole day there, a day so freed from time that when he disengaged his bicycle from an elder bush it seemed to him that the twigs had lengthened over the saddle and ripened their berries from red to purple since he leaned the bicycle there on his arrival.

The winter barn was swept out of sight, and with it went wish and motive to go on looking out of the window. Ransomed by remembered pleasure, he settled himself to sit comfortably, and stretched out his long legs. As he did so, he saw the lady hastily withdraw her feet. Catching his eyes, she smiled, and remarked, 'Still unhurt.'

It devolved on him to offer some ensuing politeness, and as she was not dressed as if to enjoy a ham sandwich or Hardy's poems, he asked if she would like the window opened.

She shook her head, and a smell of alembicated summer brushed his nostrils. 'I don't like fresh air unless it's warm.'

Just as the unhurtness of her feet had been presented as a matter of mutual concern, the lady's views on fresh air had a quality of being confidential. If confidences do not repel, they beguile. He said, with morosity, that he was travelling from one blast of fresh air to another, since at home his stepfather was always opening windows and at his school windows were never shut. This remark, too, was no sooner said than he regretted it—by an ill-considered knight's move he had exposed his queen. But the lady ignored home and school alike, and asked him what he had been looking at with such pleasure a few miles back. Out of his reply, it was the smell of the clover field she took up. They talked about scents, about fruits, about summer, about cats, and all the things they spoke about seemed an aspect of the lady, and in praising them he was also praising her.

They made no reference to their fellow-men. Even stories of eccentric aunts, the natural standby of the becoming-acquainted English, they avoided. The instinct that presides over the matings of wild animals and teaches birds the choreography of their courting dances warded them away from any evocation of what might reimprison them in their incompatible realities: a boy going back to school, a woman returning from an interlude of country air and dieting to her stern career of courtesan; the one in terror of his inexperience, the other dreading the first folly of the over-ripe. After a stage in which they devoured every detail of each other's appearance, each had become almost unaware of what the other looked like, as though the nuptial darkness had closed about them. In that darkness they fell silent, lost in a watchful, dreamlike attentiveness to each other's existence.

But with a sigh of responsibility she glanced down at her wrist-watch and knew that there would not be time. If she did not hurry, they would not even kiss, and she was too far gone in passion for hurry and scheming to be anything but a vulgarly exorbitant purchase of something not meant for the market. Buildings darkened the outlook, sheds close on the railway track flashed by, and then others went by more slowly, and the train ran into a station and came to a standstill. From overhead, a voice of inhuman refinement bellowed through an amplifier, 'This is Peasebridge. This is

Peasebridge. Change here for the London train. Change here for the London train. The train for Wittenham, Clewhurst and all stations to Market Beaton is now at Platform Four. Passengers for London will—' Under cover of that voice she gathered together her gloves, her handbag, her wrap of moleskin. 'I must say goodbye. I am so sorry. Will you help me down with my things?'

He helped her to alight, lifted the luggage from the rack, and got out after her, the luggage in either hand, and set it down on the platform. Raising his voice above the amplified voice, and ignoring its information, he shouted, 'Porter! Which platform for the London train?'

'Due in here, sir, soon as this one goes out . . . Thank you, sir. I'll be back when the London train comes in.'

'Well, that's very pleasant and easy,' he said, looking down on her affably. From the moment they were on the platform his whole manner had changed. It seemed almost as though—but it could not be!—he were feeling an immense relief at the prospect of getting rid of her.

'Thank you for getting me that porter. I hate scrambling with my bits and pieces.'

'You won't need to. I shall see to all that.'

'But the London train comes in after yours has gone on. He said so.'

'Yes. But I'm coming to London.'

'That you're not!' she exclaimed, the motherliness and vulgarity of the class she was born into coming suddenly to the surface of her manner. Squaring her shoulders, she looked shorter and almost stout.

'Yes, I am,' he insisted.

'Show me your ticket, then.'

'The ticket is out of date. I've changed my mind, and I am coming with you.'

'I never heard such nonsense. And suppose I don't want you?'

'I'll chance that.'

'A boy of your age—I heard your father seeing you off, to your Eton or Harrow or whichever it is.'

'As it happens, he is not my father.'

'No, no! Your grandson, of course.'

'And I am coming with you.'

'You're doing no such thing.'

Though she knew that every contradiction put them on more of an equality and strengthened his claim to insist, she was too flustered to use her advantage of sophistication. They stood on the platform, wrangling like man and wife.

His train was getting up steam. All along it, doors were shutting, and now only the door from which they had alighted still hung open. The guard slammed it to.

'Guard! Guard! Don't do that! My son hasn't got in yet. He can't miss the train, he's got to go back to his school.'

To obliterate the look of triumph that she knew she must be wearing in his sight, she threw her arms about him. 'Goodbye, my darling!'

Awkward as a schoolboy, he let himself be embraced, he let himself be released, he let himself be jostled into the moving train. His face, as he turned it away, wore the same

44

expression of frozen abhorrence that it had worn when she saw it first.

Horrified at the deed, she asked herself what else she could have done. If he had come with her, what sort of life could he have had? If after a night he had returned, it would have been to all the rows, inquiries and indecencies that the old keep up their sleeves to abase the young with. As it was, he would lick his wound and forget her. Sooner than she would forget him, she told herself, trying to adjust the weight that lay on her heart. The London train was signalled, the porter had reappeared and was looking invidiously at her suitcases—or, rather, at one of them. Large and shabby, it stood out among the rest. It was Evan's; he had set it down among hers, and it had been overlooked.

A Priestess of Delphi

Mary Glasscastle would have stayed quietly in his memory's cold storage if she had not been murdered. Charlton Mackrell almost said to himself 'got herself murdered,' but this would not have been just, and Charlton Mackrell specialized in being just—in seeing both sides of a question, giving the Devil his due, stating the other man's case, allowing that to err is human, and never committing himself to any opinion till he had made quite sure there were no signs of error or prejudice about it. It was by this caution that he had attained such eminence, both as a judge of Shorthorn cattle and as a literary critic. It was this that made his damnations so damning and his approvals so icily divine. A man often spoken of as the nearest thing to Thomas Aquinas since the death of Thomas Aquinas could not allow himself, even privately, to exaggerate or misstate the facts. Mary Glasscastle had been murdered— very brutally, very regrettably, very conspicuously. And the murderer was still at large.

With wrongheaded zeal, the police had arrested a tramp so ignorant of the sumptuary laws of the Church of England that it was not until the case was being tried and the noose hanging over him that the witness to his alibi could be produced in court. The tramp had persisted in saying that on the night of the murder he helped a gentleman to push his car out of a ditch some hundred miles away from where the murder was committed, and that the gentleman wore old-fashioned boots with buttons. The gentleman was, in fact, a gaitered Dean, a humane and scholarly man, who, after inattentively reading about the case in *The Times* and deploring the spread of violence, happened to see the tramp's photograph in a cheap newspaper which the fishmonger was wrapping round a purchase of shrimps for Melusine, the deanery cat. Recognizing the man who had pushed the car, the Dean realized his own part in the story and gave evidence. But the mischief was done; a murderer, an ignoramus, the police and the Dean had amongst them kindled a blaze of sensationalism, and there was not a daily paper that did not rake up the fact that, thirty years before, Mary Glasscastle had been 'a celebrated poetess and a well-known figure in London's Bohemian circles'.

Thirty years before, Charlton Mackrell was also writing poetry and figuring, though obscurely, in those circles. Mary Glasscastle had called him Stiggins, a dreadful Dickensian endearment, but this had not prevented him from becoming her lover—one among many—or from writing her a number of very long letters. He was already through with her, and only writing apologies for overlooking her invitations, when, because of some illness or other, she became stone-deaf. Too vain to be seen wearing a hearing aid, she had gone back to her native Midlands and set up house with an aunt. After the publication of a novel, which Charlton had an opportunity to review and chivalrously didn't, nothing more was heard of her.

Presumably, she and the aunt were badly off. When the murder happened, the aunt was in a public ward of a local hospital recovering from an operation, and Mary was alone in a bungalow called Buttercups, living in a manner that the press described as quiet and that evidence at the trial revealed as squalid. She was eating her supper in the kitchen when she was attacked, and a tin of pilchards was open on the table. Charlton did not know much about pilchards beyond their cultural association with Cornwall, but he knew that by the time they are tinned they are low. Besides eating pilchards, Mary was reading through old letters.

The Shorthorn side of Charlton's character steadied him against this reminder of the past; even if the murderer had stolen those letters to Mary with a project of blackmail, second thoughts would have shown that such blackmail would lead to identification and a death sentence. But a few weeks after the tramp's acquittal, the aunt, Mildred Glasscastle, wrote to *The Times* asking for the loan of any relevant material for a proposed biography of the late Mary Glasscastle. This threw Charlton into a panic. Though he could not remember everything he had written to Mary, there had been enough authorship on his side of the correspondence for a great deal to recur to his mind, and what recurred was deplorable. Not content with praising Mary's bosom, etc.—such praises do not get into commemorative biographies—he had praised her poetry, and the writings of other people who had been about at the time, committing himself to approvals that would be death to his reputation

as an Aquinas, and to enthusiasms—he recalled a headlong approbation of that Blue Horse—that would make it
impossible for him ever again to pronounce on a pedigree
bull. It was the more painful to be thus menaced by the
sins of his youth, because he had not merely grown out of
them, as most of us do; he had turned his back on them.
From the hour when an unforeseen legacy gave him an
income, leisure and a small estate in the country, Charlton
Mackrell had repudiated the shame and frustration of being
an unregarded poet who was liable to be called Stiggins.
His ambition, and a genuine longing to be responsible for
a perfection, had turned him to cattle breeding. He bred
some almost perfect animals; he established himself as an
authority. From there, he had reinserted himself into literature as a critic. He was creditably placed in two worlds.
Now, because Mary Glasscastle had been murdered, he saw
himself being hissed out of both of them.

So there was nothing for it but to be humble and to
be intrepid; he must be humble enough to visit Mildred
Glasscastle, and he must be intrepid enough to get hold of
those letters. As he was still rather afraid of his new car, and
as all the special reporters had concurred in making their
way to Buttercups by a series of stiff climbs and rugged
lanes, he decided to go as far as he could by railway and
then hire a taxi. A taxi, too, being anonymous, was more in
keeping with the simplicity of his errand. To render its simplicity more apparent, perhaps fortuity should be added.
He would not write beforehand; he would simply, quite
simply, arrive. This decided on, Charlton had to exercise

all his self-control to wait till a week had gone by after the letter in *The Times*.

It was a lowering May day, cold as March and flailed by an east wind. Slashes of sunlight gave a false drama to a landscape scabby with old mine-workings, a landscape that seemed bold for no worthier reason than that it was small in scale with sharp contours. Gusts of wind rattled the ill-fitting windows of the taxi. Tossing and swaying, the newly leaved ash trees in the hedgerows looked hysterically green. It seemed a landscape fit for treasons, stratagems and spoils, and, for that matter, murders.

As the taxi turned from bad roads into worse, Charlton tried not to judge Mildred Glasscastle too harshly for continuing to live in a house where a murder had been committed. After all, she must have reasons; empty houses at low rents are hard to find, and yet not so rare that a freehold blood-stained bungalow might not be quite difficult to dispose of—the more so if it were approached by such roads as these, and named Buttercups, and had no telephone. This last concession was prompted by seeing a public telephone booth at a crossroads, the only thing in sight that was not cowering under the onslaught of a violent hailstorm.

A hundred yards further on, the taxi halted, and the driver said, 'It's up the bank. Folk have to walk the rest of the way. I'll wait here.'

Peering through the curtain of hail, Charlton saw a red-brick bungalow at the summit of a precipice.

It had been no part of his intention to arrive breathless from scrambling up a rocky path, muddied to his knees, and as wet as though he had climbed out of a river. Yet it eased the introduction, for Mildred Glasscastle's first attentions were given to his coat, which she hung on a clothes-horse, and his hat, which, she said, she would pop into the bread oven. These kind offices obliged her to turn her back on him, and while it was turned, he tried to compose himself before another inspection of a face so like Mary's that thirty years seemed to have been stripped off him with the coat. Like Mary, Mildred Glasscastle was tall and heroically built. Her yellow hair had the same corn-straw glitter, and she wore it twisted around her head like a helmet, as Mary had done in the twenties. The same round grey eyes, blindly bright, protruded like glass ornaments from the same large, stupidly noble countenance. Only her total lack of sexual bravura differentiated her from Mary and established her as an aunt. The thought exploded in his mind how very hard that unknown man must have worked to kill Mary, how violent and furious the struggle must have been, spattering these very walls with blood; for this, as he realized from the newspaper accounts, was the kitchen where Mary had sat with her letters and her pilchards.

The room was hot and full of white linen that might almost be shrouds. Mildred Glasscastle gathered an armful of linen off a chair, saying, 'Sit down. I've been ironing.' She spoke as though she had known him all her life, and as he sat down he found himself falling into a dream that it was the aunt who had been murdered and now he must condole with a stranger who was also Mary.

'Better take it easy. The wind's about knocked the stuffing out of you,' she remarked.

Momentarily dizzied, he had closed his eyes. When he opened them, it was to see her in profile. He realized that she was not so identically like Mary. Her nose was flatter, and she had a long upper lip. Her clothes, too, were tidy and sturdy, as Mary's could never have been. His heartbeats steadied, the fumes of his hallucination cleared away, and he was left bleakly aware that he was at the beginning of a difficult conversation.

'It is very kind of you to receive me like this,' he began.

'I'd do as much for a dog in this weather,' she said. While he was trying to find the right answer, she added, 'Wouldn't you?'

Had Mary perhaps received her murderer with the same graceless humanity?

Leaping over both questions, he said, 'I must introduce myself, Miss Glasscastle. My name is Charlton Mackrell, and I knew Mary when she lived in London.'

'Did you? Well, I suppose you know what happened to her. It was in all the papers.'

'I read about it. I was deeply shocked.'

'I daresay you were. And they haven't found the man yet. Poor girl, she was killed in this very room.'

'I believe you were in hospital at the time,' he said, endeavouring not to seem as though he had come merely out of an interest in Mary's murder.

'I was. What's that to do with it?'

'I was thinking of the shock to your nerves,' he said.

Hearing the ineptitude of his speech, he added, making it worse, 'It must have retarded your recovery.'

She looked at him, with Mary's grimace of the lower lip sucked to one side, and said nothing.

'You must have remarkable powers of recovery,' he continued, driven into developing some of his own, 'to have set about collecting material for a biography already. But you are quite right. It should be done.'

'Yes. It ought to sell like hot cakes if it comes out while people still remember the trial.'

This vulgarity reclothed him in dignity, and he said, with calm, 'That was not what I had in mind. Your niece was a proper subject for a biography, quite apart from how she met her end. Are you going to write it yourself?'

'I'm writing it now.'

'May I ask if you have found a publisher?'

This was the first question he had come to ask, and if the answer had been propitious, he might not have needed to ask further, for he knew many publishers, and was known as a power by every publisher in London. It was quite likely that if he questioned the need for a life of Mary Glasscastle, they would follow suit. But the answer was not propitious.

'Naturally, I've seen to all that. It's being done by Argus, in Nottingham. They're quite used to publishing. They did a cookery book for the Women's Institute. I've got a proper typist, too.'

'I'm glad to hear that,' he replied. 'So much depends on the typist.'

'That's what the typist says. But do you know the old saying? "It all depends on me. And I depend on God." '

Squirming inwardly, Charlton made the appropriate small guffaw.

They sat on either side of an old-fashioned coal-burning range, and between them his overcoat hung on the clothes-horse and steamed. The temptation to put it on and go away was strong, but something told him that if he were to do so, he might be considerably more uncomfortable in the future than he was now. There was a pause, and this time she broke it.

'And what might you be doing in this part of the world? For you don't look as if you belonged here.'

It was an opening, but he turned away from it, judging that if she knew he had come in search of his letters, she would withhold them. His memory, a well-trained servant, proffered him a name he had seen on a signpost, and he replied, 'Primarily, I'm here because there is a bull I want to look at. When I discovered that Spixworth is only a few miles short of your house, I ventured to come on.'

'A bull? I shouldn't have thought Tom Drury had a bull worth looking at, unless he's bought one to palm off. What sort of bull?'

'I can't tell you, for I haven't seen it. I came here first. When I read your letter in *The Times,* it occurred to me that I might be of some small service to you about this life of Mary. As I told you, I knew her in London, and I also knew many of her friends. I might be able to elucidate passages in the letters, allusions to other writers and so forth. It's important to get these details right. Literary people are absurdly touchy, and our laws about libel are so inviting to anyone with a grievance that you might find yourself with half a dozen law-suits on your hands. I expect your publisher has explained to you about paying damages, and your liability.'

She was hooked, for her hand went towards a large carton near-by; but lightly hooked, for she converted the gesture into taking up the poker and giving the fire several angry prods.

'I gathered that you have a good deal of material already—letters written to your niece by various celebrities,' he said.

'More than enough, if you ask me.'

'Indeed? The mere deciphering of them must be quite an undertaking. Mary used to scold me about my handwriting, but really I wasn't the worst.'

'So you were one of them, were you?'

'Yes, I was one of them.' He spoke almost gaily, feeling now almost gay. Before she could answer, he went on, taking pains to be looking neither at her face nor at the carton, 'If by any chance she kept letters from me—of course, I don't think it at all likely, I was not in the least a celebrity—I would dearly like to read them over.' This was a moment to say something about Auld Lang Syne, but he really could not ask that of himself, so he insinuated it into a sigh.

'I don't see why you shouldn't,' she said. 'What would they be signed?'

Staring at a frightful water-colour, he mastered his reluctance.

'Stiggins.' The east wind seemed to flout him with its hoo-hooing.

'*What* did you say?'

'Stiggins,' he repeated, this time firmly.

'I thought you said your name was some sort of fish.'

'My name is Mackrell—Charlton Mackrell. But Mary called me Stiggins. It was a fashion to use nicknames then.'

She took a notebook out of the carton, opened it at what he saw was a list of names, and ran her slow red finger down the column. 'No Stiggins here,' she said, smiling like a schoolmistress. 'No Mackrell, either. Mary must have thrown you away.'

The shock of relief was so violent that it was as though a mine had been sprung under Charlton's feet. It was, undoubtedly, relief. The strain had gone on for some time, and must have been worse than he realized. It is a commonplace that any sudden relief is unmanning. Of course it was relief, and when he had recovered from the shock of its impact, and from this disabling sensation that he was about to burst into tears, he would know how glad he was, and be thankful that he had nothing worse to trouble him than the slight shame of having got into a fuss about nothing.

His nerves steadied, he was himself again. And instead of feeling relief, he confronted a gaping humiliation. Mary had thrown him away. She had hoarded letters—more than enough, the woman had said, and the list of names down which the red finger had promenaded was a long list—but his were not among them. He had not been thought worth keeping.

'Perhaps you'll be luckier with that bull.' Pleasure at inflicting humiliation made her voice exactly like Mary's. It whipped him back into the former kennel, where he used to sit trembling, a resentful, would-be assertive, half-grown, and not in the least gay young dog. Mary then, and now Mildred.

It was a long time since he had been so rawly in contact with a woman; he was out of practice and had forgotten how intensely disagreeable a woman can be when she is not tamed into her duty of being agreeable. He half rose, for why should he extend the pretext of hoping to be service-able to the biographer? He would take himself off on that other pretext, the Spixworth bull. Even if it had been a real bull—some wretched, ageing barnyard animal, out of con-dition and peering with dull, imprisoned eyes—he would still have found it more tolerable to stand in cold mud with the gale clawing at his overcoat than to sit any longer in a room where one woman had been murdered and another woman was being disagreeable. But she had got his hat in her oven, and somehow he could not abase himself into asking for it. He sat down again, barely able to contain his rage and beyond making any attempt to conceal it. A burst of smoke was driven down the chimney. As it cleared away, he saw her looking at him. Her regard was steady, cool and enlightened. There was a kind of hideous welcome in it, and he knew, as plainly as though she had said it aloud, that he had been revealed to her as Mary's murderer, dragged back, as murderers are, to the place of the crime.

She was probably quite as strong as Mary, and might go off at a touch. The most sensible thing to do—the only thing to do—was to make conversation, and so give her time to settle down in her conviction, if he could not lull her out of it. The conversation must be on some calm, uncontroversial subject, and the less part she took in it, the better. It should, in fact, be a monologue. During the years while he was falling out of practice with women, he had become versed in the technique of lecturing. He lectured on literature, but that would be a dangerous subject just now, so he would lecture on bulls.

That bull at Spixworth, he said—opening with that proved device, a concession to superficial judgments— might not be a good specimen; it might be quite a poor one, but nevertheless he felt he should go and look at it. In the matter of long-term selective breeding, a positive deficiency could always (provided that the deficient beast was pure bred) be made the means of adjusting a better balance in a future animal. These corrective adjustments are best made through the sire, for a defect or a particular excellence in a cow can become quite uncontrollable in that cow's progeny, and therefore he always preferred to work with a cow who was no more than a first-class typical specimen, relying on his choice of the bull to develop and stabilize the traits he had in mind. But it was unlikely that the bull at Spixworth would turn out to be the bull he wanted, for he had reached a stage where he was, so to speak, working to a hair's-breadth of excellence, and it would be nothing out of the way for him to inspect and reject a hundred animals before he could be satisfied. Feed, too, should be dealt with in the same spirit of rigorous selection, and he really had no patience with people who supposed you could build up a first-rate herd on a third-rate soil. At Burton St Laurence, he was fortunate in having a fair amount—say, three hundred acres—of almost faultless pasture, and by keeping a few hives of bees he had much improved his clover hay. Even so, he now bought hay from Berkshire. He had met Charles Tufton at the Bath and West Show in 1950—Tufton was a man whose ideas were usually worth attending to—and Tufton had asked him why Latona, a heifer that Tufton had been much struck by when he visited Burton St Laurence earlier in the season, was not being shown. He had explained that Latona had been kept back because of her eyelashes—there are few things more disembellishing to a cow than scanty, irregular eyelash growth—and Tufton had said at once, 'Give her upland hay,' and recommended a man on the Berkshire downs. He had followed Tufton's advice, and Latona's eyelashes soon became all he could wish. There was certainly something in upland hay. Tufton was an enthusiast for artificial insemination, but there Charlton could not see eye to eye with him. Undeniably, it might raise the general standard, but to raise a general standard was also, in a sense, to lower it. Tufton, too, had at one time a leaning toward electric fencing, but afterwards recanted. For himself, he had kept Burton St Laurence a hedged farm; though it had been necessary to grub up all the original hedges, he had immediately replanted them. Few things afforded him greater pleasure than to stand on some spring morning admiring the sharp green leaves and the masses of white blossom on a hawthorn hedge while hearing his beasts contentedly grazing on the yonder side of it. He was also rather proud of his avenue; he believed it was the only avenue of Turkey oaks in north Wiltshire. The house itself was small, and its garden front had been modernized in 1790. But it suited him very well. A plain English farmer—he did not pretend to be more than that—could not in reason expect the whole of his house to be unspoiled Palladian, and even modern central heating does not resolve the incompatibility of an English climate with the style of the Villa Malcontenta.

Having glided from lecturing about bulls to boasting, having boasted a little longer, and with his literary cards still discreetly up his sleeve, he asked for his hat and took his leave.

She seemed so normally willing to let him go that he allowed himself to remark, 'Perhaps we shall meet again,' to which she replied, 'Perhaps.'

The wind, and the brambles it lashed across his insteps as he made his way down her breakneck path, recalled Charlton to a sense of real life. Even so, the thought that he had been a suspected murderer made him glad to remember that his alibi, if it should get as far as that, depended on more than one frail Dean. Higher dignitaries than Deans had been among the picked, small audience who, together with the representative best of the British Broadcasting Corporation and outer thousands, heard him deliver the first of his lectures on Dante's *Il Convito* at the hour when poor Mary sat eating her pilchards.

He got into the taxi. It was cold and tomblike, but, thanks to Miss Glasscastle's attentions, his overcoat was delightfully warm. As the car gathered speed, he looked back for a last sight of Buttercups and saw Miss Glasscastle running with a swift, sure foot down the precipice. Continuing to watch her through the back window, he saw her enter the telephone booth. But the poor, savage, stupid creature could do him no real harm. At the worst, the hand of the law would only momentarily impede him. She had shot her bolt with those releasing words, 'Mary must have thrown you away.'

Looking steadily at the driver's innocent red ears, he repeated the words (though not so loud that the ears would catch them), for they were words he would have to get used to. Said in his own voice, they ceased to be an insult and became a statement. He was scarcely to be intimidated by a statement. He was always making them; they paved his reputation. Very well, then, let it be a statement: 'Mary must have thrown you away,' he said again, and a tree toppling toward him under the wind seemed to bow its head in assent, like a member of an audience. It was, moreover, an ancillary statement; it described a subsequent action; for he had been the first to throw, discarding Mary, abandoning with resolute relief a career of being negligible and ungainly and a poet only by the pang.

Mary's throwing was no more than a womanly 'You're another.' And yet he felt himself discarded, shrugged off into purposelessness and purposelessly conveyed towards trees that reiterated a gesture of acquiescence. The young man who wrote the letters would have been glad enough of a little acquiescence, a little homage, but he didn't get it; he would never have got it; he was not worth the keeping.

At this present moment, Miss Glasscastle was probably eating a revengeful high tea, and he was going home to Burton St Laurence with the very assurance he had set out to obtain. There were no letters, all his alarms were scotched, and after being briefly incommoded at a railway station he would resume his harmonious twin careers and forget the young man who allowed himself to be called Stiggins. His youth—why should he wish to recall it? And yet how could he not recall it, looking out from his hurrying box at this cold and cruel spring? And why, at this late hour, and without even one letter to revive him (surely she might have spared him one of those many, many letters), must he become aware of how irreparably he had impoverished himself when, in weakness and despair, he had thrown that young man away?

At the Trafalgar Bakery

'Penelope! Pe-*nel*-o-pe!'

For a moment the girl hesitated, arrested on the doorstep, in her hand a small suitcase and before her the suburban street running straight as a rule, straight as her intention, towards the railway station. The habit of biddability proved too strong for her. She went back into the house, put down the suitcase, and entered a room where a middle-aged woman was looking at a half-made dress.

'Yes, Mother?'

'I've been thinking it over. And these buttons definitely won't do. They looked all right on the card, but they are too small. Now, do you remember those barrel-shaped glass buttons I bought at Selfridge's—the ones on my blue taffeta?'

'Barrel-shaped buttons?'

'Barrel-shaped. When I say barrel-shaped, I mean barrel-shaped. When I say Selfridge I mean Selfridge. I want you to go there and buy me two dozen. But I see you don't remember them, and ten to one you'll bring back trouser-buttons, or glove-buttons, or hooks and eyes. So I'll give you one to take as a pattern. I'll just get the dress and cut one off, it won't take a moment.'

'I'll go,' said the girl, and was off in a flash. When she came back, she was panting.

'You look as if you'd run a mile for it,' her mother commented. 'I suppose you're worrying about your train. If you miss it, I don't suppose it will kill you. They go every twenty minutes, don't they? And it's not as if you had any particular appointment, the British Museum won't fly away. Here's the button. Two dozen, remember.'

The girl stared at the button as though she might read her fortune in it.

'And if they haven't got any, look about in some of the other Oxford Street shops. It won't take up much of your valuable time, it isn't as if I were asking you to go to Paris for it. Why are you looking at me so funnily? Is there any-thing wrong with me?'

'Two dozen,' said the girl. 'Goodbye, Mother.'

'Take care of yourself, pet. And bring back that button.'

There was a narrow full-length looking-glass in the hall, strategically placed where Mrs Ludham could take a certify-ing last glance before going out. As the girl picked up the suitcase, she caught sight of herself in the glass. 'Goodbye,' she whispered, pressing her lips to the lips of her reflection. Her clouding breath had not faded from the surface when she shut the door behind her. As the door closed, the whirr of Mrs Ludham's sewing-machine began, it was as though the one noise had set off the other.

Penelope Ludham was twenty-two. For several years she had been going three days a week to London, where, in the manuscript room of the British Museum, she copied illuminated capitals from missals and psalters for a firm of church furnishers who specialized in high-class Christmas stationery. People receiving Penelope's hand-painted cards would remark that they were really quite good enough to frame, and then put them away with a feeling of doing something more later. But to-day she was going to elope with Robin Jones, who worked in the same firm's stained-glass department, and whose wife was too religious ever to divorce him. Penelope was also religious, too religious to go to bed with a man unless she could do it openly and habitually, which would, at any rate in the case of a couple who had fallen in love so deeply as she and Robin, constitute a marriage in the sight of heaven. She was so sure about this that earlier in the morning she had gone fasting to the early service at St Jude's in order to set out in a state of grace. The suitcase was an outward and visible sign of the inward grace, and she had carried it downstairs without a qualm, hearing the sewing-machine and knowing that her mother was only interested in departures that were made in best clothes. But now she began her walk to the station stiffly trembling at the thought of the danger that had lain in wait. If her mother had gone to fetch the blue taffeta dress she could not have failed to notice the suitcase just inside the door. Though this danger had been averted, it still vibrated in Penclope's mind, and seemed to be like an explosion, itself smothered, which could yet fire a train of other dangers. Milk was being delivered at Avondale, and the pony who drew the milk-cart was standing as usual with his forefeet on the pavement, canvassing to have his nose patted. Suppose as she went by he turned suddenly and bit her arm? The elm tree in front of the Memorial

Hall, brooding in its late summer foliage, might drop a limb on her. The Owen girls might come out of Lindenlea, announce that they were off to town and insist on accompanying her. Even the paving-stones lay in wait to do her an injury. They seemed to rise up and thump her feet, so that she was in peril of making a false step and spraining an ankle. All this was but a mild suburban prelude to what London might have up its sleeve. 'I will concentrate on getting to the station,' she thought. 'When that is done, I shall have finished the first stage.' *Ce n'est que le premier pas qui coûte.* The words bobbed into her mind, and immediately she conceived the ridiculous hallucination that she was carrying her decapitated head under one arm, like Saint Denis. 'Why are you looking at me so funnily?' her mother had asked, having equally funnily referred to Paris. Suppose she knew, suppose everybody knew, and all were in a conspiracy to watch her being allowed to go just as far as the station? The suitcase would be opened, the nightgown held up for sarcasm.

Seeing herself being stared at from across the road by old Mr Crutwell, who mended clocks, Penelope became aware that she was grinding her teeth with rage. She gave him an airy friendly wave with the hand which was not holding the suitcase, and hurried on. A minute later she was ravaged by a conviction that she had somehow left the letters behind, and had to stop and look for them in her handbag. They were there, tucked into her passport, the letter to her mother, the letter to her employers. There, too, was the barrel-shaped glass button. Poor Mother would not get the buttons in time to complete the new dress for Mrs Bedford Bowden's canasta party. Instead, she would receive a telegram saying, *Not returning to-night all well love Penelope,* and subsequently, after the letter, a parcel of much more elegant buttons from Paris. Poor Mother, it was a pity she could not be told beforehand in some painless way. She loved excitements, and had so few of them beyond those she contrived for herself out of dress-lengths bought at sales and improvements on the pictures in *Vogue*.

The acid assay of love told Penelope that these reflections on her mother were mere pasteboard in comparison with the vital apprehension of being bitten by the milk-cart pony. She discarded them, and wrestled with a new conviction that she had packed the old bedroom slippers by mistake. She was now near enough to the station for her shortsighted eyes to read the station clock. It showed her that, as she had hoped, she had set her wrist-watch so extravagantly fast that there was ample time for her to catch the train she had intended to catch. Having bought her ticket, she bought a *Times,* in case any acquaintances should get into the same compartment. People do not hesitate to interrupt the reading of a three-halfpenny daily, but they respect *The Times* on which the reader has spent fourpence.

She saw no one she knew, and as the train pulled out a sensation of fearless tranquillity descended on her. Her heart left off thumping, her limbs relaxed, the skin on her face felt limber and released, as though an actual mask had been lifted off it. After a series of reviving yawns (the first was spontaneous, the rest self-indulging) she began to look out of the window. All that she knew so well was duly on parade: the tennis-courts, the Wesleyan chapel, the old pear tree in the builder's yard, the swivelling perspectives of Olga Road and Dagmar Road, the dumpy tower of the parish church, the five poplar trees and the two gas containers. Because she might never see them again, they already partook of the inexpressiveness of something seen in passing. By this time to-morrow, Robin and she would be approaching Paris, having breakfasted in the train. Her hair would be limp and salt-scented after a night spent romantically and economically sitting on deck, and they would have breakfasted ravenously, drinking coffee out of squat lavender-blue cups. Though she had never been to France, this prospect of tomorrow morning was more conceivable than the fact that ten minutes before she had walked down Laburnum Road. After staying for a couple of nights in Paris (there went the rubbish-tip with the pond beside it, fringed with derelict willows, where the girl who escaped from a reformatory had drowned herself), they would go on to that village in the Auvergne where Robin's friends, none of whom would care a snap of the finger whether you were married or no, were making a film. Robin would be doing something technical. She would look on, or sit among autumn crocuses.

The train drew up at a station. Instantly she felt blinded, deafened, intimidated by the harshness of being brought to a halt. When the train went on she wondered why there should be this sudden chill in the air that blew on her from the open window. A sweat of fear had broken out on her forehead. She lit a cigarette and felt sick. How could she possibly recapture that sense of fearless tranquillity, knowing that there would be nine more stops before the terminus, nine more buffeting arrests in the process of being conveyed towards her love? After the fifth stop came the cemetery, the new end first, dabbed with bunches of marigolds and bright asters over the remembered dead, then the older part, interminable, where trees thickened their shade over a density of old-fashioned gravestones, urns and obelisks and broken pillars and altar tombs caged in iron railings. Her eye was caught by a heap of yellow clay. The shade badged it, it looked like a tiger lying among the graves, and was the raw earth banked up where a family pit had been reopened for some delaying grave-fellow. To protect herself against omen-watching, she opened her *Times* and read the leading articles through the remainder of the journey.

'Taxi, Miss?'

This was something she had not expected, for she was not of the taxi class. The porter's voice was cordial, his glance rested on her with approval and confidence, as though he were pleased with his discernment in recognizing her as some one who would not be swallowed up in the underground with the other passengers. Her spirits leaped up: it had not occurred to her to take a taxi, but now she would. The porter conveyed her to the taxi-rank, slammed the door and gave her destination, and it was like a foretaste of how, for the rest of her life, she would have Robin to take care of her. On one of her impulses she leaned from the taxi window to have another look at this proxy Robin. He was already walking away, but she caught his attention and smiled at him. He shouted, 'Cheerio!' encouragingly. For he had got into his head that the poor little thing was going to the dentist, though her teeth, revealed in her easy smile, looked too pretty to hurt. The taxi turned out of the forecourt and was immediately halted by a red light. But this delay, though it cost money and would inevitably be followed by more such delays, did not buffet her nerves as the halts of the train had done. She felt the moment embrace her. Here she was in the heart of London, cocked up in a taxi and on her way to meet Robin. It was all perfectly simple and straightforward, just as Robin had said. The stream of traffic was released, the taxi slipped in front of a van, the road seemed to gain width as the traffic gained speed, and already the six-month load of care was beginning to loosen from off her shoulders. For only now was it beginning to be simple and straightforward. To meet that interesting Mr Jones again, to please him and yet not seem to pursue him, to solace his despondencies, to contain the astounding glory that he might love her, to make sure of him if only to renounce him (by then she knew he was married), to cleave to him only and keep it from everyone else, as it practically said in the marriage service, to apply for a passport, to walk out of Holmeden carrying a suitcase, never to lose her head, or be found weeping, or be seen smiling at private thoughts, or talk in her sleep, or be run over by a bus, and all the time to reflect incessantly on the hazards to which love and the beloved are exposed—though it had been next to nothing in comparison with what she would gladly suffer for Robin's sake, it had been remarkably like walking on the slack rope in very tight shoes. One deserved a taxi ride after all that.

The quality of the light and of the atmosphere changed. The taxi shot forward on to Waterloo Bridge. On either side lay the amplitude and simplicity of water, and the silhouetting of the riverside buildings gave a sudden representation of London as a city and historical. The quality of her thoughts changed to gratitude and a filial tenderness. It was in London that she had first learned how to be solitary and unafraid. And then, London had given her Robin.

Their rendezvous was an establishment called the Trafalgar Bakery, which served morning coffee and afternoon teas in a long narrow room at the back of the shop. Here they had had their first meal together, after a concert at the Festival Hall. It pleased them (they were in a mood to be easily pleased) by being so stuffy and Edwardian, with velvet-covered benches along the walls below speckled mirrors, umbered like the glass walls of a fishmonger's tank; and Robin had commended the inveterate seamindedness of the English, baking to the honour of Nelson within a stone's-throw of the other gentleman's bridge. Often remembering it to praise, they had never happened to go back to it. But sentiment recommended it as a meeting-place, also the fact that it was handy for Waterloo Station, whence they would later take the boat train for Southampton. She walked past the counter and between the looped cotton-velvet curtains into the back room. There was no one there.

There was, however, a clock, and it showed her that between her anxiety not to be late and her decision to cut across in a taxi, she was nearly half an hour earlier than the time they had agreed on. There was no reason to imagine that Robin had changed his mind, and no pressing reason to suppose he had been waylaid by his wife or had met with an accident. To realize this was such a relief that she walked quite steadily to a table at the end of the room, where the suitcase would be in no one's way, and sat down prepared to enjoy an interval of blamelessly remaining in one place. Now, if she had not left her *Times* in the taxi, she could have read not merely leading articles but the Correspondence and the Personal Column without exposing herself to the ominous; for she had done her part, she had brought herself safely to the Trafalgar Bakery, and all she had to do was to wait.

This she could do quite inconspicuously, as the two women in the shop were busy with customers. The shop-door (it had a small old-fashioned bell attached to it) was continually being opened and closed, and as there was still twenty-five minutes before Robin could possibly appear, she need not attend to the bell. A card dangling under the clock informed her that Minerals were Served Here, as well as Morning Coffee and Afternoon Teas. (Why, she had said to Robin, was coffee a solitary drink and tea a community one?—and he had replied that coffee, the kind of coffee served here, was in the category of the sins that are done by one and one, and from that they had somehow alighted on the subject of life-saving dogs and the pictures in their respective nurseries.) Farther down the room was another notice saying Sandwiches Cut. That sounded genial, more genial than Minerals. Yet Minerals had this much to be said for it, Robin had pointed out, it was a good Edwardian term and preferable to Soft Drinks. In France, of course, they would drink wine. Her eyelids had closed while picturing the table under a striped awning at which Robin and she would drink wine; she felt her head jolt forward and discovered that she was about to fall asleep. She would order a Morning Coffee—she was quite accustomed to drinking bad coffee, in fact she almost preferred it; and there was quarter of an hour before Robin could arrive to find her disgracing herself.

The doorbell was still ting-tinging, the shop full of buyers. What a vast amount of bread must be eaten in London. One did not think of these things until something impressed them on one's mind, like the drays loaded with nothing but parsley which she had seen in Covent Garden Market. The patrons of the Trafalgar Bakery must all be regular customers, for the shop was full of conversation, several people had remarked that autumn was in the air already and one forward-looking spirit had added that she was beginning to think of crumpets. Not yet, the contralto behind the counter answered, amending this to Not Quite yet, to soften the blow. Meanwhile, neither shopwoman was paying any attention to Penelope. This was ridiculous. They could scarcely suppose that she had come to the

Trafalgar Bakery in a taxi for no other purpose than to sit hungering at a table with a sugar-bowl on it. She coughed. Her throat was startlingly dry, and it needed resolution to cough again. Neither cough elicited a response. A woman with far too many children of the same age was now asking for doughnuts. The shopwoman answered that doughnuts were sold out. 'They're gawn,' said the mother to the children in a voice so inertly despairing that the second woman behind the counter, who was a soprano, exclaimed righteously, 'You shouldn't have come so late if it's doughnuts you wanted.' Too late for doughnuts, it was high time to get that coffee. Her wrist-watch was hysterically too fast to be worth consulting, and she would not look at the clock just now, for it is petty to be forever looking at a clock; but if she were to get coffee before Robin arrived (and now she wanted it desperately because of the dryness in her throat), she must assert herself.

She got up and walked towards the archway. 'Coffee, please. A coffee for one.'

The soprano behind the counter, in the same putting-down voice she had used to the mother of too many children, inquired, 'Take it with milk?'

Milk gives one stamina. Penelope agreed that she took her coffee with milk. Turning back, she could not evade the clock's statement that Robin was now over ten minutes late.

Seated once more, and concentrating her patience on the non-appearance of the coffee, she noticed for the first time that she was not alone. On the bench opposite there was a cat. It was a large cat, a tabby, and it lay curled in a boss with its nose in its flank. The curve of the boss globed and flattened with the cat's regular breathing. It was asleep.

Nevertheless, she said in an undertone, 'Puss! Pretty puss!'

Like a frond of weed in the depth of ocean, an ear stirred, but the cat did not wake. She continued to look at it in silence, and the cat deepened the profundity of its slumber, as though the intensity of her gaze were pushing against it like a tide, and it knew this and resented it, and was subconsciously resolved against waking. At last she crossed the narrow room and sat down beside the cat. Still it did not move. She sat as motionless beside it. A little later the contralto brought a cup of coffee on a tray, with a plate of biscuits. Seeing the cat, she said, 'Shoo, Monty!' Her voice was tolerant, it was obvious that she was merely complying with a professional convention.

'Please don't! I like him here.'

Penelope's controlled tones were so utterly without tolerance that the shopwoman gave a start of surprise. Looking more carefully at this customer, she said assuagingly, 'We call him Monty because he was got for the rats. Not that he goes after them, for he don't. It's cake he likes.'

'What sort of cake?'

'Anything so long as it's rich, any sort of wedding-cake mixture. As for a simnel, he'd give his whiskers—' She would have gone on, for she could see the poor girl needed distracting from whatever was biting her, but at that moment the soprano called out, 'Mrs Barry. Shop!' So after moving forward the sugar-bowl, she went away. Penelope sighed with relief.

At the end of the room was the suitcase, coyly peeping out from under a tablecloth. On the table in front of her was the coffee, steaming. In the opposite mirror, this way and that reflected, was a girl waiting. The cat, whose tenure had been defended, now, being a cat, got up, and considered going elsewhere; but on second thoughts it lay down again with its back against her thigh. How haggard I look, she thought. How haggard, and how harsh! Though she continued to stare towards her reflection, she was too far lost in the maze of endurance to notice when the reflected countenance softened. The cat, lying against her thigh, had begun to impart its warmth to her and to receive hers in exchange. A process of communication had been set up between them.

A man's tread in the shop recalled her to the actual. She noticed that the coffee was no longer steaming. Her glance slanted round to the cat and dwelt with a copyist's attention on the pattern of its tabby markings. Presently, her forefinger began to inscribe on the air the scrolled stripes of the central ebony that tapered down over a maplewood gold which, as it rounded the curve of the belly, became a pure sulphur yellow. On the haunch was a design like the eye on the wing of a peacock butterfly. It was hither that her finger was drawn and descended into the thick fur. Her hand bedded itself in repose, and presently she began to stroke the cat with a regular impersonal pressure, meeting and remeeting the variations of texture which corresponded, like changes of vegetation on the globe, with the different colours of its coat. The darkest fur was also the sleekest, the maplewood gold was softer and more airy, and where the peacock eye of the haunch included a half-circle of drab, the texture changed to a feral roughness and crudity. Her hand did not venture so far as the sulphur yellow of the belly, but she knew that to do this would carry her into yet another zone, an innocent and youthful fur which was almost fluff.

Quite suddenly the cat transcended a passive pleasure and rose to its feet beside her, arching its back and rubbing its head against her sleeve. Where its warmth forsook her thigh, she felt a physical desolation that corroborated the desolation of her thoughts. She looked at the clock and the cat went on rubbing itself against her and kneading the velvet of the bench. She felt incompetent to deal with such ecstasy, but she continued to stroke it and presently she began to praise it.

'Lovely Monty! Lovely glorious Monty!'

It was that it wanted. It wanted to be talked to. It climbed on to her lap and sat erect, purring, and gazing at her with brilliant golden eyes, proudly tranquil like a hawk on the falconer's wrist.

'Oh, my kind cat!'

For it was kindness she needed. Robin was nearly an hour late, and she had plumbed to below the false agonies of thinking him faithless, or dead, and now only acknowledged that it was perfectly to be expected that he should keep her waiting, since that was the kind of young man he was.

She would wait, and in his own good time he would arrive. She had pinned her life on him, and henceforward her life must include these intervals, like the drab-coloured parts of Monty's coat, of neglect and negligibility. Meanwhile she went on talking to Monty.

'Such a kind cat, such a wise cat! What would I have done without you? But you were here.'

Leaning forward, she said, 'I see how it is. You are really my bridesmaid. I didn't expect to have one, and at first you were not sure of it either, because I didn't look the part. You are quite right. It is much more comfortable to have the sort of wedding that has bells and a wedding-cake, as dark and rich as you are, my darling. Unfortunately, I haven't managed that. I'm not at all a good manager, and heaven only knows what will become of me. But whatever happens, I shall always be able to think that I had a bridesmaid. Or would you rather be a page? No, you are too dignified for that. A bridesmaid, a bride's-cat. All dressed in velvet, my beautiful one, and wearing white gloves and black velvet boots. And when I set out this morning, so long ago, I thought I should have no one to stand by me, no one at all.'

The cat was asleep again, lying warm on her knees, when Robin came in. Her face had achieved a look of childish abstraction and repose, and the thought sparked in his mind, Now I shall often see her like that. The cat sat up, she looked round. But he was too intent on her to see that her brief beauty had vanished.

'Have I kept you waiting? Have you been thinking me a brute?'

'I knew there was plenty of time, so I didn't worry.'

'Plenty of time? That's all you know about it. Where are your traps, darling? Haven't you brought any?'

'There's my case, under that table.'

'Good,' he said, picking it up. 'Now we'll be off.'

'But I must pay for my coffee.'

'I'll see to that. Come on, the taxi's waiting, there's no time to lose.'

'But the train doesn't start till—'

'We're not going by train.'

She had risen, but she sat down again, clutching her heart.

'Not going?'

'No, I've changed all that. We're flying. I've rung up the hotel, everything's perfect, and to-night you'll go to bed in Paris.'

He leaned forward across the table. Unsmiling, with shaking hands, he straightened her hat.

'To-night, Penelope! How could I go on waiting?'

Swept on by her destiny, she was half-way to the airport before she remembered that she had meant to buy Monty a slice of cake. She had not done it, she had not even said goodbye.

Shadwell

At Hyde Park Corner, Robert Laidlaw halted his taxi, telling the driver that he had changed his mind and would walk the rest of the way. 'Don't trouble about the change,' he added.

'Thank you, sir! *And* I don't blame you. It's a wonderful afternoon, we shan't see many more like it, this year.'

To bestow such an ample tip, and to be assured that the taxi-driver did not blame him, gave Mr Laidlaw's self-respect a fillip which just then it badly needed; for he was bound on a painful errand. That was why he had decided to walk the rest of the way through the park. Not because walking would postpone the moment of climactic painfulness—he was only too anxious to get it over; but he hoped that by immersing himself in the serenity of the autumn afternoon he might achieve a corresponding peace of mind, and a larger outlook on the disagreeable. It was late October. The trees had already shed most of their leaves, which were quietly consuming in bonfires. Those which remained hung motionless, their colours burning against the deep blue of the sky. All the shabbiness of late summer was gone. The grass had renewed its green, the plane trees had stripped off their sooty bark, the picnicking parties contained no inelegant nudes or panting dogs. It was as though summer, after a purgatory of equinoctial rain and gales, had come back ensainted. And despite the taxi-driver's Cockey mistrust of good fortune, there seemed no reason why this spell of Indian summer should not continue for some while yet. For in autumn there is a steadfastness lacking in the other seasons. Autumn is an apple, it is a keeping fruit. The park-keepers thought so, at any rate, for they had brought out the canvas chairs again.

He would have liked to repose his mind on the chairs, but the current of his thoughts swept on, allowing him no dalliance with distractions. Mrs Probus had also been a keeping fruit, persisting in a timeless suspension of old age, gently shrewd, sub-acidly kindly. Early that morning she had died in her sleep, the death that with an unimpassioned confidence she had proposed for herself. As her lawyer and exccutor, he had been rung up with the news by Shadwell, her servant. After an interval of grief and recollection— quite apart from her wealth and her hospitality, he had been attached to the old lady—he told his clerk to bring him Mrs Probus's will. And now it was too late to do anything about it. Unchangeably, unanswerably, Mrs Probus had left her ageing trusty servant an annuity of £52 *per annum.*

He was more than half-way across the park, and the noise of traffic along the Bayswater Road swelled in his ears. As though it were a challenge to which he must retort, he said aloud, 'But what could I have done about it?' He had not drawn up the will. That had been done, nineteen years earlier, by his Uncle James. At his uncle's death he had inherited Mrs Probus, and the remains of their long friendship, and had been appointed executor in his stead.

At the same time he had inherited many other executor-ships and trusteeships, for Laidlaw, Larpent and Laidlaw was an essentially testamentary firm. Mrs Probus's will was one among dozens of documents thus refurbished, and no doubt he had read it through, since that was part of the routine. It was no part of the routine to query or suggest, the obligation of an executor is but to execute. In fact, he was already going outside his obligation in the matter by walking across the Park to break the news to poor old Shadwell.

Even in 1934, a pound a week was less than Shadwell's due. Now, it was a mockery. One could not keep a cat on it. At the time when the will was made, Mrs Probus was newly a rich widow, and as such she would naturally consider herself on the verge of starvation. But there had been time to revise that opinion since, and though she had continued to live luxuriously secluded from the life around her ('As far as I am concerned, Mr Laidlaw, there has not *been* a coloratura singer since Tetrazzini. If you want to listen to little English-squeaking kittens, you must go without me. Leave the old woman to her mem-ories, you know.' 'Flying-bombs, Robert? I have forbidden Shadwell to go out, in case she should be killed and I left. I really don't see what more I can do about them'), she had remained sufficiently cognizant of the changes taking place to give up her house and servants and move into a small flat which Shadwell could run single-handed. She was capable of that much revision, and if the rise in the cost of living had been tactfully pressed home . . . There should be a law compelling people of property to bring their wills up to date every five years.

He was now out of the park, and a bus went by him with disgusting speed, as though enforcing the fact that this is a rough world, woe to the vanquished! No doubt wills more unjust, more ungrateful, were made every day, and Shadwell not the only old woman, rendered semi-imbecile by devoted service, to be thrown into the gutter. But they were not this particular will, and did not oblige him to go on this painful errand. Callous, or careless, which? Summarized in *The Times* (for Mrs Probus's fortune was of the dimensions to be summarized in *The Times),* the will would present a rather noble Ancient Roman appearance. Five thousand pounds to a family in Belgium, whose parents had befriended her son, killed during the First World War; to him, her portrait by Wilson Steer, and to his co-executor, a diamond ring; and the rest to be divided between the National Trust and the National Portrait Gallery, subject to an annuity to her servant, Bertha Shadwell. If the amount of the annuity were not disclosed (and he was in honour bound to see what he could do about that), it would seem an exemplary will. But the amount of the annuity must be disclosed to the annuitant, and in less than five minutes he would be doing it. He had no option, the co-executor of the diamong ring being engaged in archaeological research in Sicily, confound her!

The block of flats rose up before him, dowdily sumptu-ous. 'Twenty years younger than I,' Mrs Probus remarked, when he had incautiously commented on the marbleness of its halls. He entered, and the smell of steam-heating and brass-polish obliterated any sense of the autumn afternoon. The porter got into the lift with him (it was that kind of lift), saying, as he pressed the button, 'A wonderful old lady, sir. A great loss.' He agreed, and the lift was stopped at the third floor with a condoling smoothness and exactitude. He got out, the doors clanged to behind him, the lift went down into its pit unblamed. There he was, on the same level of air as Shadwell and only four doors away. 21, 22, 23, 24. He rang the bell.

Shadwell opened the door, looking just as usual, rubbed unobtrusive as stones are rubbed smooth. She wore her afternoon uniform of black serge, and a short black apron, a form of vestment denoting superior servitude. Her eyes, which that morning had looked on death, retained their shallow brightness, her anteroom appearance was unchanged, her air of being a preliminary to Mrs Probus. So she still considered herself, for her words were, 'You would wish to see Mrs Probus, sir,'—and she preceded him to a door, and opened it, standing back for him to enter. But it was a different door.

Death is a leveller. Irene Probus, lying wrapped in fine linen on her Louis Seize bed, looked like an old peasant woman, or, even more, like a masterpiece of peasant art, as though some village craftsman, with only the truth to guide him, had carved her, with every wrinkle, every blemish of age, and the overall plain statement of death, superlatively rendered in some smooth yellowish wood. This is equal to anything by Epstein, he thought, scarcely able to restrain himself from exclaiming in delighted admiration at the way the heavy wrinkles of the cheek enfolded the plane of the cheekbone and threw into relief the pure sailing arch of the aquiline nose.

'I hope you approve, sir. Mrs Probus did not wish anyone but me to touch her.'

He turned to Shadwell, saying, 'Did *you* do it?' And it was as though he had turned away from the imperious vitality of the work of art to the inadequacy of real life, for Shadwell seemed extinguished, a shabby and negligible dummy, not very firm on its legs. 'It is beautiful, it could not be done better,' he added. She replied, 'I am glad you approve, sir. And I am glad that someone has come to see her.'

It was inevitable, his errand being what it was, that Shadwell should wring his heart, but he could not have foreseen this particular pathos of the neglected artist. He said, before any more assaults could be made on his feelings, 'Shadwell, we must talk a little business.'

With her trained sense of what was befitting, she showed him into the dining-room, and pulled forward a chair.

'Sit down, Shadwell. The business is this. As you know, I am one of Mrs Probus's executors. The other is Miss Grainger, but she is in Italy, so for the present I shall do all that needs to be done. This morning I looked over Mrs Probus's will, which is in our office. I found that she has left you an annuity. "To Bertha Shadwell, if still in my service at the time of my death, an annuity of fifty-two pounds *per annum*"—in other words, for the rest of your life you will have an income of a pound a week.'

'Thank you, sir.'

Preparing himself for what he had to say, he had taken into account what he might have to say next, and how best to reply to shock, to wounded feelings, to resentment, to fear of the future. To this, he could find no answer. Yet he lifted his gaze—it had been resting on Shadwell's long, flat, neatly shod feet—and looked at her searchingly. Perhaps there had been irony in that reply. A woman who could lay out a corpse with such majestic insight must be an artist, and as such, capable of irony, scorching irony. Gladly would he have been scorched. A sprinkle of unmerited suffering would have been positively welcome to him. But the hope was vain. Realizing that he had come on purpose to tell her of the annuity, she was thanking him for his trouble.

'Have you any plans, Shadwell?'

'No, sir, I have no plans yet.'

'Then I hope you will be able to stay on here for the next week or so, at any rate until Miss Grainger has come back and seen to the disposal of Mrs Probus's clothes, and so forth. The executors will pay your wages and your expenses. What are your wages, by the way?'

'A pound a week, sir.'

His last sneaking defence, that Shadwell must have salted away some useful savings, went down. He got up from Mrs Probus's table, where he had enjoyed so many *tête-à-tête* dallyings from clear soup to port, and said, gobbling his words a little, 'Well, well, now of course you will be on board wages. They are always rather higher. You will be paid ten pounds a week.'

'It's too much, Mr Laidlaw. I wouldn't take it.'

Feeling as though he were a fishmonger who had asked Shadwell to pay ten shillings for a lemon sole, he climbed down.

'Seven pounds then. A pound a day. You'll need it. Now, Shadwell, don't argue with me. I won't hear another word from you.'

He heard his imperfect imitation of the imperious familiarity with which Shadwell's mistress had been wont to utter such words. Possibly Shadwell heard it too. Her face flickeringly escaped from its respectful composure, and she replied, obliquely quitting the contest, 'May I make you a cup of tea, sir?'

'No, thank you, no, thank you! I must get back to the office. By the way, the valuers for probate will probably come to-morrow. I will let you know when to expect them.'

'Thank you, sir.' She showed him out, and rang the lift bell for him. By the mercy of God, the lift ascended immediately, he was out of the worst of his agony and could go away, with only the painfulness of a painful mission done. As he emerged from the seasonless opulence of the hall, the plenitude and calm of the autumnal dusk overwhelmed him, for he was obliged to compare it with the prospect of Shadwell's wintry decline. He stooped his head, as if under a reproach, and hurried towards the nearest Underground.

Returning to the dining-room, Shadwell straightened the two chairs and removed a few withering blossoms from a potted begonia. These she took off to the trash-bin in the kitchen. Dropping them in, and hearing the lid fall-to with its usual tinny exclamation, she put by her thoughts for the moment, and began looking briskly into canisters, ascertaining what stores would last out for Mr Laidlaw's next week or so, and which would need replenishing. This roused the old canary. He searched himself for lice, and then broke into an abrupt flourish of song. There was a black bow tied to his cage. He had been Mrs Probus's canary until age harshened his coloratura, when he was retired to the kitchen. It was not too harsh for Shadwell. She listened admiringly till he grew tired and gave over. Now there were only the clocks to listen to. The clock on the kitchen dresser rattled on at a cheap gait, and was counterpointed by the soft whirr-whirr, whirr-whirr, of the French clock in the dining-room. From the street below, the noise of traffic rose up like steam from a cauldron. She laid out a cup and saucer, and clasped a spoonful of tea in the infuser, and put on the kettle. Then she left the kitchen and went into the bedroom, her feet suddenly noiseless on the thick carpet, so that she entered like a ghost.

At the foot of the bed, she paused, and looked appraisingly at the brief masterpiece that in a few hours would be hidden in a coffin. 'He didn't think to bring any flowers,' she said to herself, and shook her head disapprovingly. Old Mr Laidlaw would not have omitted that due courtesy. Her bunch of white carnations, bought that morning, was all that Mrs Probus had. But so it had to be.

From the foot of the bed she went with her ghost's footfall to the dressing-table, massive and ornate as a shrine. Pulling out a drawer, she pressed a hidden spring. The looking-glass slid aside, and disclosed the doors of a little cabinet, which in their turn opened at the twirling of an ivory pillar. There were the jewels, the rings, the brooches, the bracelets. She knew them as well as she knew the contents of her kitchen drawer. She had always taken care of them, cleaning them once a fortnight with jewellers' rouge and putting them back in their velvet lair. Now she took them out for the last time, holding them to the light, watching the coloured flashes leap from the diamonds, feeling the sharp facets of the emeralds and the faint greasiness of the rubies. But they did not tempt her. She examined them only for the pleasure of admiring them, and for a sentimentality of farewell. She laid them back, one by one, and took out the thing she had in mind, a long gold chain on which, at wide intervals, diamonds were set like dewdrops. It was an ornament that Mrs Probus had not worn during her memory; but like the rest, it had been cleaned every fortnight, and once, years ago, while she was polishing it, Mrs Probus had glanced at it, calling it by some foreign name, and saying that it was an old-fashioned thing, which she would never wear again, and really ought to sell; for the stones, though not large, were of a fine water, and Meux would certainly give a thousand for it. Sold one by one—and it would not be difficult to tweak them out of their light claw setting—they would not bring so much, Shadwell supposed; for part of the beauty of the ornament was the exact matching of gem to gem. But by taking a diamond from time to time, sometimes here, sometimes there, and sheltering in her indelible appearance of respectability, she would be able to dispose of them with very little risk. Even if she had been sure of selling one of the more valuable pieces without being detected, she would not have done so. She wanted no more than her due—enough to ensure that she would end her days still retaining her independence and self-respect. As it had not been granted, she had taken it.

She closed the cabinet, pressed the spring. The looking-glass slid into place, offering her the image of her narrow bust and dull, dutiful face, and behind her, the bed, and Mrs Probus lying on it—her hands, with no ornament but the gold wedding-ring, folded under the single bunch of white carnations. Reflecting again, with censure, on Mr Laidlaw's omission—what could he have been thinking of to forget the flowers? He brought them regular enough while Mrs Probus was alive—Shadwell walked over to the bedside and, after consideration, slightly adjusted one of the carnations. Then she went back to the kitchen, where the kettle was now boiling, and made herself a cup of tea.

Under New Management

When the young man at the Peacock Hotel was charged with murder, the townspeople of Dunwater expressed a moderate surprise. They would not, they said, have thought it of him—a convention of speech, since few of us really entertain such uncomfortable speculations. There was one person who might have raised a dissentient voice and said that it was very much what she thought of him. But when her cue came, an accident had silenced her, and the only invocation of her hypothetical testimony came from the accused man, who asked his lawyer whether that Miss St John would be called as a witness. The lawyer shook his head. 'Was the old lady a friend of yours?' he asked. 'Friend? *Friend?* If it hadn't been for her driving me crazy— Well, anyway, I wish to God I'd never set eyes on her!' 'You won't again,' said the lawyer. 'She's dead.' 'Dead!' said the accused man incredulously. 'Do you mean it? Dead? Christ, what a swindle!' He burst into furious laughter, and the lawyer averted his eyes from a client he already deplored.

Since 1936 Miss St John had lived at the Peacock Hotel, occupying bedroom number five on the second floor and, between 8.30 and 8.50 a.m., the second-floor bathroom, eating breakfast, lunch, tea and dinner, going to the Abbey Church on Sundays, the cinema on Tuesdays and Fridays, and the Public Library whenever she wanted another biography. The biographies she preferred were those of diplomats, sovereigns, bishops, generals, royal academicians and approved educationalists. Herself leading a regular life, she liked to read of regular lives—lives of well-conducted prosperity closing in well-attended funerals. In autumn, however, when swallows migrate to Africa and the more delicate public shrubs are wrapped in sacking, she allowed herself to read the lives of opera singers and royal favourites. Such a change was in keeping with the seasonal change from cress sandwiches to buttered crumpets.

In all these years Miss St John had made no friends, and only necessary acquaintances—such as shopkeepers and the public librarian. Other visitors at the Peacock she ignored, unless they disturbed her, when she put them down. They were Transients. She was a Permanent. In 1941 inferior Permanents appeared, people who wished to get away from air-raids or had lost their homes. They took up the attention of the management and seduced the servants with ostentatious tips (Miss St John could only afford modest tips, though she made up for this by taking an interest in those who served her, remembering to ask after their parents and to wish, if their afternoons out were wet ones, that they had been dry ones). But foreseeing that Britain would win the war—how could it be otherwise?—Miss St John also foresaw that these people would ultimately go away and that everything would proceed as before.

1946 showed how right she had been. The last bogus Permanents had left, the war was won, Mussolini had been hanged head-downward by the mob, Hitler had killed himself, atomic bombs had obliterated Hiroshima and Nagasaki, and Miss St John remained at the Peacock with some new biographies to look forward to. Biographies are a fruit of war. The only thing she had not foreseen was a change of management. The Potters were leaving. The new people would take over at the Michaelmas quarter, and were called Fry.

Miss St John had never known what it is to be a slave. Britons never do. She was therefore unaware that her feelings at this piece of news were slavish. She told herself that it was grossly inconsiderate of the Potters, and that the Frys would certainly be a change for the worse. Once or twice she varied the assessment by hoping that the Frys might be a change for the better. The hope was quite as slavish as the dread. Both sprang from the unadmitted realization that she was being handed from one ownership to another, and could have no say in it. Yet when Mr Potter begged to introduce Mr Fry, Miss St John was curtly condescending to her new owner, and opined that the Fry fellow would now realize her value as a Permanent of long standing, even if he had not been made aware of it already.

The Fry fellow was a large pale man with heavy eyelids and a low slow utterance. When he referred to his wife he did so with a particular husbandly smile, as if to admit she was a weakness. Mrs Fry was of the type known as bright. She walked briskly, she smiled often, her head was always bound up in a bright-patterned scarf, and from under the scarf jutted two careful tinted curls whose position never varied by a hair's-breadth from day to day. There was a Dennis Fry, too: an only child, who would shortly be demobilized from the Air Force. Both Frys talked of him constantly, and exhibited photographs. It was plain they doted. Miss St John allowed this to be natural. She herself had been an only child and doted on, once.

Assured that the Frys were, to all intents and purposes, Potters, Miss St John went on being as Permanent as before: snubbing the Transients, occupying the best chair in the lounge, and frowning at anyone who smoked a pipe in that apartment. Cigarettes she had no objection to; she sometimes smoked one herself. So when she returned from a Friday cinema to find a young man sitting in her chair and smoking a pipe, she settled herself on an inferior chair with a kind of bellicose placidity, sure that she would soon cook his goose.

Betty, the waitress, coming in with Miss St John's tea-tray, saw the position, and hesitated.

'Put it down by my usual chair, Betty. Thank you. That will do.'

Betty removed a tobacco-pouch to the mantelshelf, put down the tray, and went out. The tea-tray sat on the usual table. Miss St John sat on an unusual chair. This state of things had gone on for some time when the young man put down his picture paper, smiled at Miss St John, and remarked, 'I say. Won't your tea get cold?'

'As it is not in the nature of tea to remain hot indefinitely, I should suppose it has already done so,' replied Miss St John. There was a pause, during which the young man knocked out his pipe and began to search through his pockets, rolling from side to side of the deep chair. When he had abandoned the search, Miss St John remarked, 'It's on the mantelshelf.'

He rose to get it, and sat down again.

'I hope it won't spoil your tea if I smoke?'

'You may in course of time observe that I am not taking tea.'

'I wonder whose tea it is, then.'

'Mine.'

He stared at her. At length, with the most brilliant of his smiles, he got up.

'I say—I'm so sorry and all that. I'm afraid I have been keeping you off your perch.'

'You have been sitting in my chair,' she said, and sat down in it.

The chair was unpleasantly warm. The tea, on the other hand, was unpleasantly cold. The young man, standing with his back to the fire, looked down on her, and whistled under his breath. Even if the toasted bun had remained hot, it would have been impossible to enjoy it. Miss St John left it half-eaten, and took a slice of cake. The cake was stale, and so dry that she could hardly swallow it. It seemed to be moving about her mouth like a sandstorm. She gulped it down. A crumb lodged in her windpipe. Angrily and secretively, she began to choke. The young man thumped her on the back. At last, searing as a clinker, the crumb shot up again.

'Well, now we ought to be friends for life, Miss St John,' he said. Raising her flushed face, she glared at him through

involuntary tears. Even more intolerable than facetious-
ness from a Transient was the fact that this Transient had
somehow possessed himself of her name. 'You *are* Miss St
John, aren't you? I'm Dennis.'

She said 'Oh,' and added, 'Indeed,' and picked up a biography. Soon after he had taken himself off, in came Mrs
Fry, who collected the tea-tray, hemmed once or twice, and
said, 'I really must apologize for our Dennis being in your
chair when you came in. I'm sure the poor boy was ever so
sorry. But perhaps it was a bit of luck, all the same. Suppose
you had been alone when you happened to choke!'

Miss St John was of the opinion that if she had been alone
she would not have choked. 'The cake was stale,' she said.

'Anything can happen with a choking-fit. But I do hope
Dennis didn't hit you too hard. He's strong. He doesn't
realize how strong he is.'

Miss St John said briefly that Dennis had not hurt her
in the slightest, and resumed the biography. She had had
quite enough of Dennis and his strength. Shrug as she
might, she could not shrug off the sensation of his masterful unembarrassed hand. That evening she sat up later than
usual, turning page after page of a deceased headmaster of
Eton with a deliberate consciousness of peace and quiet. It
was almost midnight when she left the room. That odious
young man was still dawdling at the foot of the stairs.
He stood back for her to pass, but she remained in the
doorway, adjusting a book-mark in the headmaster, until
he was forced to precede her up the stairs, with no more
than a 'Goodnight, Miss St John.' Even this was enough

to recall the sensation on her back. Glancing up, rather against her will, she sought and found a glimpse of his large pink palm.

'And that's all the thanks I get,' he said to himself. Really, he did not wish for thanks. He had a disagreeable impression that in some way he had compromised himself by relieving Miss St John of her crumb. The act, no larger than the crumb, stuck in his gizzard. Perhaps it symbolized too plainly his return to civilian life—the come-down, from loosing death, yourself in danger of extinction, on a hundred people all glitteringly unknown, to being obliging to old hags who would be better dead anyhow.

Yet he continued to be obliging. Obligingness was enforced on him by his appearance. His curls were the genuine gold his mother's pretended to be. His smiles were as frequent as hers, but naturally much fresher, since there had not been so many of them. He obliged as nimbly as Ganymede, a militarized Ganymede with a toothbrush moustache.

When a similar moustache, but occupying at least ten foot of the screen, was presented to Miss St John's gaze on the following Tuesday, it quite broke up her usual calm conviction that she was enjoying herself at the cinema. Normally, Miss St John's afternoons at the cinema did not involve her in feelings of participation. Love-stories and crime-stories passed indifferently before her eyes. She was not interested in love, or in crime. What she looked for on the screen was continuity, one thing happening after another, as in the biographies, and, as in the biographies, handsome backgrounds with expanses of marble, or table-damask, or the Pacific ocean. But from the moment of apprehending a moustache like Dennis's, Miss St John's attention was engaged. Whether it lowered for a kiss, twitched in anger, was halted in a close-up or darted about no larger than a hornet among cactus-groves and religious processions, she watched it and watched nothing else. On her way out she saw Dennis also leaving the cinema. She hastened on, to make sure, at least, of her rightful chair; for it seemed to her inevitable that her tea would be spoilt by Dennis's company, and that he would try to talk to her about the film. 'I shall say it was a bad one,' she said to herself.

But no one came into the lounge except a wretched woman with a cold in her head. A few glances, a raising of the eyebrows whenever she sneezed, was enough to keep her well away from the fireside. After a leisurely tea Miss St John lit one of her infrequent cigarettes. The chair was deep, and dry logs crackled in the grate, contrasting pleasantly with the patter of rain against the window. Even the gasps and snuffles of the woman with a cold became tolerable. To their accompaniment Miss St John reflected on the advantages of Permanence. She had been prepared to say a few words to Mrs Fry about that boy of hers hanging about in the lounge. But no words had been necessary. Mrs Fry could take a hint. The cake, too, had been fresh. Miss St John opened her book. Just now it was a royal favourite. Coming on the photograph of a general, his moustache seemed to her no more than a detail of military discipline.

A Fry Christmas turned out to be so much richer than a Potter Christmas that Miss St John, exhibiting the seasonal goodwill, almost felt it, too, and mingled with hollyish sprightliness among the Christmas visitors. Mrs Fry certainly talked too much: 'Our Dennis's first Christmas in Civvy Street,' but as her doting expressed itself in a chestnut stuffing for the turkey, Miss St John allowed that the young man had his uses. After Christmas, no doubt, he would go away.

After Christmas he did not go away. Commenting on this to Betty, Miss St John learned that Dennis was remaining at the Peacock in order to study the trade under his father's guidance.

The shock she felt at this piece of news was in itself disquieting. To dislike a person because you choose to is one thing—because you have to, quite another. The compulsion to dislike Dennis began to menace Miss St John's peace and quiet. His features again began to seep through the films and the biographies, and he completely spoiled an otherwise most promising life of a Balkan sovereign. Rather than allow herself to be put upon like this, she would move to one of the other hotels in the town. Then the long frost of 1947 set in, and immobilized any such project. It grew colder and colder. People talked of nothing but the cold, and the radio prated of fuel economy and crisis. Miss St John postponed her walk to the Public Library and spun out an Edwardian bishop, reading every word of his correspondence on such subjects as Disestablishment, the Licensing Laws, and the Doctrine of the Atonement, as scrupulously as though they were letters to his wife about dining-room carpets. Just as she decided she could suck his bones no further, it began to snow.

A dusky pallor brimmed up every room. No sound came from the wadded streets. It was as though one were a corpse, and lay under a white sheet amid a respectful silence. Traffic was at a standstill, no Transients broke the long silences of the lounge, the weather forecasts on the radio liturgically reaffirmed that the cold weather was likely to continue. If it had not been for Dennis, Miss St John would have read her Bible (she had, of course, a Bible). But Dennis strolled in and out of the lounge as boldly as an undertaker, and somehow she did not wish him to find her reading the Bible. She had just embarked on a fourth voyage through the bishop when Dennis entered on a pretext of making up the fire.

'Still reading, Miss St John? You read a lot, don't you?'

'It saves me from conversation.'

'That must be a fascinating book you've got there.'

Encountering yet again the bishop's callow indecisions about his fitness to be ordained as deacon, Miss St John was jolted into candour, and said, 'On the contrary. But it's all I have till I can get out and change it.'

'Why not try some of mine? Needs must when the Devil drives, or so they say.'

'What sort of books are they?'

'Crimes.'

Presently he came back with half a dozen brightly bound volumes, and tossed them into her lap.

'Two international gangs, three killers and a dog-track. Take your choice.'

After he had gone, she began to look through them. Discarding the dog-track, she settled down to one of the murders. She had had no idea that such books were so well printed. Two hours later, Mrs Fry found her absorbedly reading by a dead fire.

'And he promised me he'd make it up! What a boy! Sometimes I think he'll never give his mind to anything. But I suppose it's natural. While he was in the Air Force he got into the way of living like a gentleman, and one doesn't get out of such ways in a hurry.' Still reading, Miss St John muttered that she supposed not. After an assaying glance, Mrs Fry continued, 'And that reminds me, there's something I've been meaning to ask you. Now that we're all alone, wouldn't it be more cheerful for you if we shared the lounge in the evenings?'

Miss St John looked up. It was as though she had heard, a long way off, a very loud noise. Mrs Fry hurried on.

'They keep on telling us to save coal, you know. As a matter of fact, our own stocks are running low. We've had to give up having a fire in our own little room, as it is. We'd only look in for half an hour or so, just to warm up before bedtime.'

Supremacy disables the victorious. Miss St John had for so long imposed her will on the mild Potters that she had grown unaccustomed to dealing with any overt proposals to cross it. She could think of nothing to say beyond No. She said it. Mrs Fry deftly took it as meaning that Miss St

John had no objection, gave a final pat to the rekindled fire, and hurried away.

Thereafter the Frys came into the lounge every evening— Mr Fry, a methodical man, remarking, 'Still deep in crime, Miss St John? Don't be alarmed. We aren't the police.' It was his little joke. But after her first abandonment, Miss St John found that she did not really enjoy crime-stories, and now she only read them to shelter herself against Dennis's questions and repartees. The shelter was not reliable. His manner of speech was so closely modelled upon the style of the stories that there were times when she felt that she was being addressed by the gangster on the page instead of the young man at her elbow, and this impression was strengthened by his choice of subjects. It seemed to Dennis that he was amusing himself by talking to the old stick-in-the-mud about murders and fornications. In fact, he was yielding to a much deeper compulsion. With the savage morality of the young he discerned that Miss St John's immovable law-abidingness expressed nothing more than the indifference with which one well-cherished vice can afford to disregard the flimsy satisfactions of crime. Completely selfish, she could afford to be completely virtuous. It was with a kind of proselytizing zeal that he set himself to force on her attention acts of lust and violence which she would always be too cautiously and coldly self-regarding to commit. He tried in vain. Her toughened self-satisfaction was more than a match for his young fury, and his attempts to open the old cat's eyes opened them to nothing more perturbing than a recognition that Dennis was bored to extinction, and cramped by a manner of life quite unsuitable for a strong young man. The male subjects of the biographies, while strong and young, led active lives: they climbed mountains, they hunted foxes, they worked devotedly in slums; if their financial circumstances did not permit of such doings, they split rails or worked devotedly in foundries. The doted-on Dennis did nothing but stroll about with his hands in his pockets. Admitting this, and even feeling a kind of rusty compassion, she continued to find him almost insufferable, and snubbed him whenever an occasion offered. But the presence of the elder Frys protected him like a wadding. Mr Fry sat as though at the head of a table, fingering the coins in his pocket and smiling with manly condescension. Mrs Fry blunted the snubs by exclaiming, 'Now, now, Dennis! You'll end by making yourself unpopular.'

Even for a mother, Mrs Fry was uncommonly thick-skinned. Nothing could disabuse her of the notion that to know Dennis was to love him, and as the mother of the loved object she now presumed a considerable degree of love towards herself. Her manner had become far too affable by the morning when she said, 'Hubby and I are so delighted to see what a liking you have taken to Dennis. You and he will be like old friends when the time comes for him to take over.'

'Take over?'

'Yes. Dennis is going to take over the Peacock as soon as he feels ready. We are just keeping the place warm for him.'

While she chattered on about a little bungalow to retire to, and the delights of keeping a few chickabiddies, Miss St

John stared at a vase of daffodils. They were already wilting in the sun; for spring had come suddenly, alien after the long winter.

That afternoon Miss St John set out to find new accommodation. Of the other hotels in Dunwater, two were booked up till the autumn, and all demanded twice as much money as she was paying or could afford to pay. At the Crown and Anchor, the humblest hotel in the place, the landlady asked how much she could afford. Miss St John named a sum, making it ten shillings more than she paid at the Peacock. 'I can't think of anywhere that would take you for that,' said the woman. She did not speak unkindly, but Miss St John turned her back and stumped out.

The next day Miss St John went by bus to the neighbouring town. It was a low place compared to Dunwater, but the prices were no lower. Returning, she remembered a stationer's window where she had seen notices of furnished rooms displayed, and went to look in it. The advertisements were for the most part written in curly illiterate handwriting on shabby cards or cheap envelopes. When she went to inspect the rooms, they matched the shabbiness of their advertisements. Even so, they were all beyond her means, except for one bed-sitting-room, and that was so fusty, so wretched and so hedged about with stipulations that she rejected it. She framed an advertisement herself. LADY, *elderly but active and healthy, requires* . . . She wrote it out with particular care, but behind the dirty glass it looked much of a muchness with the others—the prams, typewriters and reliable daily women required, the fire-irons and fur necklets for sale. No answer came to her box-number. Stifling her memories of dirt and squalor, she went back to the house where she had seen the cheap bed-sitting-room. It was let.

Now, when she visited the public library, the wide floors, the bright windows, the apparatus of sober civic luxury intimidated her. She felt herself unrelated to them, just as she was unrelated to the flawless weather of the finest summer England had known for years. New biographies, the fruits of war which she had foreseen, were on the shelves. But new or old, books had become no more than something to hold up between herself and Dennis, and which at his bidding she would put down to listen with shamed bare face to his chatter about rapine and bloodshed. For his savage whim to violate her decorum had persisted, and matured into an obsession. Each was the other's victim: her cold and stockish respectability had become a rubbing-post against which, willy-nilly, he must rub himself frantic, and the realization that she was living at the Peacock on terms which no other hotel would accept laid her at his mercy, since her conscience, being entirely materialistic, would not allow her to show fight where she knew herself to be under an obligation.

To escape, she must save money. She gave up her visits to the cinema and sat in the Borough Gardens instead. Passers-by glancing at the old woman dumped on a bench (chairs cost twopence), supposed she was a tramp; for in her desperate ambition to amass every possible penny she wore her oldest clothes and economized on the laundry and the cleaners. She was the more tramp-like because she had now fallen into a trick of talking to herself, muttering scraps of poetry learned in childhood, testing her memory of dates and foreign capitals, or commenting to herself on those who walked past. These assertions of a mind at liberty were of the nature of exorcisms: they warded off the frightful consideration of how she would fare later on, when there was no more fine weather allowing her to sit out of doors, and no more summer visitors to the Peacock to stand between her and Dennis. If people in the Borough Gardens supposed her to be a tramp, visitors at the Peacock knew her to be a bore. She encumbered them with attempts at conversation, had nothing to say, and could not be shaken off. Besides, she smelled.

One afternoon she was intercepted on the doorstep by Mr Fry. He had, he said, a little something to request, a little adjustment. Her heart began to bang like a door in an empty house.

'The fact of the matter is, Mrs Fry and I, we've been talking things over with a view to what's fair to all and will disoblige none. And we've got a little proposition to make.'

He had never spoken so slowly.

'Business is good, this summer. Things are looking up.'

'No doubt the fine weather has something to do with it,' she answered, suddenly enabled to be cunning.

'Exactly! Which being so, we must make hay while the sun shines. So what we have to suggest, Mrs Fry and myself, is that for the present you should take your tea in the little room.'

'In *your* room?'

'Ours in a manner of speaking. But during the afternoon you can look on it as your own. You'll find it very snug. By so doing, the lounge will be left free for Transients.'

He paused. His hand stirred the coins in his pocket.

'I'm sure you'll see our point of view, Miss St John. Being here as a Permanent, and on such special terms, I am quite sure you will see our point of view.'

Bewildered by relief and ignominy, and the ignominy of feeling relief, she turned mechanically towards the lounge. Mr Fry coughed, and opened the door of the little room.

He had been so sure of her assent that the tea-tray was already set on the partially cleared table, and a small bent-wood chair drawn up. For the rest, the little room contained a desk, two filing-cabinets, a linen-press, a sewing-machine, a dressmaker's dummy robed in a faded cretonne wrapper, a safe, two stuffed armchairs and a wicker one, all greasy and familiarized. She sat down, and immediately became conscious of the noises in the room. The blindcord bobbin tapped on the window-pane. A newspaper thrown down on the floor rustled intermittently. Two bluebottles, caught on the dangling flypaper, buzzed on different notes. One buzzed more feebly than the other, being nearer exhaustion. Ravenous with shock, she devoured bread and butter which was bread and margarine, till only one slice remained. She mastered herself then, and left it. Sipping her tea, she looked at the trade calendars on the walls: horses ploughing, a child feeding a parrot, a thatched cottage . . . Suddenly, there was a new noise in the room. The wicker chair had creaked. As she listened, it creaked again. She sprang up and touched the cushion. It was warm. She knew infallibly that Dennis had been sitting in it.

That afternoon she was left in peace. The next afternoon she found Dennis in the wicker chair, smoking his pipe, and reading the evening paper. The tobacco smoke drifted round her. It made her throat dry, and with that, and her haste, she began to cough. Remembering how she had choked, and how he had thumped her back, she broke into a sweat, thinking that he would hit again, but this time more roughly and shamelessly. But his reading absorbed him, and it was not till some minutes later that he laid down the paper and began to talk about a murder reported in it. The murdered woman was a street-walker, and elderly. This conjunction of age and profession enabled him to torment Miss St John very piquantly.

For the next few days she went recklessly to a teashop. But having been tempted by a sixpenny ice, she panicked at the thought of further extravagances, and went back to the little room. The little room faced west, and was stiflingly hot. It wilted even Dennis's powers of dis-agreeable conversation. But he could torment in silence, too. Sometimes he would walk slowly round the table, staring at her as though she were on exhibition in a cage. Sometimes he feigned to make love to the dressmaker's dummy, tweaking at the wrapper, and snuffing the brown holland bosom. Miss St John tried another expedient. This was to abjure her tea and sit in the Borough Gardens till dinner-time. Parched with thirst and stupefied with headache, she sat watching the tennis-players and the slow clock. Sometimes fragments of passing conversation lodged in her ears, and rang on there, meaningless as music. Then, one afternoon, the word *murder* alighted on her hearing. 'Did you see that another of those wretched women has been murdered? It's as bad as Jack the Ripper.' 'Oh well, I suppose the poor creatures expect it.' The shadows of the two speakers flicked over her, and were gone. The words remained, and she sat nursing them, a figure of such self-forgetting and abject misery that a young man on his way to the tennis-court turned back and laid a half-crown on the bench beside her hand. Miss St John instantly rose to her feet and walked away.

After ten days' resistance, she gave in, and told Betty, forcing herself to speak unconcernedly, that she would have her tea served in the little room as usual. 'The old cat's come back to her saucer,' commented Betty, reporting this to Mrs Fry. Mrs Fry did not even smile. The heat and the busy season had knocked the spirit out of her. She looked careworn and listless, only her two curls retained their spruce appearance. 'I know someone who won't be best pleased,' continued Betty. 'Poor Mr Dennis, he doesn't seem to be in the best of spirits anyhow, and I should think this'll be the last straw.' 'Nonsense!' exclaimed Mrs Fry, suddenly alert. 'There's nothing wrong with Dennis. He overdid himself on that week-end in town, that's all.'

Dennis was there to witness Miss St John's return to the little room, getting up to bow ceremoniously, and saying, 'Miss St John, I presume? Why, you are quite a stranger. May I have the pleasure of dusting your chair?'

The taunting manner was just as usual, but he stared at her as though she had suddenly taken on a meaning for him.

'And where have you been all this long while?' he continued. 'What wonderful weather we are having, are we not? It really seems quite a pity to come indoors.'

It was plain enough that he knew she had been sitting tea-less in the Borough Gardens. Keeping up his pretence that her return to the little room was a return from an authentic absence, he expatiated on the benefits of a little change. He, too, had been away for a few days, seeing life. Enduring his mockery, and telling herself that it was nothing new and no more than she expected, she was presently driven to entertain a most fantastic surmise: that Dennis was glad to see her.

She was too much bewildered by the notion of such a development to speculate whether it would make things better or worse. His loquacity saved her from having to answer him, that, at any rate, was so much gained. She bundled away her impression of having been welcome, and hoped he might not be there next day. He was there. When she entered, his expression was so savage and morose that she hastened to sit down with her back to him, opening the book she was too nervous to read. *On his return from Switzerland Canon Edgeworth took up once more the project of furthering the establishment of an organisation designed to promote the welfare of those engaged in the boot and shoe trade . . .* The words were still dancing about the page when Dennis began to talk. Again she received this extraordinary impression that during her exile in the Borough Gardens their relationship had changed. His familiarity, which had been as formalized as an obscene gesture, assumed an almost boyish quality of gush and self-commendation; it was as if he were sitting up to beg for a lump of sugar off her tea-tray; and when he resorted to his threadbare jest of imploring her not to choke herself, he grew quite sentimental as he recalled their first encounter, when, as he said, she might have died if he had not intervened. Resigned to this new variety of persecution, she drank and munched, munched and drank, giving more attention to the recovered solace of her afternoon tea than to his rigmaroles.

Though she had lost any real hope of her advertisement at the stationer's, she continued to call there once a week. Doing so gave a regularity to her days, and replaced the Friday visit to the cinema. One afternoon, interrupting her usual, 'I have called to inquire,' the stationer handed her a card, saying that it had been left five days before, and that it was a pity she had not called sooner.

'Where is Albion Terrace?'

'Behind the slaughterhouse.'

Her bedraggled dignity reared up, and she said severely, 'That is out of the question.' But after she had left the shop, she turned about and went in search of Albion Terrace. Though it lay in the poorest quarter of the town, it had retained a kind of jettisoned gentility. Miss St John noticed that the windows of number six were cleanly curtained and that its doorknob was polished. She was telling herself that one would soon grow accustomed to the smell from the gasworks, when a girl ran past, jostling a perambulator and screaming. Heads popped out of windows, more people came running, children darted among them like firecrackers, and a cow charged down the street, dragging along two men who were wrenching at her horns. Miss St John hurried into an alleyway. The alley branched into further alleys; before she could feel herself in safety, she knew herself to be lost. Her tongue was so swollen with fear that she did not feel able to ask her way. She stumbled on, tossed from street to street, rebounding from blind alleys, pursued by bursts of laughter, stared at by impassive men on doorsteps, and bewildered by a growing sensation that she was not in Dunwater at all. When at last she caught sight of the Minster spire it seemed to belong to another life.

Nearly an hour behind her usual time she walked into the little room. It was so homelike, so securely familiar, that she scarcely troubled to notice if Dennis were there.

'I thought you would never come!'

His voice was so warped by impatience, and fatigue had put her so much off her guard, that she replied, 'Why, did you want me?'

'Did I want you? My dear Miss St John, you know I cannot bear to miss a moment of your society. No one appreciates me as you do. There is no one else I can tell my little secrets to. Besides, you make me laugh, you keep me fresh and jolly.'

It was as though he did indeed depend on her, and now meant to punish her for keeping him waiting. But the tea-tray was still there. Her hand shook so much that she could barely lift the pot. She sat impaled between Dennis behind her and the headless watchfulness of the dressmaker's dummy in its corner by the door.

She realized that for some minutes she had been hearing only the buzzing of the flies on the flypaper. She drew a long breath, and poured out another cup of tea. Instantly the wicker chair creaked.

'I'd give a lot to know how many cups of tea I've seen you put away since our first merry meeting. What an introduction! Fate threw us together, as you might say. That little crumb that took the wrong turning . . . that's what set the ball rolling! If I saved your life, Miss St John, you've certainly changed mine. It's been a mutual . . . *What's that?*'

The door opened. Mrs Fry stood on the threshold. Her face was grey and brittle as if something had withered it.

'Dennis! Dennis dear, you're wanted. They want to have a word with you.'

There were two police officers behind her, and now they came forward.

'Dennis Fry, I am going to arrest you for the murder of—'

There was a crash of breaking glass. Sitting with her eyes fixed on the teapot, Miss St John disassociated herself with the struggle behind her.

'I'll come, I'll come. I'll do anything in reason. God rot the whole beastly lot of you! And as for her, sitting there . . . Well, it's goodbye, Miss St John!'

Panting, and with blood streaming from his hand, Dennis was led past her.

'I suppose I can take my hat.'

Mrs Fry held it out to him.

'Oh, Dennis, Dennis, it can't be true! I know it must be some ghastly mistake. I can't believe such a thing!'

'More fool you, then,' he retorted. One of the officers said, as though he were continuing an interrupted sentence, 'You need not say anything at this stage, but if you do so, it will be taken down and may be given in evidence.'

After they had gone, Miss St John rose softly and nimbly, and closed the door, which had been left open. The little room seemed to be spinning round her, and she must keep its excitement to herself. For she was alive, saved by a miracle. Not only was she not murdered, not only was she still here—but Dennis had been taken away. Nothing remained of him but the sighing wicker chair with its lap spotted with his blood. In step with the spinning room she perambulated round the table, holding a slice of cake in her hand. A phrase swam into her mind: *The bread of freedom*. A quotation from a biography, no doubt, for it was not the sort of thing that anyone would actually say. She took a bite of cake. A pistol shot cracked out. It was so immediate a sound that it seemed to her she must have been wounded by it. *Oh!* she exclaimed, with her mouth full. A moment later she exclaimed again. A silly crumb had gone the wrong way. She set herself to cough it up. How tiresome! It was still there. She did not seem able to cough as vigorously as usual, the energy of her coughing only drove the blood into her head. She attempted to beat herself on the back. Her hands, flapping ineffectively, drew no strength from her heavy arms. A swallow of tea would do it. But the cup was empty. Well, that could be overcome, she must pour out another cupful. The essential thing was to keep one's presence of mind. She saw her hand take a lump of sugar and drop it into the cup. That was a waste of time, and silly. But the teapot was there. She had only to lift it, it could not be as heavy as all that. She took a firmer grasp, and raised it. But a dart of anguish ran along her arm, the pot tilted, all that was left of the tea poured on to the tray. The milk-jug was empty, they never gave her enough milk. Oh, she was dying, she would choke to death, unless she could get help! She went on all-fours, trying to vomit. She saw the leg of the table, and in a frantic attempt to attract attention, she pulled at it. The table swayed, and toppled, and very, very slowly the tray fell off with a clatter of crockery. The sugar-basin spun like a foolish top, and came to a standstill under her nose. Beyond the closed door everyone was talking, a noise like waves on shingle, but inside her was an even louder noise, a noise so loud and awful that the tea-things had seemed to fall in silence. And now, but this time in the back of her head, more pistol shots were going off, exploding with black flashes behind her eyes.

Momentarily recovering consciousness, she looked round the little room and saw with perfect lucidity that she was alone in it.

At a Monkey's Breast

The visitor—who came so regularly that one might almost call him the patron—sat feeding the old monkey—which should, in strict biology, be classified as ape, had it not lacked so completely the intellectual earnestness of the ape that monkey was the only word for it—with cherries. He was an oldish man, with grey hair, and wearing a suit so well tailored and well kept that it seemed like a civilian uniform. His countenance, too, was set in an expression of adequacy and composure which made it seem to be on parade; though parading in some subaltern capacity, for it was without the lineaments of authority. Indeed, if closely examined, it revealed marks of frustration and some distant timidity beneath the healthy colouring and the pompous mould of the lips.

There was nothing in his appearance to account for the degree of intimacy which obviously existed between him and his *protégée*. As a rule, those who practise these odd, these almost romantic, assignations with captive animals bear, or come to bear, a physical likeness to the creatures they frequent. The woman on whose knee the eagle perches, sits with drooping shoulders and responds to the eagle's sad scrutiny with the almost blinded gaze of extreme far-sightedness. The man who grasps the bars of the buffalo's cage is thick-set and burly, and stares in, round-eyed, with an expression of clouded wrathfulness. The giraffe and the lanky poet who extend their long necks towards each other exchange identical glances of supercilious sensibility and mistrust. But the man with the cherries bore no resemblance whatsoever to the creature he visited so punctually and indulged so patiently. One might even think that he had taken pains not to look like a monkey, and that in dress and manner he had exerted himself to obliterate the inherent simianity they had in common.

If this were so indeed, and the discreet fraternity badge on his lapel a symbol of how far he had travelled in the flight from the ape, he must have needed to retrench his vitality and abjure some natural instincts—a policy which could have imposed the traces of restriction and timidity which qualified his general air of calm prosperity. Certainly the old monkey looked much the livelier of the two, though she (it was a female) was so plainly aged and rather out of condition. Life seethed and pulsated under her shrivelled skin, life tensed the hand that scrabbled among her white hairs or clutched at the woollen shawl that was perpetually falling awry from her restless shoulders. The cherries he offered were snatched at, and conveyed with an odd rapid daintiness to the working mouth. The cherry-stones, which one by one the mouth returned to the paw, one by one were tossed gaily into the air, with an aristocratic disregard where they might fall. So many of them were spattered against the knees or the waistcoat of the visitor, or even hit him in the face, that one might have thought they were deliberately aimed, and with apish mischief and malice, but any such surmise was disallowed by the unwavering direction of her glance. Like dirty diamonds in their red sockets, her eyes remained steadfastly fixed on the cherries still in the basket.

Unoffended by the cherry-stones hailing upon him, the man continued to feed his favourite. From time to time he broke the silence, remarking, 'Here's a nice red one, darling,' or 'Look, what a big one!' But these speeches seemed to be attached to the act of giving rather than addressed to a receiver. And though he sat facing her, he did not look at her with any persistency of awareness, certainly not as intelligently as he glanced from time to time at his wrist-watch.

His stay seemed to be more measured by cherries than by minutes. As the basket emptied, and her gaze clung more devouringly to the diminishing mound of pink and scarlet, he began to hasten a trifle, and to speak rather more and rather louder—as bath-water, running away, begins to chatter and gurgle when the bottom of the bath appears. Perhaps the smell was becoming too much for him. The old monkey was well cared-for, her bedding was plentiful and clean, the walls of the room were painted with white enamel, an electric fan whirred overhead; but for all that, the smell of old animal was oppressive, and like a direct defiance to the freshness and sparkle of the cherries. Now that the cherries were so few the smell seemed more prevailing—as if the power of an exorcism were running out.

The last cherry had been eaten. Frowning slightly, and with a natural embarrassment, the man said, 'No more, my darling. No more just now,' and rose to his feet. Diverted to a secondary pleasure, she snatched the empty basket and began to tear it to pieces. In trying to take it from her, his glance fell on her left hand, which clung to its toy. His features sharpened. He gave an exclamation of angry alarm—not loud, but so charged with feeling that the old monkey caught the infection of his tone and began to thresh up and down excitedly. There was a bell-push by the bed. He pressed it, and an attendant came in, her white apron rustling, her starched white veil standing out round her wholesome red face.

'What's the matter?' she asked. 'I hope nothing's gone wrong with the old lady. What is it, ducks?' she continued, bending over the bed.

'Nurse,' he said, and his air of dignified perturbation almost supplied the authority he lacked. 'Nurse! My mother is not wearing her wedding-ring.'

'Oh no, Mr Hardy, I know she isn't. She plays such tricks with it, we've given up trying to make her keep it on. But it's perfectly safe, Mr Hardy. Matron has it.'

'I would prefer her to wear it. I would very much prefer her to wear it. It must be put back again, nurse, and somehow or other, she must be persuaded to keep it on.'

Addressing herself to the old monkey, the nurse said, 'You've been enjoying yourself with those cherries, haven't you, you naughty old pets!'

Colouring like a child, he said in a diminished voice, 'After all, it's a wedding-ring, you know. A wedding-ring. I don't wish to be troublesome. But as her son, you see, and in my position, it is not pleasant for me to see her without it.'

Absalom, My Son

Having escaped the fall of high explosives, incendiaries and guided missiles, and having been preserved from requisitioning or billeting because of the age and reputation of its owner, in 1948 Matthew Bateman's house in Kent was totally destroyed by an ordinary civilian fire. It was empty at the time, and the cause of the fire was never ascertained. A farm-hand, on his way to the morning milking, noticed smoke rising from the valley, and a moment later saw a trophy of flame leap up as the thatched roof fell in.

It was a roof which in earlier years had sheltered many visitors. The headlines, 'Well-Known Writer's House Burned Down: Total Destruction of Kenton Mill-House,' revived memories of rooms darkened with books and lit with the tremulous reflection of water, of a reedy voice, and a bony hand stroking a jackdaw, and of a quantity of slightly macabre bric-à-brac—blotched shells, scowling daguerreotypes, the Emblems of the Passion in a bottle—placed with old-maidish precision on fringed mats. Several such readers wrote to condole, to offer hospitality or to search, even, for that white blackbird, an empty house. These offers were politely refused by Miss Loveday Patterson, writing on Matthew Bateman's behalf.

And so, at the age of seventy-three, Matthew Bateman found himself possessed of the clothes he stood up in and those in a small leather suitcase, two pairs of spectacles (those on his nose and those in his pocket), a watch, a fountain-pen, a pistol, a signet-ring, a note-book, the mss. of two novels which, published in the early twenties, had established him as a man of letters, and the ms. of an unfinished novel, earlier in date. These mss. had been lent to an exhibition in Maidstone, which he had opened afterwards, spending the night on which his house caught fire at a hotel there. He also retained Miss Loveday Patterson, who had accompanied him to Maidstone, and had been his secretary for so long that she really might be counted as part of his personal estate.

He heard the news of his loss in silence, and bore it with acid stoicism. 'It is your *books* that I grieve for!' exclaimed Mrs White, the lady who had got up the exhibition. 'It might be worse: at least, I have read them,' he answered. Condolers, reporters and friends in need came to the hotel in quantities, and after two days of this he told Loveday Patterson to go in search of a furnished house without neighbours or telephone and not to come back until she had found it. Thirty-six hours later she returned with news of a bungalow (called High Hope) already rented, coals delivered and a charwoman arranged for. 'It's on a hill,' she said.

'I hate hills,' he replied.

'And I found out in the village that the two ladies it belongs to tried to run it as a café, but couldn't make it pay because they kept such large black dogs—they bred dogs, too—that strangers were afraid to go near it. Then all the dogs died of distemper, and one of the ladies had a nervous breakdown and is in a mental home, and the other has gone to work in a hostel near Birmingham.'

'Did they bury the dogs in the garden?' he inquired.

'Yes. But I wouldn't call it a garden. It's just a patch of rough ground, with horse-radish all over it.'

'Horse-radish is practically ineradicable. I like the horse-radish.'

She had mentioned the horse-radish and the deaths of the dogs on the established principle of mentioning the disagreeables first, in order to get them over and wipe them out with the subsequent agreeables; and also because honesty is best. She had been with Matthew Bateman for twenty years, at first as secretary and housekeeper, then, as time went on and times worsened, as cook and partially laundress and sometimes nurse. Statistically and clinically, she knew him thoroughly, and if she had been less conscientious, she might have known him humanly. But devotion to duty browbeat her intuitions and imprisoned her in a state of cautious astonishment. Intuition now told her that she could not hope to improve on the dogs and the horseradish, but to herself she only said that Mr Bateman had a sense of humour, and that with a sense of humour one can overcome anything—so she could go off with a quiet mind and buy him winter underclothes.

On the day they moved in, seeing him get out of the hired car and walk resolvedly unnoticing towards what would now be his front door, she was thankful that she had bought them thick. The wind of the autumn equinox plied the macrocarpus hedge that sheltered High Hope from its total absence of neighbours, and the lean sinewy branches bowed as if in a grotesque homage to the new owner. A plane flew over. The cloud hid it, but the gusty wind carried its noise like an intermittent shouting. As they entered the house, they heard the first spikes of rain hit the windows.

'It won't take me a minute to get tea,' she said. He did not answer. He had walked towards a bookshelf, and stood staring at it. When she came back with the tea-tray, he was standing in the same place, a book in his hand.

In her first visit of inspection she barely glanced at the books, only noticing that they were battered, miscellaneous and not Mr Bateman's kind of book. Mr Bateman's kind of book would have to come from the London Library, wrapped in the darkest and toughest brown paper. How nice it would be if Mr Bateman, nourished by the London Library, should spend the winter comfortably making extracts about astrologers, complying with Mr Crocker the publisher's wish for a companion volume to the book about almanack-makers which had sold so well during the war. Mr Bateman had called it a potboiler; but as far as she could see, it had cost him quite as much pains and needed retyping quite as often as the books that were all out of his head. And it had sold much better. Meanwhile Mr Bateman, book in hand, had sat down to let his tea get cold; and only his surroundings, and the social category of the tea-cup, and the nature of the book divorced him from the process of letting his tea get cold at Kenton Mill-House.

Book by book, reading with unswerving, unsmiling attention, Mr Bateman traversed the High Hope bookshelves. He read *The Scarlet Pimpernel* and *The Green Hat* and *The Blue Lagoon* and *The Lilac Sunbonnet,* and *The Revised Prayerbook of 1927* and *Lassie* and *Rin-tin-tin* and *The Memoirs of Marie of Roumania* and *The Story of San Michele.* He read the works of Barrie and Milne, and old copies of *Vogue* and *Good Housekeeping,* and bound volumes of *The Girl's Own Paper,* and *Gone with the Wind,* and *The White Cliffs of Dover.* Roused to helpfulness by news of his burned house, or possibly aware of the increased sales value of anyone publicly pitiable, editors wrote and asked him when they might have another article, even if they had never had one, and publishers suggested that he should write introductions to their reprints of lesser classics. These letters, having typed envelopes, were opened by Loveday Patterson, who was pleased to see them. Mr Bateman's finances had suffered by the ebb-tide which catches all writers who have become well known without ever having been popular. Keeping her voice suitably impartial, she read them aloud. But barely raising his eyes from *The Intimate Life of the Tzarina* or *Opening a Chestnut Burr,* Mr Bateman asked her to write to the fellow and say he'd think about it.

He's relaxing, she thought; and having found this benign explanation, settled down to do a little reading and make herself some new clothes; for her possessions, naturally, had been burned with his. As secretary to a distinguished man of letters, Loveday made a point of reading high-class books, and got them from a lending library. She could only afford the cheap subscription, so by the time she got them they were a year or so out of date, but they were still high-class.

He read, she read and knitted. And then, with laceration, like one startled from a deep dream, Matthew discovered that he had read every book in the house. Awakening with a sigh, he looked round on his new surroundings. There, exhaling in a long perspective, was the landscape of yet another autumn; and here, so close at hand as to be almost perspectiveless, was Loveday Patterson, growing old in his service, but still fresh-coloured, prompt and trim.

'Loveday, who was the fellow who wanted an introduction to *Peter Wilkins*?'

'To *Peter Wilkins*, Mr Bateman? I think it was Butler and Bugler.'

'Tell him I'll do it.'

For Peter Wilkins, creature of an eighteenth-century romancer who wrote but this one book, being shipwrecked on a desert island, wooed a feathered mistress, half woman, half bird; and having mastered his first mistrust of such a being, got children on her and put her into European dress. Just so, thought Matthew, writers substantiate their first amours with poetry, and make novels, and publish them. All this is a parable, and should be written down. But as usual the first impetus was caught and strangled in thickets of analogics and qualifications. Poor Loveday typed and retyped, and each revision was a stage further away from his intention. The Introduction to *Peter Wilkins* was limping towards its final stage of completion and nausea when the postman brought a registered packet. The Maidstone exhibition had closed, and Mrs White returned his three manuscripts together with a letter aptly hoping that he was at work on another of his delightful books.

'Tell her I wish she were at work in a soap factory,' he commanded, and later in the day signed unprotestingly a note of polite acknowledgment. In the interval he had begun to read the unfinished novel—his first child by his feathered love, begotten before he had put even a rush ring round her finger or tied an apron before her sex. Oh dear, thought Loveday Patterson, there he is with a manuscript—so unsettling! For while in a state of being in manuscript, Mr Bateman was always quite unlike his usual self: only an attempt at dictation had been worse. This was a manuscript out of the past, and unpacking it, and noticing that it had come back from the exhibition with its pages a trifle jostled, she had felt as calmly about it as if it were a shirt come back from the laundry with a ravelled cuff: she would set it to rights and put it away. But he had taken it, and now it had taken him. There he sat, straining his eyesight over the waning ink, his cheeks flushed, his lips moving, his hand with the veins standing out on it trembling with impatience as he turned over two flimsy pages for one. She stood with the signed letter to Mrs White in her hand, looking down on him, and it was as if she saw the rash coming out. If only he would let her type it!—for that is why a properly established writer keeps a secretary—to wash and clothe and cradle these reeking fragments of creation. There was not much of it, she could rattle it off in no time. But it wouldn't do to say so now.

He became conscious of her, and glanced up. His expression was brilliantly serene, a glance from another world;

as if he were a boy going fishing. 'Is that you, Loveday,' he said. 'Off to bed? That's right, that's right.' She went to her sitting-room, took the cover off her machine, and sat down to write to her married sister in Canada. 'You will be surprised at my new address,' she wrote, half-knowing that Phoebe would omit to notice it, 'but it does not mean what you might think, for I am still with Mr Bateman.' Canada was a long way off, but the man on the yonder side of the wall was further away than Canada.

Before going to bed that night, Matthew strolled out among the horse-radish. It was the first time since the arrival at High Hope that he had felt an interest in the weather. The wind was blowing from the south-west, the air was soft, the sky overcast. It smelt of rain. He went to bed deeply satisfied, knowing that the following day would be wet and stormy, the most propitious weather for his purpose, which was to write. This time, he would really write: freely, dashingly, leaving out all the stuffing and nonsense, observing nothing but his own intentions, going where he pleased, even if it meant going where he had notoriously gone before, unharnessed to any purpose except to please himself, as he had written when he lived in the harsh Arcadia of youth. He would take up the unfinished story, and finish it, and nothing of his doubtful later self should get into it, except the technical skill of the practised hand. Not for nothing had his middle years vanished in smoke. This negligible little box he now inhabited was, in fact, the perfect container for the deed he proposed. As for Loveday, he would put her under hatches. She could be sent off on excursions of pleasure.

The following day was so extremely wet that he could not in conscience pack Loveday out to enjoy herself. He told her not to bother him, and she obeyed. The gale whirled him into the dusk before he remembered to feel hungry. During the night the storm blew itself out.

'Loveday, have you ever been to Rochester?'

'Yes, Mr Bateman. I've been there several times, to a dentist.'

'Ah! Well, have you ever been across the Thames on the Gravesend Ferry? No? Now that's a thing everyone should do. This would be an excellent day for it. You'd better start at once.'

Smoke, shipping, the pale estuary horizons: the mind's eye prospect delighted him, he would have gone himself if he had not had better fish to fry. 'To-morrow,' he added, 'you might go to Canterbury. I know you've been there before, but one cannot go too often to Canterbury.'

The weather continued implacably fine, and after a couple of days it became necessary to send Loveday for a breath of sea air at Ramsgate. He was getting to a stage when the combination of a high barometer and Loveday fidgeting about on tiptoe might be fatal. When he was over this precarious bridge, where the inexperience of the original narrative had to be underpinned by knowledge of real life and yet preserve its air of fortuitous infallibility, things would be easier. Loveday could stay at home and the woman could come to scrub.

'I think you had better spend a night at Ramsgate, while you are about it.'

She put on her look of being a bear that can dance no longer, and said that if it were the same to him, she would much prefer not to. He had to give way. But the thought of her return that evening irked him. It shortened the day. Two separate interruptors, a gipsy selling clothes-pegs, and a man coming to read the electricity meter, shortened the day still further. When he had eaten the tray luncheon that Loveday had left for him, he realized that for the moment, only for the moment, he had written himself to a standstill. He would have coffee, and then he would go for a walk.

The coffee-pot was on the stove, it only needed heating. This time, instead of leaving it to boil, boil over, and boil away, he remained in the kitchen. One of Loveday's lending library books was on the window-sill. Without looking at the title, he opened it at random and read on till the coffee boiled.

The recollection of what he had read stayed pleasantly with him as he walked. The book had shadows in it: though what Norman Leigh (he had noticed the name as he put the book down. it was a name unknown to him) meant by calling such an unbedizened piece of work *Reverse the Sun* was another matter. Perhaps it was something astrophysical. Titles change like women's hats. He must find a title for his old story made new, for *The Bride of Smithfield* smacked of the twenties and wouldn't do. His mind went back to his own affair. He hit on a possible answer to a difficulty which had hampered him all that morning, and he turned home.

He saw a bicycling woman dismount at his gate and walk with a dreadful positiveness up the path. Instantly deciding on the worst, he foresaw his afternoon laid waste by Mrs White. She had come to 'look him up', her car had broken down, but at the garage, inflexible as a tiger on the trail, she had borrowed a bicycle . . . It was the girl from the post-office with a reply-paid telegram. Loveday had met a friend at Ramsgate, and would spend the night there if he had no objection. He scribbled his permission, went jubilantly into the house that was now so much more his own, and settled down to work.

His hand was out. The expedient he had carried back did not fit. Words lay on the page like drowned flies. All his renounced obesities came back to him, qualifications and evasions muddied every sentence. It was worse than the Introduction to *Peter Wilkins*. He threw the day's work on the floor, washed his face and hands in cold water, and began again, leaving the botch to clear itself, and taking up the narrative farther on where the manuscript petered out. He fell into a conversation, and three hours later the conversation was still going on, weakly sparkling like a squib that wouldn't lie down and die. His head ached, his wrists were furrowed where he had clawed them. He walked into the kitchen to find himself something to eat, and immediately his spirits began to revive. Triviality released him into self-respect, and he sang to himself as he wandered about collecting the ingredients for a curry. Carrying his tray into the sitting-room, he turned back, daunted by the smell of smoked tobacco and labour-in-vain. The kitchen smelled gaily of onions and India, and he would eat his supper there. His hand went out for

Loveday's book. This time, he would begin at the beginning, and find out what the young man was up to—he was bound to be young, nowadays they were all young men. Seeing the first page so branded with over-anxiety, and finding the curry so accomplished, he muttered to himself that malt does more than Milton can, that if he consulted his own pleasure, he would drown his books, dismiss Loveday, and devote himself entirely to the satisfactions of cookery. After the first few pages—quite properly a little stiff, for if you cannot begin like Byron it is much better not to try to—*Reverse the Sun* seriously delighted him. He began to match his reading to the book, pausing to consider, turning back to compare one stroke with another. After those annihilating gallops over the High Hope course, just to be reading so was pleasure in itself. At times he stopped quite uncritically, halted by sheer astonishment at finding something so unforeseeably well managed. Yet though the book astonished him, it was congenial too, the fruit of a congenial mind: a scrupulous, searching, disdainful mind, with a vein of black bile. It was against this Calvinistic melancholy that the details of the narrative stood out with such brilliance, as though they were reeds and dragonflies taunting the vision of a drowning man. He read it to the end, and went to bed thinking of it, and thinking of the letter he would write to Norman Leigh. Words slipped through his mind, a little greasily from having been fingered by every reviewer. Rare . . . judicious . . . distinction . . . originality . . . authenticity . . . Plagiarism! That word didn't slip! It seized on him, as ice is welded on a warm hand. The fellow was a plagiarist, an aper, a purloiner! And how near he had been to writing to congratulate his ape! He sat up in bed, shaking with fury. 'Blast his impertinence,' he said: and the exclamation doddered, because he had taken out his teeth.

He lay down again, stiffly humiliated, and tried to compose his feelings. These things happen, he told himself. Young hawks pick out old hawks' eyes, each generation begins its course with such a stirrup-cup; and at the end of a career of honest work with small thanks for it, there is even a sort of compliment in being found worth stealing from. 'Dear Mr Leigh'—the letter might be sent, after all—'Thank you for your kind attention to my writings. I am gratified to find that they have been of use to you.' But his resentment could not be sneered away. It had too much grief in it. He grieved for the brief duration of his pleasure in the book, he grieved for his dreamily decaying wits, and his grief was made weightier by a sense of bereavement. For the time was gone by when he had enjoyed his reputation of singularity, of being the only writer to write like Matthew Bateman. In *Reverse the Sun* there had been something corroborative, a look of kindred—so he had thought, till the look of kindred was reshaped into a pasteboard mask held before a thief's face. How could he have become so dull that he did not recognize his own imitation? Loveday herself could not have failed to notice it. Everyone must notice it. His anger, once more charging ahead, plunged him into another morass. Why should anyone notice it? He was known by his reputation, not by his books. At best, a few people reading Norman Leigh might remark on a slight influence of Matthew Bateman, which it was to be hoped would soon be shed.

He could bear it no longer. He had drugs beside him, and in the next room there was alcohol, but for him there was only one reliable form of dramming. He got up, dressed and went grimly to his desk. With the beard poking from his jaws, he sat till the first blade of sunrise thrust through the curtain-chink. Writing fluently, he had covered a dozen pages. He drew them together, astonished to find so much accomplished. Perhaps, after all, he might live to be grateful to Loveday's lending library author. Mettled by jealousy, roused from being the unique Matthew Bateman into being a competitor, he had not done so badly. He sorted the new pages into order, and was laying them down, when a sentence caught his eye. It wouldn't do. He was ringing it, when another sentence grimaced at him from further down the page. He read more attentively. Everything he had written that night smelled of Norman Leigh.

Too tired for any more rages, he groaned, and looked out of the window, rubbing his cheeks. Here was another day. The sky was clouding over, the macrocarpus hedge twitched before an oncoming wind. It would be a day to write in; but as things stood, it was the day when Loveday would come back. Before she came, there would be brewers, bakers and candlestick-makers coming to the door, and he must shave and spruce himself. That meant the electric kettle. He walked into the kitchen. It retained the previous night as a bed retains an act of carnality. The meal was still on the table, the unwashed saucepans stood hardening on the stove, the sink was littered with onion peelings and grains of rice. Lying in the crumpled cretonne lap of the armchair, and occupying the whole kitchen, was *Reverse the Sun*.

He heard time falling like drops of water from the clock on the wall. Time cannot be put back, the book was there, and he had read it, and it could never be unread. But it remained that the deed should never be known, and so he would put the book back on the window-sill whence he had taken it. Holding it at arm's length, he crossed the room with it, and stiffly set it down. He was turning away when a further initiation into criminality told him that he might have left a crumb in it, or a shred of tobacco. He took hold of it by the covers, and gave it a shake. The action tossed him into bodily fury, and he shook it long and savagely. It was only when the noise of the fluttered pages reminded him of a bird's wings that he was able to control himself and put it down. The paper jacket had slipped awry. He straightened it, and before he could stop himself he had begun to read the publisher's note on the inside flap.

Norman Leigh, whose death from poliomyelitis at the age of twenty-six cut short . . .

It was as if he had heard his whole being utter a shout of triumph.

Slowly, an agony of shame overwhelmed him. He did not know what to do.

At last something stirred in his cavernous discouragement, and was remorse. He turned to the first page, and began to read. There it was, that rather stiff, rather defensive opening: the scabbard, with the blade of a purpose lying in it.

The postman, and after him the woman who brought the milk, passing the kitchen window saw Miss Patterson's old gentleman standing within, reading a book. When they knocked and got no answer, they concluded that Miss Patterson's old gentleman must be deaf, and left parcels and milk on the doorstep. Later, when his legs began to tremble with fatigue, he went down on his knees to read. By then, however, there were no more daily comers, to conclude that he was praying. When cramp began to eat away his power of concentration, he hauled himself to his feet, drank some cold coffee, and settled down in the armchair.

For a long time after he had finished the book, he sat thinking. One thing still perplexed him: whether the evocations of himself (and a second reading made them unmistakably plain) were deliberate imitation or the expression of a mind like his own and working with a similar intention. He would have liked to know this; but he never would know, and, after all, it was not so very important. It was more significant that Norman Leigh, writing like Matthew Bateman, had written a better book than ever Matthew Bateman had set his name to; and would not write another. He was dead, this young man who had already matched and surpassed him. Matthew Bateman, so long and complacently a man without a match, lived on, a man without an heir. Putting the book down on the table, he laid his cheek against it, and fell asleep.

Waking much later, he retained a steadied sense of bereavement and a steady knowledge as to what must be done. First, the kitchen must be put in order. Then he must straighten his bed; finally, his desk. He went at it calmly, too much fatigued to be conscious of any additional effort. Once only he was impeded by an uncertainty of purpose, and that was when he came to the manuscript on his desk. But after a glance at the bookshelf, he let it be. Those deplorable favourites had taken their chance, and so should this. He took the pistol from the drawer, and checked that it was in order. A minimum of oil and attention will keep such things in condition, though they lie for years unused and unthought-of. The habit of carrying it with him when he travelled had conveyed it to Maidstone, and now it was here. A last thought struck him. He went from room to room opening the windows. The air flowed in, impartial and absolving. Air flows in, soul flies out. But that is for the housebound deathbed; for his part, he had no notion to die anywhere but out of doors. Blood, so unseemly on a carpet, soon assimilates itself to earth.

He went out, and into the patch of ground at the back of the house where the dogs were buried and the horse-radish grew. Frost had already touched the strong-grown serpentine leaves. Their edges were fraying, their green was blotched as if with rust. Rubbing one against another in the slow wind, they made a grating noise, one might almost call it clanking—or would that be a Gongorism? One must be on one's guard against . . . He remembered that the obligation to be on one's guard was now at an end. All he had to do was to decide whether to shoot through the eye or the ear. The eye is infallible, yet most people flinch at that who flinch at nothing else, and prefer to blow their brains out through the ear. He would wait for the robin to end its little stanza, and then he would shoot himself through the eye.

The robin flew up. Loveday's voice, a little out of breath, said, 'Oh, Mr Bateman, are you after that rat? He's about here every evening. But you won't get him now, for I saw him run into the hedge as I came out.'

'Oh! Did you? Well, so here you are. Did you enjoy yourself at Margate?'

'Oh, yes, Mr Bateman. I had a very nice time. The sea looked so calm, I quite wanted to go on it.'

Ramsgate was where he had advised her to go, Ramsgate was where she had been. But Loveday knew that this was not a moment in which to be geographical. It was enough that she had come back, found all the windows open and that manuscript blown all over the floor, and Mr Bateman up to no good. Up to no good: she would not allow herself to think more explicitly. To do so would not help him or her. Talking of the blueness of the sea, the whiteness of the cliffs, the devastations of war, the unexpectedness of sitting down on a bench and finding Lucy Petter, whom she had not seen for years, sitting at the other end of it, she stood conversing among the horse-radish, wearing shoes that had become too tight for her and a hat like an apple-turnover.

'You really ought to go to the seaside for a few days yourself, Mr Bateman. It's wonderful! When I woke up this morning, and heard the waves—I can't describe how I felt; but somehow, it did seem so extraordinary.'

Little by little, she got him indoors, and sitting down, and fed. He shivered; and when he spoke, though what he said was ordinary enough, his voice sounded as if it had not been used for a twelvemonth. It looked to her, she said, as if he might have a cold coming on, nothing likelier than that he should have got chilled waiting about for that rat. The pistol was still in his trouser pocket. When she had given him a hot whisky and seen him settled in his bed, she carried off his suit to give it a good brushing.

'No waves to-morrow, poor Loveday,' he called through the closing door. A weight fell off her heart: he was not planning any more excursions for her. Whatever it might be that she had been sent out of the way of, whatever the solitary drama whose last act she had interrupted, it was at an end. But, to be on the safe side, she dropped the pistol into a larder crock containing haricot beans. The larder looked as if a hurricane had raged in it. He must have been putting things tidy: but she would leave it so until to-morrow. To-morrow. She sighed, stooping to take off her shoes. At this time yesterday evening she and Lucy Petter were sitting in the ice-cream parlour, and Lucy was saying, 'Secretary? It strikes me that you're nothing but an old man's darling. What future is there in that, my girl? The future—that's what you should keep your eye on.' 'But Mr Bateman is a very distinguished writer, Lucy.' 'Distinguished writer? He must be, if that's all he pays you, and gets away with it.' Lucy's diagnosis had frightened her. During the journey back she had reasoned fright into prudence, and she entered High Hope quite resolved to tell Mr Bateman that she needed to find another post—a post where she could keep in better practice and use her shorthand. Now all that was out of the question. She could not think of leaving anyone who looked as lonely as he had done, standing in that derelict patch you couldn't call a garden. She would write to Lucy, telling her that High Hope would continue to be her address, but giving no reason. And before going to bed she would finish that book from the library, and have it done up ready for the postman to take in the morning, so that she could get another.

A Kitchen Knife

Rachel and Trevor Gilman had been married for almost three years before they got into a house of their own. Till then, they lived with Trevor's parents. In post-war conditions this was nothing to wonder at. Nor, since the war had levelled class distinctions as well as dwelling-houses, was there anything very odd in the fact that her husband's home should remind Rachel of seaside lodging-houses where she had stayed as a child—except that there was no sea.

But in the seaside lodging-houses she had taken a spade and bucket and gone out to spend a day on the beach. Now it was Trevor who went out, taking a small attaché-case containing sandwiches and a thermos of milk coffee, to spend the day at a bank. At first—for they were very much in love with each other—Trevor's departure only initiated a delightful process of waiting for Trevor's return, the snatched embrace before the others got at him, his regular inquiry, 'Well, my darling, how have things been going?' Nothing had gone at all, she would reply. Life had been a blank. As time went on and the inquiries continued, it became apparent that another kind of answer was now due and must acknowledge the Gilmans. The acknowledgment was no sooner made than it seemed a guilty acknowledgment. The guilt was evasive and obscure, for it did not lie merely in occupying a bedroom which had previously been occupied by Topsy Gilman (who now doubled up with Patricia) and occupying it with Trevor (since Trevor's parents often and amply expressed their confidence that Rachel was going to make Trevor a wonderful little wife), nor in being penniless and without useful relations (since it was a Gilman axiom that money was not everything, and a Gilman tradition that what can't be got through unassisted effort is not worth having), nor even in speaking with a different accent and calling a serviette a table-napkin (since every Gilman knew that it takes all sorts to make a world). It was a guilt compounded of finer elements, such as not knowing the way to the fishmonger's. Any Gilman labouring under a similar sense of guilt would have known and applied the remedy: to live it down. Rachel did not feel that she possessed enough stamina to undertake a process with so much perspective in it. She compromised by redoubling her acknowledgments of the Gilman way of life, their cheerfulness, their unselfishness, their goodness and sterling worth, their devotion to fresh air, good nourishing food and traditional laxatives, their abounding, resounding, unremitting obsession with a home that reminded her of a seaside lodging-house. She was becoming quite good at this, when her participation in a thorough Gilmanlike merry Christmas brought on a miscarriage.

It is among the weaker and more feather-pated animals that one finds the most resolute capacity for self-mutilation. Discovering herself irreparably an alien among Gilmans, she proceeded to cut herself off from all her former friends; and knowing that childless couples were the last to be aided by the Borough Housing Committee, she refused to be got with child until that child could be born in a house of its own. That was how she phrased the stipulation. In fact, it would have been more closely expressed if she had said, until it could have a father of its own. Trevor at home could not fulfil that stipulation; at best, he would only be instrumental, Mrs Gilman's eldest boy who had acceded to her natural longing to be made a grandmother. So everyone concerned went on being uncomfortable and frustrated till Mr Gilman senior exerted a masonic grip on a friend in the Council Offices and got the young couple into a bungalow on a new housing estate. The plaster was still damp on its walls when they moved in, and Trevor immediately caught a cold, which went, as all his colds did, to his chest. To be nursing Trevor unaided, and hearing milk boil over without an accompanying, 'Rachel, dear! The milk!' from her mother-in-law, imparted a sensation of such prowess and amplitude that it seemed to her that henceforward nothing could dash her spirits, not even the suite of two armchairs and a sofa—all alike brown, shiny, vast and unyielding— which the Gilmans had given as a parting present. Now only one thing was needed to make her completely happy—for Trevor to recover and go back to work, leaving her free to repaint all the interior woodwork.

Presently that too was added ('No one could say that our Trev isn't obliging,' as Mrs Gilman was wont to remark). The new housing estate was on the outskirts of the town, it now took Trevor over an hour to travel to and fro. But the return journey was sweetened by the meat extract advertisements in the evening paper. These represented a young husband returning to a young wife, and though they changed slightly every month or so, their gist was always the same, the young husband commenting, playfully and appreciatively, on the delicious smell that the meat extract had given to a soup, a stew, or a plate of rissoles. During the years of living at home these advertisements had made rather wistful reading—not that he wished for better soups, stews or rissoles than those of his mother's cooking, but he would have liked to be praising Rachel for them. Now he could enter a home of his own, exactly like the young husband in the advertisement; and Rachel, turning off the Third Programme, would jump up and become the advertisement's young wife, and after supper and washing up would sit on the glacial arm of his easy-chair, looking forward to the day when they could have a television set, and being interested in the assorted womanly bits read aloud from the evening paper.

'What about this, Ray? "Special offer. Brighten your table with plastic salad-servers. Choice of art shades in pink, blue, or old gold." '

Rejoicing in a home of his own, he also rejoiced in his now domesticated Rachel, the wife he had looked forward to, cooking almost as well as Mum, thirty years younger than Mum, and getting ready to be a Mum herself—for Rachel had honourably observed her bargain, and was again with child. He expressed his joy and approval by bringing home little presents, presents of a kind that would please a domesticated young wife: plastic fruit-dishes, rayon tablecloths, chromium-plated toothbrush-holders, and—an acknowledgment of Rachel's more extended culture—an Old English brass toasting-fork. His elation pursued her into the kitchen, endowing it with every kind of patent labour-saving device for peeling potatoes, slicing beans, whisking eggs, saving soap, removing pips from grapefruit and unstopping sinks. All these were shiny, fragile and clattering; there was even a kettle that whistled when it boiled. Rachel reflected that she could not have a home of her own that was not also a home of Trevor's. And, after all, she did not have to use these kitchen comforts; she had only to keep them dusted and displayed, and to refer to them.

She was now appreciably pregnant. Being sick was part of the daily routine, and when she was lucky took place immediately after waving off Trevor to his bank. Trevor longed for the baby, irrespective of its sex. Rachel hoped it would be a boy. Pink salad-servers, armchairs like glazed brawn, and Mrs Gilman as a grandmother would not matter so much to a boy. She hoped so devoutly that it would be a boy that she did not often allow herself to consider that it might be a girl. To live, during some hours of the day, like a young wife in a meat extract advertisement (she had recognized the source of those sprightly compliments) was perfectly tolerable, since Trevor was not only so good and so sterling, as became a Gilman, but also was lovable, and the man she had elected to love. For her daughter to grow up like the young girls in the advertisement of How to Glamourize your Hair at Home was a different matter.

One day, considering this more attentively, she broke into a cold sweat. She wrote to Celia Hanson, asking her, if the child were a girl, to be its godmother.

Celia Hanson was the only one of the old friends whom Rachel had not been able to lop off. Ten years older than Rachel, Celia was unmarried, rationally wealthy, sociable and managing. With a number of friends to be managed, she found time for Rachel too. Disregarding Rachel's insistence on being no more to her, she continued to send birthday and Christmas presents, admirably non-committal, and at Christmas she sent presents to Trevor also. She had met him during the brief engagement, and he had been much taken with her, saying that it was really a pity that she had not found anyone to marry her, she was not the attractive type, but he could see that she was the soul of kindness and a wonderful mixer.

The provisional invitation to be a godmother remained unanswered for some weeks. Rachel had left off being sick, and was quite sure that the child would be a boy, when a letter from Celia appeared. The letter opened with delight, congratulations and a blanket acceptance, passed on to some maternal advice and inquiries, and culminated in Celia's own news. Celia had been slaving like a black, renouncing the world, selling the lease of her London house, buying tweeds and thick woollen stockings and settling down as a rustic; for old Aunt Hester had died, leaving Celia her house and furniture—the house a little Georgian box, just large enough to hold the aunt's collection of Rockingham poodles. That was delightful, wasn't it?——but what was even more delightful was that Celia had just realized that the house was in a village only twenty miles from where Rachel lived; ideally adjacent for a godmother, and meanwhile, would Rachel and Trevor come to lunch next Sunday? There was a bus.

Feeling for some uninvestigated reason scornful, Rachel read out this invitation. The feeling of scorn persisted, even into the bus; and as they left the town behind and travelled into a landscape that was like the music of Gluck, she remarked how extraordinary it was to think of Celia, of all people, settling down as a county lady. 'I suppose she will join the Women's Institute, and boss the village Flower Show.'

Trevor, for once not attending, exclaimed, 'Look, Ray! There are lambs in that field. And that church, too! It must be genuinely old. I had no notion there was anything like this within a bus-ride. We must come out oftener. And just look at the size of that hedge!'

'It's a bullfinch,' she replied. There was no time for explanations, as the bus stopped, and the conductor told them that the lane branching off on the left was the lane to Chipgrove.

It was the latter, the enriched half of May. The hawthorn blossom was whiter than anything that could be achieved by delighted housewives in the advertisements of patent soaps, the bluebells and the rose-campion were beyond all plastics. Trevor exclaimed, 'I've made up my mind! When my time comes to retire from the bank, we will buy a cottage in the country.'

She did not respond, since at that moment Celia hallooed, and opened a newly painted gate between brick gateposts with stone balls on them. Her tweeds, her shoes, her wrist-watch on a leather strap, were all perfectly in keeping, and she held a small trowel in her large white hand. It must be marriage, so Rachel decided during lunch, that renders one so pure from minor materialisms, and teaches a Stoic poise among graces and comforts. She looked on Celia Hanson with calm approval, admiring her tact, her flow of conversation, the white streak that had somehow been persuaded to remain no more than a magpie flash in her black hair. With the same detachment, she exclaimed at Celia's good fortune, the charm of her house, the lofty rooms with narrow windows, the two Bartolozzis and the one Bonington, very much as though Celia were one of the Rockingham poodles in the display cabinet. A good choice . . . an excellent godmother. Perhaps she would be just as suitable if the child were a boy. Perhaps she would be even more suitable. Celia's new and tweeded bonhomie might grate on a girl; but on a boy—judging from Trevor—it would fall like manna.

For Trevor, after his first disappointment at the plain brick exterior of the house, was all eyes, ears and admiration. It was as if he were in church, she thought, but playing a more concurrent part than is usual on the part of a congregation. Praising a soup that he would have thought neglected at home (surely it should have been put through a sieve or something?), carrying the tray into the kitchen without more than one startled glance at the condition of the sink, remarking that he had never thought a valuable picture could look as clean as the Bonington did, laughing at Celia's jokes and refraining from making any jokes himself, he was . . . he was . . . The words were supplied by memories of Mrs Gilman. Trevor was as happy as a sandboy and as nice as you could wish.

After observing this, Rachel spent the remainder of the visit burningly resenting Celia's contemptuous affability towards a genuinely happy guest.

Walking towards the bus, with Celia's brisk adieux still warm in his ears, Trevor looked sideways at his wife. She must be feeling it. He himself, with so little claim to do so, was decidedly feeling it; and Rachel, to whom all these confident luxuries, these soups and satins, were natural as a birthright, must be expected to be feeling it much more. But Rachel was smiling, and looking unusually pleased with herself. And immediately, Trevor knew why. Rachel, to put it vulgarly, knew which side her bread was buttered; comparing her lot with Celia's, she realized how much better it was to be walking away with a husband of her own, and felt a womanly satisfaction. During the years of living with the Gilman family, Trevor had on several occasions slunk off to the Marriage Guidance Bureau—alone; for Rachel had never wished to consult that organization. The Marriage Guidance Bureau had always assured him that the moment his wife had a little home of her own, everything would come right. And it had turned out exactly as they said it would.

Rachel opened her handbag, and peeped in.

'You needn't worry,' he said. 'I've got the return halves. No sensible husband trusts his wife with the tickets.'

She laughed, and pulled something out of the bag. 'Look,' she said. 'Look what I've got!'

What she held out towards him was a knife.

It was a common kitchen knife, and not even a new one. The bone handle, yellowed and battered, seemed disproportionately long for the blade, which had been worn down to a couple of inches by long use and countless sharpenings.

'What a curious thing for Celia to give you.'

'She didn't give it to me. I stole it.'

'Rachel! You can't mean that! You don't mean that you actually—*stole it?*'

'I stole it, all right. I saw it the moment we went into the kitchen, and waited till neither of you were looking. A real old-fashioned kitchen knife! . . . Look, Trevor!'

She pressed down the thin blade with her thumb and released it again.

'There! D'you see? It's as supple as an eel. I expect it belonged to that aunt. I tell you, this knife is going to make the whole difference to me.'

'But how? What do you want it for? You've got a set of cook's knives, and a potato peeler, and the curly knife for grapefruit, and a bean-slicer, and I don't know what beside. Everything—and all new, and stainless steel.'

'Yes, and all fit for nothing but a doll's house. This is a real knife. *It will cut!*'

Dodging the affront to his feelings as a giver, he concentrated on the issue of theft.

'Really, Ray, I cannot make you out. I don't think you know what you are doing.'

'I know a good knife when I see one.'

'But you've stolen it.'

'Of course I've stolen it. How would I have got it otherwise? No woman who does her own cooking is going to part with a knife like this.'

'If you really wanted it so badly, why didn't you ask her?'

'Because I wouldn't have got it. She'd have made some excuse, and fobbed me off with a silver toastrack. I know my Celia.'

'But now, if she misses it—'

'She'll miss it all right!'

'She'll blame some innocent person. Her charwoman, or the gardener, or some one of that sort.'

'No, she won't. She'll know I took it.'

'Well, that's quite as bad. I don't know that it isn't worse, really. How can you ask her to be godmother now?'

'Oh, Trevor, do leave off making mountains out of molehills. You don't understand these things.'

'I understand the difference between right and wrong.'

She threw the knife in the air, caught it, and put it back in her bag. The action, so light, carefree and flirtatious, was at variance with her encumbered body. The discrepancy alarmed him. He said, and his voice was stiff with anger, 'I'm sorry, Rachel, but this can't be allowed. Give me that knife, and I'll run back with it, and explain. I can say it was a joke.'

But, as he spoke, she saw him glance at the watch on his wrist, and knew that his whole life, fastened to timekeeping, must enslave him to catching the bus. Filled with scorn, and elated as though scorn were a sharp wine, she said, 'We shall miss the bus.'

He submitted, and they walked on in silence.

The bus was crowded, they saw with thankfulness that there was no possibility of sitting side by side. Trevor inserted himself beside a middle-aged woman who took up more than her share of the bench because she was carrying an enormous bunch of bluebells. The two women beyond her also carried bunches of wild flowers. They talked cheerfully amongst themselves, and he gathered that they were cousins, and had met for a day's outing. They informed each other of how they would dispose of their flowers when they got home, how some were destined for friends in hospital, and others for graves. Their talk was full of the dead, the dying, calamities past or foreseen, and they spoke with cheerful interest, as though such things were part of daily life, to be heartily dealt with, like washing-days. Not one of them, he knew, would do such a thing as steal. And though in class they were almost as far behind him as Rachel was beyond him, he felt a wistful filiality towards them—as though they were beds on which he had slept as a child. But now, no such reposes were possible. Solitary and adult, he must deal with this business of Rachel and the knife. Acting gently, and with regard for the vagaries of her condition—he had understood it might be pickles or apricots, a kitchen knife was something he was not prepared for, but no doubt it must be classed as a vagary—he must assert his authority, and send it back by post. A simple matter, really, and there was no reason to get upset by it. There would be a little tussle, and then they would be happy again. So he would tackle it this evening, and to-morrow, on the way to the bank, he would post the parcel, and that would be the end of it.

He leaned forward to look beyond the bluebells, and saw Rachel. She stood out from everyone else in the bus. She was sitting bolt upright, and her face was the face of a demon.

I might just as well make up my mind to it now, she was thinking, here in the bus. I should never be able to explain to Trevor why I took the knife; and what's more, if I could, I wouldn't, for I don't want to. This is what one gets oneself into by play-acting. Play-acting that I esteemed the Gilmans for their bloody good qualities, play-acting that Trevor wasn't like the rest of them, play-acting that I wanted my little home, play-acting that I liked it when I got it. I hate my little home, and Trevor is exactly like all the Gilmans. And then, after that intolerable lunch, with Celia being affable to him over an invisible counter, I must needs see that knife, and play-act on, as if it were a talisman, as if, because it was the real thing and could do its job, I should be able to do my job too, cook interminably well and enjoy doing it, turn into a real wife instead of a meat-extract bitch. Oh, my God, what a fool I have been! What a fool I was to give in and marry him, when all I wanted was to go to bed with him! Now here we are, going home after our little outing, with Trevor knowing the difference between right and wrong, and me knowing that I can't go on fooling myself any longer.

When they got out of the bus, she was surprised to find that it was still afternoon.

The three women also alighted, and hurried towards a teashop, carrying away their warrant of spring and green fields. Trevor and Rachel waited in silence for the bus that would take them within walking distance of the housing estate. It was an infrequent bus, and they waited for a long time. When an empty taxi went by, Rachel hailed it. As she got in, she said to Trevor, who was holding open the door, 'Why don't you go off and see your family? You'd still be in time for their tea.'

'Well, yes, I might. Perhaps I ought to. We haven't been there lately. What a pity I didn't think of picking some flowers. Mum would have liked some of those buttercups.'

'You'll do quite as well.'

An obligatory smile slid across his dulled face. He gave his little bow, and turned away. Watching, she saw him quicken his pace, making his way with neat alacrity through the crowd of Sunday strollers. Already in his mind he was home, running eagerly up the flight of clean doorsteps.

The taxi quitted the bus route, and now took her by an unfamiliar way through a quiet residential quarter where mid-Victorian houses, each with its own peculiarity of porch or bow-window, stood amply in rather neglected gardens. Trees of the period, mountain ash and ailanthus, waved their boughs over wide pavements, and she found herself thinking that here would be a good place to wheel a perambulator. It would also be a good place to throw out the knife. Dust to dust, vestiges to vestiges, with no hope of any resurrection. She opened her bag. Holding the knife in her hand, she realized that it would be ridiculous to throw it away. Though it had done its work already, severing her from her illusions as cleanly as it would trim off the fat from a cutlet, it was still a thing she wanted, a proper kitchen knife.

Uncle Blair

There was a distinct, if non-contractual, understanding between Miss Iris Foale and her fellow-citizens that something commemorative would go up after her death. A woman who had devoted her life to a steady puffing of the flame of education could scarcely talk about bricks and mortar, and Miss Foale often remarked that she could wish for no better memorial than the characters she had formed and the ideals she had inculcated. But the process of turning a snuffy seminary for young ladies in a decaying West of England town into a flourishing boarding-school had formed more than characters. Two school tailors had retired with fortunes. The Buffalo Inn had become the Buffalo Hotel, three garages and seven teashops of refinement had sprung up to succour visiting parents, and a derelict cloth mill had reopened, to specialize in turning the wool of local sheep into academic flannel of the proper shade and toughness. Farmers had grown prosperous by supplying pure milk, market gardeners had enjoyed a steady market for their cabbages and tomatoes, the town drains had been put in order, a fire engine of the latest kind had been bought, and Anchor Yard, Tittingham's modest red-light district, had been expunged and buried under the school sanatorium and the school laundry. If all these benefits had been brought by a stranger, they might have been less gratefully received. But Miss Foale was a local woman, with local interests at heart. It was her boast that the girls were clothed in Tittingham wool, nourished on the fruits of Tittingham clay, and took their yearly part in the White Mopselling—a traditional Tittingham ceremony, which she had been foremost in reviving. Such a benefactress had earned a memorial. She died in 1930, and the Memorial Committee was set up, within a week of the funeral, to receive subscriptions and consider suggestions.

It became known that, in a delicate way, Miss Foale had bequeathed her own suggestion. The Committee accordingly decided that the memorial should be a Tittingham Folk Museum, which would house Miss Foale's collection of eighteenth- and early-nineteenth-century boots, and shelter the Mopselling Maidens' dances when Mopsell Day happened to be a wet one. The site was soon agreed on. At the junction of Lady Street and Cow Lane there was a sizable open space, which could be enlarged by pulling down Opie Cottage—a small Georgian house in very bad repair, with a garden in front of it overgrown with lilac bushes and frequented by all the low cats of the town. Its freehold belonged to a Miss Bishop, who many years before had been removed to a Home for the Aged. Though she was senile, it was felt that she was not too senile to sign an agreement to sell the property. The Chairman of the Memorial Committee guided her hand as she did so, and afterwards congratulated her on the sum of a hundred pounds—quite a little fortune—deposited in her name in the Post Office Savings Bank.

The foundation-stone of the Museum had been laid when Aubrey Cutbush, who for the last five years had been travelling in Asia Minor, came back to his house at Tittingham Parva. Hearing of his return, and bethinking them that he was the unmarried remainder of a hoary local family, the Memorial Committee sent him a copy of their appeal for funds. He ran his eye over it, and buried it under the pages of a book of travel he was getting ready for the press. It was not until a week later that he happened to drive down Lady Street and saw that Opie Cottage was gone. Sixty years earlier, he had been born in Opie Cottage, which his parents had rented while the family dwelling was being reroofed. He had quitted it at the age of six months, but still, he had been born there. Its removal struck him as an affront.

In the heat of the moment, he did what any English gentleman would do. He went to see his solicitor. The solicitor rashly disclosed that he was a member of the Memorial Committee. Shortly after, Mr Cutbush left the office, followed by a junior clerk staggering under three brown-paper parcels; and the three japanned deedboxes lettered 'Cutbush', in which for the last few centuries the family papers had reposed, stood empty except for a few strands of pink tape and some dead spiders. A man of pure passions, Aubrey Cutbush was immune from the gentility of having to appear to behave magnanimously. He got a copy of the list of subscribers to the Memorial Fund, and spent the afternoon writing to inform various local tradesmen who had contributed that he was removing his custom. By the time he had gone through the list, he had not only severed his relations with grocers, fishmongers, butchers and so forth, but had also cut himself off from the law, the church, medicine (including dentistry) and society, as represented in Tittingham and its environs. In fact, the only links that remained were those which tied him to the Rating Committee and to the Collector of Inland Revenue, and these fell naturally into the scheme of vendetta to which he was now devoted.

Having got over these preliminaries, he settled down to the finer conduct of his campaign. The first arrow was sped from the correspondence column of the *Western Herald,* and was editorially headed 'Changes at Tittingham':

Sir,

On a recent visit to Tittingham I noticed with regret that Opie Cottage, that little architectural gem of the Golden Age of our domestic culture— 'when Good King George the Third rul'd our land'—has disappeared from its former site in Cow Lane, and is in process of being supplanted by an excavation bearing every appearance of Public Baths. If the ratepayers' money is to be spent on these gewgaws of Socialism, is it too much to ask that we should not be deprived of the relics of a happier England, in addition to paying for these so-called improvements?

I am, sir, etc.,

Devonian

As Aubrey had intended, the imputation of Socialized baths paid for out of the rates drew a dignified correction from the secretary of the Memorial Committee. *Devonian* wrote again:

Sɪʀ,

I stand corrected. But though the Secretary of the Foale Memorial Committee has courteously elucidated that the large pit in Cow Lane is to be a Folk Museum, he does not explain why the provision of this no doubt desirable amenity should have entailed the demolition of one of the few houses in Tittingham on which the eye of a connoisseur could dwell with satisfaction.

These regrets for a house known to have been infested with rats and unconnected with the main drainage system were too much for Mr Moggs, the only Socialist member of the Tittingham Town Council. He wrote to the *Western Herald* with manly wrath and verbosity about the crying need to do away with all such dwellings of the so-called Georgian epoch, designed to be the smug abodes of toadying parasites, and to replace them by a proper housing scheme for the workers of Tittingham. To this *Devonian* replied that though he feared he and Mr Moggs could not exactly see eye to eye about Opie Cottage, he entirely agreed about the foolishness of building folk museums while the 'folk' of the present day were as ill-housed as ever they had been.

After this letter, the editor of the *Western Herald* inserted: 'This correspondence is now closed.'

He spoke for his own pages. From across the county border, the editor of the *Cornubian* had watched this shindy blow up. Thankful that no such acrimony had broken into his own quiet correspondence column, he accepted, nevertheless—for one likes to be in the movement—a short article about the Cornish artist John Opie, which, after some irrefutable twaddle about Opie's birthplace and schooling, continued: 'There is good reason to suppose that Opie spent some months, at any rate, in Tittingham, then a thriving and unspoiled specimen of the Devon market-town'—Aubrey had wavered for some time between this and 'then a rotten borough'—'a sojourn commemorated in the name of Opie Cottage, long borne by a small house at the foot of Cow Lane. But those who seek him there will seek in vain, for the house, with all its interesting associations and aroma of the past, has recently been destroyed. *Eheu, fugaces!*'

Aubrey contributed this under the pen name of *Autolycus Junior.* He was meditating a further contribution—'Little Known Folk Lore'—in which the vital spark was to be the distich:

If Mopselling Maidens go under a roof
Bread will rise to a guinea a loaf,

which an octogenarian milkmaid recalled learning at her grandmother's knee, when an arrow from another hand twanged into the correspondence column of the *Cornubian*:

Sir,

Opie Cottage, that pretty little specimen of Georgian Domestick, is not the only relic of old Tittingham to have been swept away. A far more savage piece of vandalism occurred when the fine old timbered houses in Anchor Yard were demolished. These houses had long been famous. Benjamin Crispin, in *The Woolepack Open'd* (1579), refers to them as 'mansiones, nay, pleasant Palaces, newely aedify'd to match the towring ambicion of our Occidental Clothiers.' Their destruction was the more criminal, since they had retained many of their Elizabethan features.

Dulcibella Tregurtha, B.Litt.

If the editor of the *Cornubian* had not used his discretion and deleted the last sentence, which ran, 'They have since been miserably replaced by a pest-house and a wash-house,' Aubrey might have thought twice about the note, *c/o the Editor,* in which he said that if Miss Tregurtha should find herself in London, he would be very happy if she would lunch with him, a fellow-antiquarian, at his club. Aubrey's club was the Athenaeum, A female B.Litt., he supposed, would enter its portals—even those morganatic portals which admitted female guests—with a pleasing trepidation. He saw her in his mind's eye, dowdy but not disgracing, probably thinnish, and almost certainly bespectacled; above all, virginal. Only an irreparable virgin could have been on visiting terms with Anchor Yard and seen no more than Elizabethan features. Her letter of acceptance was typed, but typed on a sheet of handmade paper. Her scholarship seemed reliable—after visiting his publisher he had gone on to the British Museum and checked the quotation from *The Woolepack Open'd*. He looked forward to a harmless, kindly luncheon, which would present him with no difficulties beyond remembering not to reveal himself as *Devonian* or as *Autolycus Junior*. It had been his experience that women, proverbially at the mercy of their passions, are in fact much more likely to be run off with by their principles; and a Miss Tregurtha who had taken pains to be a B.Litt. might not readily understand that in order to get printed in a provincial newspaper one must write like a hog.

He had appointed one o'clock for the meeting. By one-forty-five, still endeavouring to feel like a gentleman and not like a thwarted hyena, he supposed that Miss Tregurtha was not good at finding her way about London. Ten minutes later, when with tolerable resignation he was picturing Miss Tregurtha as a mangled street casualty, his attention was caught by a lady who had just come in, a lady who would be able to find her way about any capital city. Quite an amphisbaena, he was thinking mildly, when she advanced on him—her dark eyes rolling, her diamond ear-bobs swinging, six feet high at least, perfumed like Araby—and claimed him as her own. She made no reference to having kept him waiting. Instead, she told him he had saved her reason. She had been in despair, she said. She had thought that no one but she cared a snap of the fingers for the spoliation of the West of England. But now there were two of them: herself and Mr Cutbush.

'We must plan, darling, we must plan! . . . No, just caviare, just plain caviare.'

There was this to be said for her: she was the real thing, though *mal tournée,* having stooped to the lure of mere academic distinction. As the real thing, she would not stay with him for long. They never do. Meanwhile, lunch was long drawn out, partly because everyone within earshot was immobilized by a natural desire to hear more about Miss Foale.

'A collection of boots, did you say? Exactly what I should expect of her! Of all the dreary, wistful middle-class perversions, she *would* take up with boots.' . . . 'The Bishop told my uncle that nothing would induce him to go near another confirmation at Tittingham. She mewed at him all through the Address. Mewed, do I say? The Bishop said caterwauled. His chaplain had to beat her back from the vestry with the crosier. Sacrilege, of course—but necessity knows no law.' . . . 'And even then the woman was such a grovelling snob that she didn't expel me!' For Miss Tregurtha was one of those characters formed by the late headmistress to be her memorial. Preservation of ancient buildings, protection of bishops, humanitarian concern for the poor whores driven out of Anchor Yard—all Miss Tregurtha's zealotries stemmed from a schoolgirl's resentment. Even the B.Litt. was a retort to Miss Foale's remark that our Dulcibella will never learn to spell. As for Opie Cottage, the pretext of this meeting, it was whirled away like the corkscrew that began the process of letting the Djinn out of the bottle.

Aubrey was not allowed to escape before she consulted her engagement book and discovered that in a fortnight's time she would be free to come down to Tittingham for a couple of hours 'to strike,' she said, 'our first blow.' But a woman of fashion, thought he, can forget anything in a fortnight. For that matter, a man of the world can have fled the country by then.

It was two days later, and Aubrey was home again, and had lounged downstairs after breakfasting in bed, and was dividing his speculations between cold partridge for lunch and Corsica, when a familiar voice cascaded through the open window. A car stood before his door. Miss Tregurtha and a young woman got out, commenting—in the main with approval—on his hellebores.

If only he had stayed in bed! Second thoughts showed him this would have been no protection. There was nothing for it but to tell Hopkins to set lunch for three. They would be ravenous into the bargain, for they must have started at cockcrow.

Like an echo to his thought, Dulcibella swept in, exclaiming, 'Cockcrow! We started positively at cockcrow. So sweet, so touching! All the little milk-carts. Don't you think there is something extraordinarily appealing about people's daily lives? I felt that we mustn't let a moment slip, so I threw myself into the car with Krafft-Ebing. And here is Jeanie. She has got the Evil Eye.'

Jeanie was a very young girl, fat and pasty, with flaxen

hair and white eyelashes. Her expression was hallucinated, and her hand was cold as ice, but so, Aubrey thought, would any expression be, and any hand, that has just been driven down from London by Dulcibella Tregurtha.

'Has Leo arrived?'

'Not that I know of,' he said, not choosing to admit that he had no notion who Leo might be.

'Old turncoat! Never mind, we can do without him, and after all he's not really interested in anything outside Byzantium. I wouldn't have bothered with him if it weren't that he can do anything he pleases with *The Times*. Anyhow, this business about architecture can wait. The more I think of it, the more clearly I see that the first essential is to establish the truth, and that the least we can do for these innocent, good-hearted burgesses of yours is to open their eyes to that woman's shameless boots. They have been hoodwinked long enough. Let them have the truth, I say, and then they can decide for themselves whether or no they will perpetuate her loathsome hoard of fetishes. Burn the lot, I say! But they must decide for themselves. This is a free country. All I can do is to open their eyes. Jeanie agrees—don't you, darling?'

'Yeth.'

Miss Tregurtha's copy of *Psychopathia Sexualis* bristled with paper markers. It was plain that she proposed to give readings—whether public or private Aubrey would know all too soon—from the section of that captivating work devoted to foot fetishists.

Jeanie, on the other hand, struck Aubrey as being shy. Overcoming a physical distaste, he set himself to be hospitable to the poor little guinea-pig. 'Have you had it long, your Evil Eye?'

'Yeth.'

'Indeed. That must be very—'

'It'th in the family. My Uncle Blair had it latth.'

Quelling an impulse to ask—for the lisp was compellingly catching—whether it had been bequeathed ath a legathy, Aubrey inquired what her Uncle Blair had done with it.

'Lotth of thingth. Onthe, he blathted a window. It wath a thtained-glath window in a church, and he wath there to dedicate it—he wath a dean. It wath a very ugly window, and he gave it one glanthe of horror, and it cracked from top to bottom and fell to piethtth during the theremony—like minthemeat.'

The purpose of Jeanie's visit was now clear, and lunch, Hopkins said, was served. Dulcibella remarked that they should not think of waiting for Leo. While Aubrey was hearing about Uncle Blair, she had been turning over his proofs, and now had some revisions and improvements to suggest. She suggested with energy, Aubrey stood up for his own, and fifteen minutes later Hopkins repeated that lunch was served. The meal was plentiful, succulent and totally unforeseen. Aubrey realized that it was the servants' lunch, nobly contributed to keep up the credit of his establishment. As he ate it, he reflected that though Mrs Trumper cooked very well for him, she cooked even better for her peers. Jeanie ate with a good Scots appetite. Dulcibella supported herself on pickled walnuts and cig-arettes—as he had expected. It was a shocking reflection that already he knew her well enough to know what she would eat.

Two hours later they set off for Tittingham—Jeanie to blast the budding fabric, Dulcibella to visit remembered darlings among the tradespeople and read to them from *Psychopathia Sexualis*. Aubrey was so negligently invited to be one of the expedition that it was quite easy to decline. He would know all about it soon enough, he said to himself. Fortunately, there was Corsica. Yet it was hard to be exiled to goat and garlic just when he had discovered how very well Mrs Trumper could cook. Hopkins, too, had never shown himself so efficiently humane. The car had no sooner snorted out of earshot than he was at Aubrey's elbow with a strong brew of Indian tea, saying that Primrose had been told to make up two beds for the ladies, and that if that Mr Leo should arrive, Primrose's mother was ready for him.

'Hopkins, would you like to visit Corsica?'

'If it should come to that, sir, I'd have no objection.'

Hopkins closed the door, but not before Aubrey over-heard peals of laughter from the back of the house. Hopkins, Mrs Trumper and Primrose, at any rate, were enjoying this incursion as a heaven-sent harlequinade.

A little before ten they returned for dinner. They were a trifle late, as Dulcibella informed him. She had been showing Jeanie ruined tin-mines by moonlight, and on Bodmin Moor they had remembered toothbrushes. A relation of all the things that had been shown to Jeanie took up the first half of dinner. When Jeanie inserted herself into the conversation, it was to ask, 'Where are we going to thleep?'

'Here, I suppose,' said Aubrey, and looked at his watch as brazenly as though he were in a railway station. His day had been laid waste by harpies, and in twelve hours' time they would be expecting breakfast, having left hairs in his bath and cigarette burns on the spare-room carpet. Such uninvited circumstances would justify any host in behaving as though he were in a railway station. Then a small salvaging impulse traversed his total resentment: he rather wanted to hear what had happened in Tittingham. So he sheathed his voice in politeness, and added, 'I hope so.' Luckily, Dulcibella had been too busy with menhirs to hear him tartly supposing. From menhirs to Druids, from Druids to erroneous assumptions about Mopselling Maidens, he would guide her to Miss Foale. He had just clutched a Druid when the telephone rang. Hopkins came in with a look of happy expectancy and said that Sir Leopold Pirkheimer was on the telephone and wished to speak to Miss Tregurtha.

As she left the room, Jeanie leaned back in her chair, shut her eyes, and began to fall asleep. It was a shame to wake the poor little wretch, but Aubrey reflected that even the most involuntary guest owes something to even the most involuntary host.

'Now, tell me all about this afternoon. How did things go off?'

'Oh, we thaw thome thweet people, and they all theemed very pleathed.'

'What were they pleased about?'

'Theeing Dulthibella. What time do you thuppothe it ith? I lotht my watch in Cornwall.'

'Still quite early. Not midnight yet. And did she read to them?'

'Yeth. She read to a Mr Vickery. He thelth booth. He thaid he knew what kind of booth, black, with buttonth and high heelth. He uthed to thell them, but he doethn't now. Not with buttonth. And he made uth look at all the booth he had in thtock, in cathe they'd do inthead. It took thome time—hourth and hourth, really.'

'And who did she read to next?'

'A man with whithkerth—a thaddler.'

'And what did he say?'

'He thaid—thomething about letting bygoneth be bygoneth.'

Aubrey made a mental note to resume his patronage of these two tradesmen. He remembered that he must also show a polite interest in Jeanie's share of the expedition. 'And how did your part of it go off? I hope it went well.'

She did not answer. He repeated the question. Out of her slumber, she replied like an obedient child, 'A man fell off a ladder and broke hith leg.' From a deeper layer of slumber, and with a more childish docility, she added, 'It wath the betht I could do.'

Nothing more was said until Dulcibella came back, when Jeanie sat up with a start and asked where Leo was, with every appearance of having been devoured with dutiful anxiety. Dulcibella replied that Leo was in the fens and that she washed her hands of him. 'He thought I said Gittingham. Apparently, there's a Gittingham in Cambridgeshire; anyhow, he must needs go there and comb it in vain for Cutbushes. In the end, he rang up the Education Office and got a list of dead headmistresses, and then the name of Foale burst on him in all its hideous familiarity and he got to us through the Tittingham police station. All the rest of it was his own tedious little concerns. Really, there are times when I find Leo too intolerably self-centred! What concern is it of mine whether or no he goes to a temperance hotel in the fens and sprains his ankle?'

Hearing his surname tossed about in the plural, Aubrey began to burn with resentment; and as it is undignified to feel resentment on one's own behalf, he burned with all the additional incandescence of altruism on behalf of Sir Leopold Pirkheimer, a fellow who had shown a great deal of goodwill and resourcefulness, and got no thanks for it. The least he could do for Sir Leopold, hungering and thirsting in Cambridgeshire, was to cut short this interminable dinner. He rose to his feet, trampled on his table-napkin, and exclaimed, 'For what we have received, may the Lord make us thankful!'

Hopkins, coming in with the pudding, withdrew.

Dulcibella heaped her plate with salad, added mustard, and remarked, 'Shouldn't that be "truly thankful"? Miss Foale said "truly thankful".'

'I do not use the adverb until I am in my bed,' Aubrey replied. 'Now we will go to the library for coffee, and I shall hope to hear all about this afternoon. I gather it was only a qualified success.'

Jeanie cried out, 'I never thaid that!'

The outcry was slavish. That the repulsive Jeanie should be cowed as well as Sir Leopold slighted added new intrepidity to Aubrey's wish to make himself thoroughly disagreeable. 'I mean as regards the readings from Krafft-Ebing. Smale, the saddler, was an unfortunate choice. He is proposing to be next year's mayor, so he is quite unable to admit the smallest defect in anyone's character. You could not have known this, of course. But if you have ever bought as much as a pair of galoshes from Vickery—I suppose you wore them during your school days?—you should have known the extent of Vickery's horizon. If an archangel, even—some really arresting figure—were to enter his shop, he would receive it as a customer. Naturally, Vickery supposed you wanted buttoned boots for your own wear. No doubt it was disconcerting. But you have only yourself to blame.'

'Smale and Vickery were not the only people I called on,' said Dulcibella, helping herself to more mustard with sinister calm. 'I also visited the editor of the *Cornubian*.'

There was no time to waste on repentance, and Aubrey hastened to deliver another blow before his shame caught up with him. 'I hope you did not go there to impart your theory why the man fell off the ladder. Chattering about the Evil Eye would be even more ill-advised than reading *Psychopathia Sexualis* to respectable tradesmen. If you are really so anxious to blast Miss Foale's reputation, you should try to be less fanciful in your methods.'

'Fanthiful? My eye fanthiful? You'll be thorry—'

Jeanie had got in first, but only to be gathered into Dulcibella's unhurried eloquence. 'Hold your tongue, my pet! Don't get excited over such trifling slanders. You and I, Jeanie'—Dulcibella here seized Jeanie's hand and patted it inattentively—'came here openly and honourably, to do what we could in the cause of truth. If we have cast pearls before swine, at least we have done it in the light of day. We have not slunk to it anonymously, and forced dirty little articles into the provincial press, for no higher motive than pique that the miserable hovel we were born in has been pulled down. "Interesting associations and aroma of the past!" What associations? Mr Cutbush was born in it. "Aroma of the past!" Mr Cutbush's infant napkins. Merciful God, what pettiness, what egotism, what utter disregard for truth! Opie was never in Tittingham in his life. No one had ever been in Tittingham except that woman Foale, who throve in it like a great proliferating pumpkin, and Mr Cutbush, who was born in it, and writes anonymously to the local press in a style of such flat-footed fustian that I would have supposed it to be Foale's own if I did not know the bitch was dead. Throw it away, Jeanie! You have nothing to reproach yourself with. Nor have I, except that in my impetuosity I gave way to his boring importunities and brought you here to be exploited and insulted. For that, I can never forgive myself!'

Though this fine tirade was addressed to Jeanie, it was delivered at Aubrey, which obliged him to go on looking at Dulcibella with an expression of serene indifference. Otherwise, he would have turned round to see where the draught was coming from. It was a hellish draught, cold as though it were blowing on him from the wastes of Lapland,

and by the time she had completed her lifelong regrets for Jeanie's sufferings, he seemed to have a square patch of ice wedged between his shoulder-blades. Earlier in the tirade, Jeanie had detached herself from Dulcibella's increasingly rhetorical pats. Perhaps she had gone out, and left the door open.

But when Dulcibella released him, breaking off to re-establish an earring, he looked round and saw that Jeanie was still in the room, slumped on a chair in the corner and looking completely exhausted.

'It's time that child was in bed,' he said.

Dulcibella got up. 'If you can still suppose that we would spend a night under your roof, I despair of making you understand anything. Come, Jeanie! Goodnight, Mr Cudweed.'

Aubrey held the door open while Jeanie gathered up Dulcibella's belongings. As she passed him, she paused to say, 'You'll thee, you old beatht! You'll thee!' Then, pale as death and riven with yawns, she staggered loyally after Dulcibella, and they drove away.

Left to himself, Aubrey felt as quiet as an oyster, and almost as cold. He wished that Hopkins would bring him another brew of that strong Indian tca, but, hearing Hopkins approaching, he said pettishly, 'That's enough for to-night, Hopkins. Leave everything, and go to bed.'

'Very good, sir. We were thinking of having a cup of tea amongst ourselves. Perhaps you would—' Hopkins in his solicitude almost said 'join us,' but he amended this to 'be glad of one yourself.'

Aubrey was very glad of the tea, though it was not so reviving as he had hoped. He certainly felt quite bowled over. But he had taken the full charge of Jeanie's youthful hatred, and it was a taxing injection for a man of his age. He slept heavily, and in the morning he had his breakfast in bed without much enjoying it. The wind had gone round to the east, and when it sat in that quarter, nothing would properly warm the house—not even the hope, rather laboriously indulged in, that Dulcibella and Jeanie would have broken down on Salisbury Plain and caught great colds in their heads. He himself seemed to be hatching a cold, for his sense of taste was dulled and the wedge of ice was still lodged between his shoulder-blades. The sky all day was a sharp, cloudless blue, and whenever he looked out of the window he was teased by the lines:

Bright Reason will mock thee,
Like the sun from a wintry sky.

Most unpleasant of all was the awareness that there was something he childishly wanted to know and childishly did not dare to ask. No doubt his servants knew, but he did not wish them to be putting two and two together, and he could scarcely go into Tittingham and hang inquiringly round the Folk Museum, even if he felt equal to going out in this wind.

The day after, the wind shifted and blew from the south, and a soft rain fell from a grey-feathered sky, and Aubrey felt well enough to work on his proofs again. Late in the afternoon, the Tittingham police sergeant called about the yearly renewal of the gun licences. When this had been seen to, Aubrey said, 'By the way, what was all that I heard about a man falling off a ladder at the new Museum? I didn't think it was high enough for such doings yet.'

'I wouldn't hardly have thought so myself, sir. But fall off he did, and what's more, he sustained a considerable fracture. It was young Rex Shillibeer.'

Aubrey asked if this was one of the Milk Street Shillibeers, and was told that he was correct. His hand was quite steady as he took a note from his case and gave it to the sergeant to be given to Mrs Shillibeer with his condolences.

Bright reason told Aubrey there was nothing in it. One of the tribe of Shillibeers had fallen off a ladder—probably he had been gaping at Dulcibella. There was nothing in it at all, except that it confirmingly accounted for the way his servants were behaving. A household of devoted Devon-bred servants makes a bad climate for a gentleman engaged in pooh-poohing the superstition of the Evil Eye. Aubrey was beset with four-leaved clovers, the garden walks were infested with horse-shoes and bits of old iron, he could not put his hand into a pocket without meeting a rowan twig, and one night when he happened to be lying awake and turned the pillow for its cooler side his cheek was scratched by two pins neatly stuck into the linen in the shape of a cross. A persistent faint odour of something disagreeably roasting suggested that a bullock's heart, stuck with more pins and representing Jeanie, was hanging in the kitchen chimney. Mrs Trumper was doubtless reinforcing his food with anti-malefic herbs, which would account for the fact that his meals now disagreed with him, and Hopkins encompassed him with a haggard cheerfulness, like one keeping up morale on a sinking ship.

'I tull' ee vor zhure: he'm overluked.' The assurance came in through the bathroom window, and rose from Primrose's mother, who was now a daily backdoor visitor, as if for bulletins, though on a pretext of new-laid eggs.

These attentions were the more depressing since they could only be offered as precocious funeral tributes. Everyone concerned knew that there is only one way to turn back the curse laid by an Evil Eye, and that is, to draw the blood of the bestower. But the rowan twigs, the four-leaved clovers, the horseshoes, the pins and all the other sad assiduities continued, and so did Aubrey's state of feeling not quite the thing, until he decided that, even at the price of raising blood-thirsty hopes in vain, there was nothing for it but that he should drag his old bones to London.

Eating an unphiltred railway lunch and reading *Erewhon,* Aubrey congratulated himself on the decision. He felt better already; he was going to London for conversations with his publishers and a little final research needed for his third Appendix. By the time the train drew in at Waterloo Station, he was able to admit to himself, quite rationally, that the state of his health perplexed him, and that as he had not renewed the severed link with the Tittingham doctor, he would take this opportunity to consult one of those Harley Street fellows. It would be too absurd to allow oneself to become the prey to some genuine disease just because one's servants were the prey of superstition.

The first Harley Street fellow did all that is customary. He took a piece of Aubrey's flesh for a biopsis and some of his blood for a test, and analysed his sputum and his urine, and asked him if he had disliked his father; he also took a good many of Aubrey's guineas, and prescribed moderate outdoor exercise. But he did not hit on a diagnosis until he learned that Aubrey had travelled in Asia Minor, at which point he prescribed a specialist in tropical diseases. Aubrey cavilled at this outlook on Asia Minor, but followed the prescription.

The specialist in tropical diseases drew off some more of Aubrey's blood and injected him with several experimental vaccines, which bore out to perfection a prognosis that they would make Aubrey feel uncomfortable. Even so, the specialist declared himself still unsatisfied, and wanted an exploratory operation to rule out any lingering possibility that he might have overlooked a splenetic aberration. Dejected as a sick cat, Aubrey resentfully began to yield. The specialist spoke of the surgeon he had in mind, a wonderful man, a real artist, and, as pills are sugar-coated, the surgeon was presented as 'old Bust-Bodice,' a soubriquet, the specialist explained, based on the initials B. B., though of course with some sly reference to incisions in the thorax. The cat being so nearly in the bag, why not, he suggested, make an appointment immediately? B. B. was only a few doors down the street. It was a door resembling all the other doors, clinically clean and flashing with brass plates. The specialist chose out a bell and pressed it. As he did so, Aubrey, who had been feeling no worse than dully afraid, found himself shaking with terror. The name on the plate above the bell was Blair.

The door yawned open. A moment later, the door of a strolling taxi had slammed to and Aubrey was driving off in it. He congratulated himself that he had saved his reason; to be in the hands of anyone called Blair must inevitably compel him to meditate on Jeanie's ridiculous confidence in her eye, and that way lay madness. His actual sensation was that he had just managed to escape with his life. In either case, he was done with doctors, and for the remainder of that day he was in excellent health.

By the next day, he felt as ill as ever, which was now intimidatingly ill. Keeping up his spirits by recalling everything he had disliked about the specialist in tropical diseases, he recalled an allusion to 'that charlatan Gregory Ionides'. He looked up the charlatan in the telephone directory and, finding that he lived in King's Road, Chelsea, decided to give him a try. Gregory Ionides was a sturdy, swarthy man with a beard and a diamond ring. Aubrey felt he was a man who at any rate could be trusted not to behave like the Harley Street lot. His trust was deepened when the consultation turned to an interchange of views about the Lebanon, and agreement as to the incomparability of its bedbugs. On these lines, he went on consulting Dr Ionides, and by their fourth meeting succeeded in reintroducing the subject of his health, artfully presenting it as an aspect of the Levant. Dr Ionides warmed to it. Aubrey warmed to it, too, answering questions that were relevant and assenting to suppositions that hit the mark. Dr Ionides passed from warmth to fervour; it was as though each detail he drew from Aubrey were an ingredient thrown into an elaborate sauce, a sauce that at every cook's sip declared itself as coming together into something superlative. When he began diving into a tin box filled with cheap notebooks, he seemed to be suspended over the spice-box. When, to a question whether Aubrey sometimes felt as if a key were being turned in his navel, Aubrey replied that this described the feeling to a nicety, Dr Ionides emitted a solemn 'A-ha!' and, as it were, took off his cook's apron.

'I thought so. I thought so. I have already had a case like yours. He was a pig-driver in Thrace. He had been treated with viper fat, toads boiled with artemisia, fumigations, wood lice, medals of the Virgin—all the usual things. I gave him *liquor arsenicalis,* camphor . . .' Dr Ionides detailed the treatment with creative fullness.

'Did it work?' said Aubrey, so full of hope that he could be natural.

'I have no doubt it would have done the trick. But just after I had taken him in hand, he was stabbed through the heart at a wedding. An unsatisfactory patient.'

A book published soon after its author's death is pretty sure of being favourably received. *Western Tartary: A Vindication of Sir John Mandeville* had excellent reviews, and continued to sell in thousands even after it had been acclaimed as a minor classic. Aubrey Cutbush was compared to Kinglake, Richard Burton, Borrow, Laurence of Arabia, Herodotus and Omar Khayyám. He was invited to join committees, promote nudist colonies, help to suppress (or defend) democracy, church schools, and blood sports; to buy a tiger skin; to write a few words that could be used in promoting the sale of a new brand of Tokay; to repent of his sins before it was too late; and to subscribe to a news-cutting agency—invitations that his executors impartially declined.

As *Western Tartary* could not be made into a film or a play, or adapted, with incidental seagulls, for broadcasting, it continued to be read as a book. Another author benefited by all this; the *Travels of Sir John Mandeville* was presently reissued in a cheap edition. Aubrey was fond of Mandeville, and would, presumably, have taken this as a good enough memorial. However, he is also commemorated in his native town. In the Tittingham Folk Museum there hangs a neat Victorian water-colour enhanced by a great deal of mount and a gold frame. Below it is a pasteboard notice.

OPIE COTTAGE, *c.* 1840
Artist Unknown

Opie Cottage, pulled down in 1930 to make
room for the present structure, was the birthplace of
Aubrey Cutbush, Traveller, and Author of 'Western
Tartary'.
Presented, 1936, by Dulcibella Tregurtha, B.Litt.

Emil

It was April 1938 and Mrs Hathaway said to Mrs Kirkpatrick, 'We are going to take an Austrian refugee.'

'Really? An Austrian? I believe they are charming. My cousin Linda adores hers. But I can't imagine you without your old Hannah. I didn't know she was leaving.'

Mrs Hathaway explained that this refugee was not coming as a domestic servant. He was an Austrian who had escaped to England after the *Anschluss*. 'It's a boy,' she said, and blushed, for it sounded so ridiculous, as though she were announcing a birth.

Emil Kirchner was rather more than a boy. He was twenty-one. He was an orphan, his elder brother was pro-Hitler. He had a high forehead and curly, mouse-coloured hair and a small mouth. He spoke English fluently. Mrs Hathaway had imagined that on their first introduction he would bow from the waist and kiss her hand, but instead of kissing it he shook it.

They met in London at the house of a friend of the Hathaways, a woman who worked in an organization called the Friends of Democracy. There had been a tacit understanding that if Mrs Hathaway did not like the looks of this refugee she could have another. But the idea of picking and choosing among the unfortunate was repulsive to her. She could not imagine herself leading Dora Welsford toward the window and murmuring, 'I should like to see another of them.' And anyhow, Emil seemed a very pleasant young man.

So Emil picked up his suitcase and they went off together and had some tea, Mrs Hathaway apologizing that it was not chocolate. And then they went to Charing Cross, and travelled to Ryebridge, and went on by bus to the village of France Green.

The village was looking its best. The converted cottages —converted to the use of the small gentry—seemed to wear looks of gentle festivity, fluttering with clean window-curtains and posied with flowers. Even the unconverted cottages, which were much more recent in date and built of red brick, had a certain comfortable glow in the sunset. As they walked along the village street, Mrs Hathaway, exchanging nods and greetings with neighbours, said to Emil, 'That is Mrs Kirkpatrick—an old friend of ours,' or 'Major Cullen. He knows Austria, too,' or 'That's Miss Forrester. You'll like her so much.'

And then she was introducing Emil to Mr Hathaway and feeling as though they were already quite old acquaintances. Mr Hathaway was a bank manager in Ryebridge. He was also chairman of the France Green Parish Council and the founder of the France Green Debating Society. Bank managers in England are usually Conservatives, but Mr Hathaway was a Liberal.

They had agreed that during the first evening they would avoid asking questions about how and why Emil had left Vienna. It would be better to keep to ordinary topics. It is difficult to keep to ordinary topics with a perfect stranger; even though Emil's English was so good, the conversation flagged, and it was a relief when he said, 'You have a piano. I, too, am fond of music.'

Now I shall be caught out, thought Mrs Hathaway. They are all so intensely musical, and suppose he asks me to play duets with him? If it were only the slow movements—but when everything gets black with semiquavers I always lose my head.

Emil showed no inclination for duets. Most of the time he played by ear. The things he played by ear were all unfamiliar to the Hathaways, but after a week or two they got to know his repertory; especially Mrs Hathaway, who had no bank to manage. The piano was clearly a great solace to Emil, even more so after it had been tuned. He played by the hour: sad melodies and dance tunes with a sorrowful hop in them. Hannah said she expected it was as good as knitting to the poor young gentleman. They all did their best to understand his position.

But it is difficult for people living in their busy, untroubled homes to understand the position of a refugee, unless, of course, that refugee is of a class which cooks or sews or looks after children. As the spring advanced, as the lawn needed mowing and the green peas needed sticking, the Hathaways hoped that Emil would find comfort in nature, but he still preferred art and remained indoors. He preferred art to politics, too. It was almost impossible to get him to talk about the *Anschluss*. Mr Hathaway was inclined to take a large view. Emil had left Vienna because he disapproved of Fascism. Mr

Hathaway also disapproved of Fascism, more intellectually, if less violently, than Mrs Hathaway. Surely, he said to his wife, a common disapproval is common ground enough.

Other people in France Green could not leave it at that. Miss Forrester, for instance, examining the carnations in the border below the sitting-room window, made Mrs Hathaway quite an eloquent speech about the sufferings of the Jews.

'Actually, Herr Kirchner is not a Jew,' said Mrs Hathaway.

Miss Forrester swept on. 'And I said to Mr Benson, I can't understand it, I said. Surely you, as a churchwarden, should realize what is meant by religious persecution. It's nonsense, I said, and it's unchristian to go on talking of Mrs Hathaway's Communist just because the poor young fellow is a Jew. What about the Bible? I said. Was that published by the Left Book Club? Oh, I was furious with him! Though I couldn't say to him, as I can to you, that I, for one, am beginning to think there's a great deal to be said for the Communists.' She glanced in the window. The music continued. 'If I met a Communist,' said Miss Forrester slowly and clearly, 'I would say to him, we have a great deal in common.'

But still the music continued and Mrs Hathaway was obliged to say, 'Actually, Herr Kirchner is not a Communist.'

Presently she was rebutting other constructions. One time it was Mrs Kirkpatrick, who, without saying anything of the sort herself, or even believing it, felt obliged to let Mrs Hathaway know that the Riddles were going about quite openly saying that the Hathaways were harbouring a German spy.

184

'There's a lot going on in France Green, isn't there,' said Mrs Hathaway, moved to satire, 'that Hitler would give his ears to know about?'

'It isn't so much what goes on,' replied Mrs Kirkpatrick, 'as what goes over. After all, we have Imperial Airways flying over us twice a day. And any amount of other planes.'

'Well,' said Mrs Hathaway, 'if the Riddles have seen Herr Kirchner running out to count airplanes and then running out to the post office to send messages in code, they've seen more than I have. My trouble has been that I can't get him to stir out of doors.'

'But you wouldn't expect him to, would you?' said Mrs Kirkpatrick. 'Spies have to conceal their movements.'

Mrs Hathaway began to feel that any movement from Emil, overt or covert, would be welcome. He did not care for gardening. He had no impulse to explore the country-side. Though he played tennis very well, he did not care for playing tennis. Throughout the summer he moped— there was no other word for it. He was polite. He was, when called upon, obliging. He played the piano, he took many baths. His stock of small talk kept up better than the Hathaways', perhaps because he did not tax it so hard. The only person in the household with whom he seemed to feel at ease was Hannah. He spent a lot of time in the kitchen, helping Hannah with the vegetables and listening to her talk of cats she had known in the past, but even this attachment seemed questionable and might have been due to nothing more than an English summer and the fact that the kitchen was the only room in the house that had a fire in it.

Refugee mentality, said Mrs Hathaway to herself. The phrase would have been more of a comfort to her if she had not been an honest and compassionate woman. As it was, she suffered a great deal, imagining how she would feel in a foreign land and among strangers. What was going on behind that high forehead? What words of melancholy and disillusionment did the small mouth shut back? She herself could hardly endure a week-end of paying a visit, and Emil had been at France Green for the whole summer and had never once crossed the moral frontiers of the spare room.

'Well, that at any rate is something to admire,' she said to her husband. 'He's not happy and he doesn't try to be. He doesn't like us and he doesn't pretend to. I call that real integrity. I honour him for it.'

Mr Hathaway looked up from the evening paper. 'I don't like the look of things,' he said.

Presently Mr Hathaway convened a meeting of the Air Raid Precautions wardens. As chairman of the Parish Council he made himself unpopular by urging that the France Green fire engine, which dated from 1895, should be overhauled. He got leaflets and distributed them. He laid in stores of brown paper and sticky paper, recommended for making rooms gasproof. He collected sacks for sandbags and made a survey of cellars. He wrote several letters asking for gas masks for the village, and, thanks to his importunity, received three. He outraged the County Education Department by suggesting that a trench should be dug in the school garden and was told that such a thing would be out of the question, as it was essential not to spread panic among children. And he called two Public Meetings, which would have been better attended, as those who did not attend them explained, if people were not getting up their potatoes just then.

Mr Benson, who was also a warden, spoke bitterly about the apathy of the working class. 'They're spoon-fed!' he exclaimed. 'They expect one to thrust a silver spoon into their mouths. They're born like that.'

Mr Hathaway wrote his fifth application for a supply of gas masks and received a reply saying that they were officially termed gas respirators and would be available in due course. He also spent some time examining into the rumour, put forward by several of the oldest inhabitants, that an underground passage, long lost, ran between the church and Manor Farm.

'Every village in England has that story,' said Major Cullen.

Mr Hathaway remarked that France Green might be the village where the story was true.

Simultaneously with Mr Hathaway's appeal for volunteers to dig trenches between five-thirty, when the men of France Green ceased work, and sundown, the Rector announced that the church would be open every evening between six and eight for those who wished to pray for peace.

'What's the use of all these precautions?' inquired Mr Riddle. 'I'm a bit of a fatalist, I am.'

Aided by Mr Cobb at the garage, Mr Hathaway spent the next to the last Friday evening in September trying to construct a siren, and on Saturday he returned from

Ryebridge with all the picks and shovels he could buy. This was timely, as on Monday everyone began to dig, everyone except the women, who were attending First Aid classes, and Mr Benson, who surveyed the diggers.

Emil dug, too. He dug extremely well. After a little wary observation by the other diggers, he became very popular among them. When it was too dark to dig any longer, he produced a mouth organ and the gang marched home with a swagger. The moment dinner was over, he tore down to the kitchen where Hannah had promised to teach him how to darn sacks. At ten-thirty he reappeared, saying that all the sacks were darned and demanding cartridge paper and red paint. He was still making posters and notices when Mr and Mrs Hathaway went to bed, and when they got up next morning Hannah told them that he had made an early breakfast and gone out with his pick and shovel.

Mr and Mrs Hathaway were so moved with relief that neither said a word to the other. To have commented on this transformation would have been a disloyalty.

Digging went on through Tuesday and Wednesday. They were making a shelter now as well as trenches. Emil had organized the workers into competitive gangs. On Wednesday the news came that the Prime Minister was going to Munich, but no one slackened for that; and that evening Emil and Mr Cobb rigged up lighting and the younger men worked on most of the night. On Thursday morning a load of timber was found neatly stacked beside the shelter. On it was a piece of paper with the words: 'Mr K. with compts. from an unknown friend.'

Emil had flashed into such popularity that when young Jimmy Barnes inadvertently dropped a pick on his foot a shout of wrath and despair went up. The First Aid detachment hurried out with bandages and the stretcher. Emil caused himself to be conveyed in a wheelbarrow to where the children were filling sandbags and worked on with them. At sundown they wheeled him home, refusing to let anyone else handle their hero, and spilling him twice.

'You must go straight to bed,' said Mrs Hathaway.

'I probably won't sleep.'

'You must. Really, you must. You are much too valuable to wear yourself out now. You must be kept in trim for when——'She stopped. The question jumped up in her mind: What would happen to Emil in a war—in a war which would make him an enemy alien?

'For when the curtain goes up, eh?' His high forehead was plastered with mud. The small mouth was open in a brilliant, breathless smile. 'I go to bed, then. Thank you very much.'

Afterwards she went to his room and looked in. He was asleep. Hitherto she had seen only his waking countenance. Sleeping, his face was rigid and melancholy. The corners of the small mouth turned down, the arched eyebrows, doll-like by day, now gave him an expression of agonized bewilderment. She glanced round the room. His clothes, his brushes, his washing things. Nothing else. Not a photograph, not a book. It was a spare room, with a week-end visitor asleep in it.

Downstairs was Henry, checking off the names of those who had been measured for gas masks.

'This awful waiting,' she said. 'I never thought I'd hope for war. I don't even know if I do. Henry, what *is* one to think?'

'It will be the news in a minute,' he answered, stretching out his hand to the wireless. She sat down, nerving herself to listen.

The morning papers carried the headlines: 'Agreement Reached, Occupation to Begin To-morrow. Mr Chamberlain Flying Back', and in smaller type, 'Prague Agrees to Further Concessions.' Like a nose-bleeding, a ghastly, warm trickle of relief began to move in her. She realized that for the last twenty-four hours she had been counting on this.

Mr Kirchner was still asleep, said Hannah. She was taking him up his breakfast. Mrs Hathaway put a newspaper on the tray. 'Don't wake him,' she said.

'Nothing to wake anyone for,' said Hannah. '"Mr Chamberlain returning." Trust him to come back! Grinning hyena—feathering his own nest!'

Presently Mr Hathaway left for his bank. The breakfast tray went up and came down again. I ought to do his foot, thought Mrs Hathaway. She went upstairs. The room was empty, the bath water was running. She came down again.

About midday Emil appeared. The Rector was calling. He proposed to hold a special service. He also proposed to give the collection to the Czechs. So he had come to ask if Mr Kirchner would do another of those wonderful posters of his, announcing both these intentions.

'We owe it to them,' he exclaimed.

When he had gone, Emil limped across to the piano. For a moment he stared at the keyboard. Then he turned and looked at Mrs Hathaway—a look of mournful, scornful, listless understanding. 'Couldn't we play a duet?' he said.

Idenborough

The car was a Rover, a 1939 model. In the December of that year Amabel's husband, Thomas Serpell, had bought it to put by, saying that at the end of a war there is no decent metal or decent leather left. It was still on blocks when, three years later, he died.

When wealthy men die, there is always a sensation of poverty, and under the stress of death-duties the executors had spoken of selling the car; but Thomas, Amabel's stepson, had cabled from Canada, where he was training pilots, that it must be kept, so it remained in the garage, draped in dust sheets and looking like a funeral trophy. Amabel also remained, living on with her mother-in-law for company, a dull, kind, preservative life, so preservative that when Thomas finally came home he exclaimed, 'Good God, Amabel, is this really you? You look like my niece!' Her smooth skin and her flowering full lips were the more remarkable for being encountered among Serpell aunts and cousins, fine large specimens of a North Country stock, brief in bloom and durable as pigskin. Amabel, an alien, had reversed this. She looked young and she felt elderly.

Her answer was defensive: 'Rather fat for a niece, Thomas.'

'Well, that will soon come off,' he said. 'You should do exercises, and swim, and play tennis.' Sojourning for so long in a new world, Thomas had brought back an embarrassing insistence on youthfulness, and smartness and spryness.

'Now we must get out the Rover,' said his grandmother, speaking as though it were a ceremonial teapot.

Thomas replied that it was scarcely worth the trouble, since in Cambridge he would use a bicycle. Thomas had also brought back a craving for culture and scholasticism and was going to Cambridge to read history.

When Thomas came north for Christmas, he brought his friend, Winter Gregory. Winter Gregory was a don, a kind of being Amabel had never set eyes on. She wished she had the sangfroid of her mother-in-law, who had never seen a don either but supposed he would eat and drink like any other mortal. After a couple of days, it was evident that he could fall in love like any other mortal, too. Amabel ceased to feel elderly, and refused his first proposal of marriage with such headlong vigour that the most cloistered and artless don might have taken hope from it. Winter was not notably cloistered. He had viewed with horror the bald solitaire diamond with which the deceased Mr Serpell had expressed his intentions of matrimony. The ring that he took with him on his second visit spelled out *Regard* with a ruby, an emerald, a garnet, an amethyst, another ruby and a quite moderate diamond. It looked very pretty on Amabel's old-fashioned small hand. There seemed no reason why the hand should not immediately become his, but she evaded marriage for over a year, and was finally routed into it by her mother-in-law's scorn for a woman of forty who hadn't the spunk to take a second husband. Her rough tongue succeeded where Thomas's encouragement had failed. Amabel had been abashed by the encouragements. It seemed to her like robbing a blind beggar to accept so much kind approval from her stepson when for the second time in her life she was violently in love, and on this occasion, too, not with his father.

The Rover preceded her to Cambridge. Thomas had given it to Winter as a wedding-present. This was so much what Thomas's father would have done that Amabel had a polyandrous impression that Thomas's father had almost done so.

Now, in the second year of their happy marriage, the car was swivelling along lanes and byroads whose banks were brooched with primroses and veined with the heavy blue of wild hyacinths still in bud. Winter had wanted to visit Amabel's birthplace in Somerset. She had not seen it since her fifth year, when her father went to a London parish, and there was very little she recognized except an archway under which he had driven her hoop. She felt a complete stranger and sightseer. It was the Cockney Winter who knew Priddy in the Mendips and the sudden violent view of the Bristol Channel from the road above Clapton-in-Gordano, and who, saying calmly, 'We shall find it down here,' turned the car down a one-in-five rabbit-run. But it was Wiltshire, he said, as they crossed the county boundary—especially the unattended-to, undramatic country north of Salisbury Plain—that he was more at home in.

'Stonehenge,' said Amabel, catching at something she could be sure of. 'I should like to see Stonehenge.'

Without comment on her geography, he began to drive south-eastward toward the smooth rampart of the chalk. On the timelessness of Salisbury Plain, Amabel suddenly became aware that the Rover looked somewhat out of date.

'You know, Winter, it's only just struck me that this car does look rather odd—spinsterish, and as if we ought to be wearing toques trimmed with autumn leaves.'

'If I had to choose between a spinster and a chromium-plated strumpet—' He broke off, and pointed ahead. 'Look!'

'Oh!' Her exclamation sounded like a cry of pity. 'Oh, Winter, is that Stonehenge?'

'Are you disappointed?'

'No! But somehow I feel so sorry for it. It is so small, so very small, and so neat.'

'Amabel, you don't know how I love you for things like that. You are the only perfectly sincere person I have ever known.'

He halted the car. Presently, he turned it and they drove away. She felt vaguely surprised. Winter's spendthrift treatment of historical monuments was something she could not get accustomed to. Thomas her husband never quitted a castle or a waterfall (he had been equally prone to both) without having, as he said 'thoroughly taken it in'. Thomas her stepson, though immune to nature and the Middle Ages, could take quite as long to absorb a portico, and talked much more. At times, she felt a certain nostalgia for the Serpell method of sightseeing. Though tiring to the legs, it was restful to the mind; there was none of this hit-or-miss, sharpshooting responsibility for saying the right thing. Having been so lucky with Stonehenge, she was the more anxiously aware of her inadequacies during the rest of the day's journey, for when they turned aside for a manor house, she could think of nothing but living in it, and when Winter stopped the car with a shout of laughter before a Baptist chapel, she asked him what he was laughing at. Above all, she was estranged by the duplicity of the landscape, so intricate and so indeterminate. After the large, hymn-tune solemnity of the North of England, it was perplexing as a fugue.

She's tired, Winter thought, and in his concern for her he lost his sense of direction, and took a wrong turning. He began to hurry, and so overshot a signpost, and had to turn back. It stood where the road branched left and right, and the left-hand pointer read, 'Great Wimble 9, Oxford 31.'

Sighing with relief, he said, 'There! Oxford. We shan't be long now. After Wimble, we shall strike a main road.' Even as he spoke, he noticed the right-hand pointer 'Idenborough! I had no idea we were so near it.'

'Ten miles,' Amabel said. 'And a dreadful road.'

'Yes, but Idenborough at the end of it. It's almost the loveliest small town in England, and there's quite a good inn. Why don't we spend the night there, instead of in Oxford?'

Amabel had read the name before he spoke it, and had been nerving herself to hear it spoken. It was at Idenborough, twenty years before, that she and Harry had spent a day, and two long autumn nights lying in a lumpy bed—so short a time, and yet outweighing all the rest of her life. She had gone there by train, abandoning her Thomases on the pretext of an old school friend just leaving for India. Blinded by excitement and sick headache, she had got out at a station on a branch line, where Harry was waiting on the platform, his face so stern with love that for a moment she had not recognized him, while he, glaring at the other end of the train, was so sunk in his conviction that she had changed her mind that she was compelled to take him by the sleeve and shake him before he noticed her. All rapture, all romance, and all leave-taking were sealed up under that word, *Idenborough,* and now it was a name on a signpost, and a place where she and Winter might spend the night.

'Oxford's only thirty miles on, and you wanted to show me Oxford.' Her voice shook as if she had been running.

Glancing round, he saw that she looked pale. Oxford be damned, with its bells and its buses, and its admirers settling with veneration on all the fakes! 'Oxford can wait,' he said, and turned off for Idenborough.

If only I could sometimes tell the truth, if only I could learn to speak out, she thought—and remembered how, earlier in the day, Winter had praised her for her sincerity. But now it was too late. Deceit must accumulate on deceit, and with her second husband she would visit Idenborough, where she had cuckolded her first one. Winter was assuring her how much she would like Idenborough, and comparing its grape-coloured roof-tiles with roofs in Burgundy, while, faithless once again, she sat staring ahead, licking her lips with excitement as she waited for the first recognition. The lane ran into a main road. Ahead was a wide, placid street, and the silhouette of a church tower, old and owlish. She did not particularly recognize anything, but no doubt that was because they were entering from another direction. The tower had been there, of course, for she remembered the bells chiming the hours and the quarters, and Harry saying that he had an uncle whose conversation was precisely similar. And, in fact, what did she remember of Idenborough? So little—only everything. But when Winter stopped in front of a porch surmounted by a mild bear painted plum colour, she nearly said, 'This isn't the right hotel.'

While he was garaging the car, she followed the servant to the room allotted to them, her legs moving under her like the legs of some other person, legs imperfectly attached and rather too short for her. Strewing her coat and gloves and bag on twin beds of blameless springs, she went to the window. Roofs of weathered tiles, fig trees and lilacs emerging from walled gardens, the leaden haunches of a church, and beyond, a row of tall poplars . . . She knew those trees. They signalled everything into place. The hotel where she had stayed with Harry must be at the farther end of the town. There was the true Idenborough. The poplars grew close to that hotel, aligned along a bridle-path that led to a cemetery and the gasworks. There they had walked up and down, in a gentle drizzling rain, saying that it was really too wet to stay out any longer and yet continuing to walk up and down. And there she had known the inexhaustible melancholy of youth, extending below her like an ocean and endlessly surrounding her while she floated onward, immortally buoyant and serene.

When Winter came in, she turned from the window, saying, 'I am so glad we came here instead of Oxford. Shall we go out for a little walk?'

'Not till you've had a drink. I only hope I haven't gone and overtired you, jaunting about all day. Besides, it's nearly dinner-time.'

'Well, after dinner, then?'

The drink mounted lightly to her head. All through dinner, she felt a detached, competent animation, as though she were behaving to music. Exactly on the beat, she said, 'What horrible coffee! Don't let's waste time on it. I'd rather walk round Idenborough.'

The direction of the poplar trees was so perfectly established in her mind that she felt no impatience when Winter set off in the opposite direction, talking of a town hall. A lion and a unicorn decorated the town hall, plump and suave as though they were in sugar on a biscuit. They were just what Harry would have liked, and she almost wished that they had come this way instead of going by bus to that rather tiresome village with a wishing-well. Winter liked the lion and the unicorn, too, and agreed about the biscuit. They walked down several streets, pausing to admire doorways and converse with evening cats, and finding a chemist's shop still open and lit up like an Elizabethan jewel with its coloured flasks and rosy patent tonics, they went in for the pleasure of buying something in Idenborough. The purchase of a small hot-water bottle led to a long conversation between Winter and the chemist that wound its way to leeches and local survivals of traditional remedies, such as stolen potatoes and fried mice.

When they left the shop, the twilight had changed to a blue dusk, and Amabel could hear doors being shut and bolted. But still she was not impatient, though it was apparent that Winter had something more up his sleeve, some special beauty that he was saving for the last. While she was waiting in the chemist's shop, it occurred to her that if this evening were frittered away, there would still be to-morrow morning. It would be easy to make an excuse of wanting to shop by herself in order to buy him a surprise present, and then all she need do would be to find the railway station and from there retrace her way to the hotel and the poplar trees, and on the way back she could buy a mug. Idenborough was full of shops where mugs could be bought, and when you have taken the first step of deceiving a husband, nothing is easier than to go on.

Reposing on this, she accompanied Winter down a street so narrow that there was no inducement to stop and admire anything. At the foot of the hill, the street turned sharply. She received a sudden impression of light and space, and felt the air freshened, and heard the slap of water against stone. They were on a quay, and before them extended a narrow bridge of many arches. Half-way across it, he stopped.

'Look, Amabel. That's why I wanted to bring you here.'

Behind them the town, catching the revenant light of the eastern sky, was a muddle of brown and mulberry-coloured velvets. The tower and the high nave of the church rose above it, and the sky showed through the clerestory windows. But she only looked at it long enough to steady herself, and then returned her gaze to the wide, pale river, whose waters swirled with a kind of sleepwalking impetus from between the piers of the bridge. So wide a river . . . How could they not have known there was this river? She looked along its course and saw on the far bank a row of poplar trees, rising lugubriously tall from an unlit, unbroken flatness of water-meadows.

Laying her hand on the parapet and finding it quite real, she asked, 'What river is this?'

'The Thames.'

Another strong swirl of water emerged from under the bridge and spread itself onward, as though in calm assent and confirmation.

'What did you say this place was called?'

'Idenborough.'

A small black dazzle flashed in front of her and disappeared under the bridge.

'A bat,' she said, fastening on a certainty.

Not hearing her, he went on, 'Idenborough Regis, to give it its full name. There's another Idenborough, in Bedfordshire. A dull place—though now I suppose it glitters with cinemas and garages, for there's an aerodrome near by.'

After a while, still looking down on the river, Amabel said, 'Is there anywhere you haven't been?'

There was such rancour in her voice that he was nearly stampeded into asking her if she felt tired. Taking his cue from an oncoming yawn, he replied, 'Bed, perhaps. Judging from my present sensations, I have never been to bed.'

The yawn achieved itself, and on its close he took her by the arm and began walking back to the hotel.

'I expect it's driving that old-fashioned car that tires you,' she said.

His car, his dearest possession (since one does not number a wife among possessions), which throughout their holiday of by-roads and hysterical contours had behaved like a duchess—not satisfied with attacking him, Amabel must needs turn against the Rover, too. This time, he asserted himself. 'With a good car, it's mileage that counts, Amabel, not years. The same with wives.'

'Yes, but it *is* an old car, Winter. One's only got to look at it to see that. And though it's very chivalrous of you to feel affection for your old dowdy . . .'

All the way back to the hotel she talked in this strain, flagellating herself under the guise of depreciating the car, condoling with him on his faithfulness to an old car and an ageing wife. It rent his heart to hear her. It appalled his heart to admit an identity between his gentle, modest, complying Amabel and this provincial harridan at his side.

She saw his grief and his dismay, but she dared not weaken to them. If she were to change her harsh tune, if for one moment between now and when she heard him grunt and fall from her into the solitude of sleep she were to let him be kind to her, she would be done for; she would give way and tell him about Harry and the other Idenborough, and how, merely by her own despicable shilly-shallying and playing for safety, there had been no more to tell. To Winter, unjudging, unblaming, possibly even approving, it would seem next to nothing, and by length of time diminished to nothing at all. Indeed, there was not much of it: two nights and a day, a rapture so inattentively, unbelievingly entertained that she did not even know what county Idenborough was in. Unbelievingly entertained, weakly lost, negligently remembered (for months at a time she did not give it a thought), yet it was all she had. Thinking this, she reversed the thought. She was all it had. It existed by her secrecy; to speak of it would be to dismiss it, like the small crystal world of a bubble, into common air. Any infidelity but that.

A Funeral at Clovie

For many years Archie Stevenson had felt that his cousin Hew's wife, Veronica, was too much of a good thing: too good, signally too good for poor Hew, who would have done better with some ordinary sinner; and too much; too healthy, too majestic and too striking. Now here she was, the first thing to catch his eye as he entered the hotel in Edinburgh, the first thing to catch any eye; for she was dressed in white from head to foot, a white sombrero on her red hair, a white cloak flowing off her shoulders, a sky-blue enamel cross swinging on her bosom, and pinned elsewhere on the bosom various denominational insignias; got up, in short, as though for a religious Ascot. She saw his start of horror—there was little that Veronica did not see with her fine rolling blue eyes—and with her customary frankness she took up the challenge.

'I'm afraid you don't think me very suitably attired, Archie dear.'

'No, no, not at all! It looks very nice. Cool. Most refreshing on a day like this. I'm afraid it's going to be a scorcher. Was it as hot as this in London?'

Scorning his poor little red herring, she continued, 'But I don't feel quite as you do, perhaps, about funerals. To me, a funeral is something joyous. A beginning, not an ending.'

'Um'hm,' said Archie, thinking of the bleak little affair that would take place at Clovie.

'And Hew's funeral . . . Poor Hew! I feel much more as though I were going to his christening. As his godmother, you know.'

Several people in the hotel entrance were pricking up ears. Courteously raising her voice for their benefit, Veronica continued, 'Yes, now I feel that I can begin to do something for Hew, something really practical. Of course, I've *always* prayed for him, but now—'

Mark the pregnant aposiopesis. A book of his schooldays had adjured Archie, in a footnote to *The Bacchae,* to do this. He did it now, and replied, 'Yes, of course.'

And in a sense, he agreed. A dead Hew could not be so demonstrably refractory to Veronica's prayers. But the words that rose in his mind were, 'hitting a man when you've got him down'. He suppressed this thought. It wouldn't do. Veronica very trustingly had asked him to squire her to the funeral, and he must begin the day in a proper spirit, whatever might come later.

As she was finding so much to rejoice in, he too would be glad about something. 'I'm glad the boy was there. Hew was very fond of Martin.'

'Darling Martin! He was always so wonderfully loyal about his father. Thank you *so* much! Goodbye, goodbye!'

Thanks and farewell were addressed to the Head Porter and one might have supposed from the unction and the tip that Mrs Stevenson had been his only interest for a fortnight instead of someone who had arrived overnight. Hew's voice sounded out of the past, observing, 'Veronica's doing her Angel's Farewell. She does it to everyone in sight, and never less than five bob a time.' Not wearing a buttonhole, not tipping anybody, Archie escorted her down the steps, put her into the car which was so sadly unworthy of her, and took the road for the north. He disliked driving in traffic, and there was something wrong with the radiator, for the car had boiled as he drove across the Lammermuir Hills to meet her at the hotel, and it would certainly boil again before they reached Clovie. He felt a strong reluctance to take her to Hew's funeral (for that matter, he did not much want to go to Clovie himself: it had been the family place when hc was a boy, and now it wasn't). But every family has its factotum, and naturally Veronica, getting herself as far as Edinburgh by train, would expect him to drive her the rest of the way. Besides, being so totally English, she most likely could not credit that the railway system extended beyond the Firth of Forth.

He drove none the better for her helpfulness in telling him of cars that wished to overtake, warning him of oncoming cars whenever he pulled out to overtake himself, drawing his attention to traffic signals and dogs about to cross the road. They had several near shaves. All were due to his misjudgment, but she made no comment, she did not even suggest that he might like her to take over the wheel for a change. It had to be admitted, Veronica lived up to her cheerful outlook on funerals: there could not be many women so nonchalantly prepared to be shot into eternity. When the car boiled—it boiled twice—she did not fuss.

There was nothing to suggest that having come all this way to attend the funeral of a husband who for the last twelve years had refused to live with her she would be annoyed if she arrived too late for it. A woman, Archie said to himself, giving Veronica her due, whom one would find congenial in emergencies; especially if one had a taste for emergencies. Hew had no such taste.

'I suppose it was his low blood-pressure,' said Archie, who had been thinking about Hew while Veronica had been talking about him.

'Low blood-pressure? I don't see why. Why should low blood-pressure make him dislike alabaster?'

'Dying so suddenly, I mean. Taken ill one day, dead the next. Fearful shock for young Martin. All the more so for happening at Clovie Shaws, miles from anywhere.'

'I always thought it sounded a most depressing spot. No view, no drains, midges and that gloomy little river. Besides, why should Hew want to live with those farming Baxters, even if he had known them all his life? Still, Martin liked it. He always enjoyed his visits to Clovie Shaws.'

'I wonder if he'll keep on going there.'

'Oh no!' Veronica spoke with decision. As if she had overheard the exclamation and thought it too trenchant, she added, 'It was only for Hew's sake. Martin has been so good about all that, so scrupulously fair to his father. Dear boy! I've always said to him, "Darling, you mustn't judge. You must just love." '

'Damn that sheep!' The car swerved violently away from a sheep that was grazing by the roadside. 'These sheep are a menace, always causing accidents. As I was going to say, Martin seems to have managed admirably, kept his head, thought of everything, even remembered to send a notice to *The Times*. But I daresay he'll be feeling a bit shaken. It's a nasty shock for a boy of seventeen.'

The pretext of the sheep had failed, and Veronica retorted to the waspish anger she had roused.

'Well, Archie, Martin rather happens to share my quaint outlook on death. He may think that a dead Hew is a happier, safer Hew than a Hew alive, shut up in that miserable self-centred existence, doing nothing, going nowhere, never able to get outside himself.'

If he were self-centred, why should he want to get outside himself? The question was so nearly jerked out of Archie that he appeared to be mastering a hiccup. Veronica gazed ahead. 'Those hills,' she murmured. 'So wonderfully, so forgivingly blue!'

'Grampians.'

'Yes, I thought so.' And she continued to gaze, with the expression of someone who would say, I am not quite such a fool as you think, but I will be patient with you as my mind is on higher things.

She might be all right in emergencies, thought Archie, but how Hew endured six years of uneventful ideal marriage with such a woman passed his comprehension. Six years of it, then Hew went off. No man could have left his wife more considerately, getting himself parachuted into occupied France and not till after the Liberation sending her evidence for a divorce. But all she did with the evidence was to grab at Hew's address and pester him with Martin. Martin must not be allowed to feel himself unwanted, Martin must not be deprived of a father, etc. Hew was an ass to give in to her. Martin had almost forgotten him, and if Hew had held out a little longer he would have got over his craving for the boy. As it was, Hew went off to Clovie Shaws, and lived with the Baxters, a bachelor for eleven months in the year and a father during the other month. It was no way for a healthy normal man to live. For that matter, Veronica was a healthy normal woman, and couldn't have found living like a widow much fun. Now, however, she was a widow in fact.

Catching his speculative glance, she said like a Mother Confessor, 'Well, Archie? What is it?'

'Now that Hew's dead—now that you needn't have any more of those feelings about marriage being indissoluble, and whom God has joined, and all that sort of thing—do you suppose you'll marry again, Veronica? Would you like to, I mean?'

She coloured. It was not a blush, nothing so impulsive. It was a slow gratified pink, blooming like a rose among her white draperies. Good God! She'd got her eye on someone already!

'I have my Martin, Archie.'

But it had taken her two telegraph posts to remember that she had her Martin. No wonder she's dressed up like a bride for her husband's funeral, thought Archie. The whited sepulchre! Probably the next one will be some Bishop or other, and she'll marry him in pink. When this natural effervescence of dislike had blown off, a residual Archie with more compunction thought, Poor wretch! She's been keeping herself waiting all these years.

He came out of a muse to discover that he had somehow failed to turn into the right road. At intervals the ridge of Clovie came into sight, the kirk and the manse set on it like sunlit toys, and the dark sycamores cloaking its side. Presently some toy figures were added, sitting on the wall of the graveyard, as was the Clovie wont with a funeral in prospect. After that the ridge did not reappear for some time, and when it did it was perceptibly farther away. There was nothing for it but to turn the car and go back, and even so, ten to one they would be late. Flustered, and with his private woe of exile, Archie was additionally vexed by a consciousness that there was something he ought to tell Veronica, something that had stirred in his mind when it took her two telegraph posts to remember Martin, and which should be imparted before they reached Clovie. Now they were nearly there. They had passed the old quarry, and he could see the river skulking along at its summer pace. What on earth was it? And what on earth was that notice at the side of the road? *Narrow Bridge.* Of course the bridge was narrow. It had always been narrow—but these new-come officials defaced everything with their notice-boards. By going very fast over the bridge one got a good start up the further slope, and they would be in time for the funeral after all. He heard the noise of the river rattling over the shoal, and remembered what it was he must tell Veronica. He must explain about Baxter. If she were thinking of marrying again it might give her a nasty turn to see Hew in duplicate walking after the coffin. She'd think he wasn't dead.

Before he had parked the car to his satisfaction, Veronica was out of it, and into the graveyard, and making for the door of the kirk. In a moment she'd be inside, and down on her knees.

'Veronica, stop! You can't go in till the corpse does. And there's something I meant to tell you. It's about Baxter. Did Martin ever happen to mention anything about him?'

'Of course he did. He could scarcely lodge under the man's roof, summer after summer, and not mention him.'

Baulked of her prayers, she was naturally irate, and what he had to impart was not likely to soothe her. But there was no time for beating about the bush.

'But did he ever say anything about Baxter's looks? No? Well, Baxter's an excellent chap. But he and Hew were as alike as two peas. Quite remarkable—but not so very remarkable when you come to think of it. He was Hew's brother.'

'Brother?'

'On the wrong side of the blanket, you know. It's quite customary in these small places,' he added.

A man looked over the wall and called out, 'They're coming.' The Reverend Mr Guthrie appeared from the manse and entered the graveyard by his personal gate. Archie pulled Veronica away, as if they had been stealing gooseberries, and hurried her back to the road. Emerging from the cover of the sycamores, the small procession came up to the bare summit of the ridge as if it were coming up on to a stage or a scaffold. A farm-waggon, with the coffin on it, and an old man leading the horse; after the waggon, Martin, walking alone; then Baxter and his three sons, and after them a small tail of Clovie farmers and graziers, and the postmaster and the policeman. The waggon halted, the coffin was lifted off, and the four Baxters shouldered it. Veronica stepped forward with a maternal gesture, exclaiming 'Martin!' Martin's glance did not swerve from the coffin as he signalled her and Archie to fall in behind him. Every face was shining with sweat, and Mr Guthrie's white hairs glittered like the dried grasses of the field which he was presently to invoke. Poor old Hew, thought Archie. Hew was no more than fifty, but nothing ages a man more rapidly than being dead.

Following the coffin into the kirk, into the mitigated light that came through windows glazed with alternate diamonds of heliotrope and sickly green, Archie kept the imprint of the round sun on his retina. He blinked it away, it reasserted itself with a milder glow, and now it was no longer the round sun he saw, but the image of Martin's face. It was a round and platter face, like the sun's, and like Veronica's. Like Veronica's, and unlike the sun's, it was totally English; except that the boy walked with a light thievish gait like every other Stevenson, Hew had not left much mark in him. The image of Martin's face continued to haunt Archie, perhaps because all that Archie could inspect was the back of his head and the rims of his ears (Archie and Veronica had been shepherded into the second pew as deftly as they had been put in the second rank of the procession). *Exalté,* thought Archie. No wonder, a boy of seventeen, and robed in his first funeral, and Veronica's son at that. But just as purple had boiled up over the green sun imaged on Archie's retina, the image of Martin's face now reappeared before his mind's eye wearing a look of intense complacence. If that were so, if the boy were in fact taking Hew's death as a subject for complacence, the bequest of Beatrix Stevenson by Raeburn should go out of the will as soon as a lawyer's pen could scratch at it. Summoning himself to keep calm and to recall what Martin had really looked like, coming out from under the sycamore shade, Archie recalled that he had looked pale, just as you'd expect after all he'd been through—and breathless, which was natural enough after climbing the ridge of Clovie with all that English puppy-fat on his bones. But he had not looked so much breathless as if he were holding his breath, holding his breath as one does when putting the last storey on a house of cards—yes, and with the complacence of one who is successfully accomplishing that delicate act.

Archie, his wits sharpened by being in the place of his boyhood again, remarked to himself, 'Something's up.'

His eye rambled on to the Baxters. There they sat in their blacks, everything that four Scotsmen at a funeral should be, grave, sternly composed, panting a little from the weight of the coffin. Their hands lay spread on their knees, and they smelled of mothballs. Nothing wrong there. And yet there was something not quite right. A conviction expanded in Archie that the four Baxters were looking as if they felt about death pretty much as Veronica did. She triumphed over it outwardly, they inwardly pooh-poohed.

Everyone else looked perfectly ordinary.

From the point of view of one engaged in research, it was a pity that Jean Baxter was a respectable modest woman and didn't go to funerals. Jean Baxter was Highland stock, truth and duplicity blazed from her face in a mingled lightning, and from such a woman one could get a dozen clues and hope to pick the right one. But Jean was at Clovie Shaws, six miles away, wrapping scones in a napkin and nursing an iron frying-pan for ham and eggs. If Veronica had not been on his hands, he could have gone back with Martin and the Baxters and sunk his sad old teeth in those scones. Veronica was doing a lot of crossing herself, Clovie would think she had fleas, but this couldn't be helped. Archie's searching eye returned to Martin, and noted that Martin was not crossing himself. There was no reason to smell a rat in this. Possibly male Anglo-Catholics don't cross themselves, or possibly Martin refrained through discretion. He was certainly discreet: he had never spoken to Veronica about the resemblance between Hew and Baxter. He was discreet, he was masterful, as witness that mastering of ceremonies behind the coffin. Whatever the card-house Martin was building, Archie sincerely hoped he'd bring it off. Still pondering on the nature of the card-house, Archie presently noticed that Dr Forbes was not one of the congregation. This might be a clue, but it might equally well be a childbed. And when they followed the coffin out to the graveside, old Forbes was standing there, a hoary pillar of testimony to the truth that whisky can't kill a man who drinks it regularly before breakfast. His face was just as red, his high head no balder, as when he got Hew through double pneumonia and vaccinated Archie with a darning-needle, forty years ago. No clues on old Forbes, thought Archie, looking with a surge of affection at the upright old scoundrel who had been, ever since he could remember, the unillusioned faithful friend of the family. He recollected Forbes stalking through the emptied house, and saying, 'You're all going, though you belong here, and I'm a foreigner and I'm staying. I shan't know myself with no Stevensons to pull out of their scrapes. Queer, queer!' Now Forbes was eyeing Veronica as if his glance would reap her down into the grave. Hew's coffin was lowered, and Veronica, her cloak billowing after her, swept forward, extricated a bit of rosemary from her bag and dropped it in. The grave-digger, with very much the air of a head-waiter who has seen some smirched diner let fall a cutlet, came up with a blank face to Martin and gave him a little handful of Clovie earth. The flints glittered as they fell from Martin's hand to the coffin-lid. Mr Guthrie took up his praying, but in that fraction of silence Archie had heard the flints ring false. Whatever was in the coffin (and his mind's eye instantly presented him with an equivalent weight of river sand and hay), it wasn't Hew.

A sham funeral! Martin once prevailed on to be a party to it, the thing could have been managed as easy as apple-pie. Forbes wouldn't boggle at such a trifle as falsifying a death-certificate. The Baxters were of the family, and Jean Baxter would have shrivelled up any undertaking person who might suggest that other hands than hers should lay out Mr Stevenson and chest him. Seven people were in the know—eight, if he counted in himself. And Hew was off and away.

The conviction was so powerful that Archie turned his head and stared across at the further hill as though he would see Hew on it, leaping and bounding like a hind let loose. Hew was young again, now that he wasn't dead. A man of fifty has a lot of life under his waistcoat, and vitality would start up, fresh and strong, in a man who by his own artfulness and election had cleared himself from one life and begun another. Asked how he'd felt when he was dropped into France, Hew had replied, 'Dropped. I lay there like a dropped calf. And then I knew I had legs and got up on them.' Deposited in a new existence, Hew would do very well and get a lot of fun out of it.

Mustn't grin all over my face at a funeral, thought Archie with a guilty start, and returned his attention to the ceremony. Veronica was again fidgeting with her bag, was she proposing to tip the grave-digger? Good God! If Veronica married again, she would be a bigamist. It seemed to be written in the stars that he would not be able to give his mind to this funeral, for now he was compelled to think about Veronica becoming a bigamist. Bigamy is worse than divorce: at any rate, Veronica, holding that nothing could be worse than divorce, would have to admit that bigamy was as bad. Unfortunately—no, that was no way to feel at a funeral, even a mock one—fortunately, she would never know. Martin was not likely to give Hew away, and nobody else would. There might be rather a fracas when the second marriage came to be discussed, but Martin would not be able to speak out his real reason for opposing it, and nothing short of the real reason would stop her. She would get her way, as usual, and live a happy bigamist ever after. What a funeral! He was amply recompensed for his long duteous career of being the family funeral hack. But the hacking was not over, he still had to drive Veronica to Edinburgh. What on earth could he find to talk about? And to sit without talking while bigamy burned in his bosom was a frightful risk, for she might say to him, as she had done on the way north, 'Well, Archie?'—and if she so much as glimpsed a cat in the bag she would have no mercy on him.

Mr Guthrie had done and was walking away, everybody was moving; they would be silent till they were outside the graveyard, conversation would then begin with a few grunts, leading to restrained commendations of the dead and acknowledgments of a common mortality. Veronica's attempts on the grave-digger having been headed off by Martin, she was now showing herself in charity towards the Church of Scotland.

'Such a dear old clergyman! Martin, darling, will you particularly thank him from me for taking the service so reverently? What struck me so much was the utter sincerity of it all. Did the flies bother him, poor old boy?' (This was the Clovie Shaws horse, for they were now back on the road.) 'Even if it wasn't quite what you and I would have chosen, Martin, it was what Hew wanted.'

'I hope so.' Martin's tone was decently confident, but it is a mother's part to understand and reassure.

'Oh, yes, I'm quite sure it was. Aren't you, Archie!'

'Haven't a doubt of it.'

'And, Martin, you have been splendid, quite splendid through it all.'

'Couldn't have done better.'

Archie was willing to be affable. His mind was at rest, for he had decided to take a leaf out of Hew's book. After a few miles, he would find something going wrong with the car. He would then drive Veronica to Perth and put her in the train—nicely, very nicely, after a cup of tea. She had eaten enormously of sandwiches on the way to Clovie, but one needs refreshment after a funeral, whether one looks on it as an ending or a beginning.

A Passing Weakness

During the summer holiday season, strangers would sometimes come half-way up the avenue, thinking that a house with
such chimney-stacks must be either a hotel or a youth hostel;
but at the turn, where the total inhospitality of Bendish Hall
stared them in the face, they beat a retreat, scolded by the
squirrels overhead. The squirrels were the indigenous red
English squirrels. Horace Winterton piqued himself on this.
His country was going to the dogs, his house was falling to
pieces, the nephew who would inherit after him had settled
in New Zealand, vowing never to return; but at least there
were no interloping grey squirrels in his trees.

He was nearing his eighties, and his income when rates
and taxes had done with it was under six hundred a year. A
few years before, carried away by the satisfaction of damning
a Labour Government, he had been fool enough to tell this
to Ursula, his sister-in-law. At once Ursula exclaimed, in
her gross, omniscient way, 'Then why go on living here?
Sell the place, and settle down in something of a reasonable
size, with some money in your pocket.'

'A bungalow. Why not come out with it and say a
bungalow?'

'Because I know you are a snob,' Ursula said. 'Though
why it should be the sin against the Holy Ghost to live in
a bungalow, I cannot imagine. I could live in a bungalow.'

'You should have gone to New Zealand, then. New Zealand is covered with bungalows,' Horace said. In his mind's eye, a geyser spurted boiling water, and Ursula was within spray-fall. Unable to put this into words, he uttered a brief, screeching laugh, like a jay's.

Ursula was twelve years younger than he and a widow, with nothing to do, since her son and his family had emigrated, but make a nuisance of herself. During the immediate post-war years she had been indispensable to something or other and left Horace in peace. Now, embellished with an O.B.E. (a decoration tantamount to grey squirrels), she had come to see what had become of him. What had become of him (since structures of flesh and blood are notoriously subject to the hand of time) was less astonishing to her than what had become of Bendish Hall. Outwardly it kept its peacock swagger of Jacobean brick and crow-stepped gables. Inwardly it was perishing from damp and penury, and smelled of rats, soot and mildew.

Since Horace would not sell outright, Ursula said, Why not convert the upper storey into a flat and let it?

The upper storey, he replied, was the worst. Some fool had machine-gunned the roof.

Then why not convert the kitchen wing? Nowadays people really preferred smaller rooms, as being easier to keep warm.

Anyone living in the kitchen wing, said Horace, would need a ladder to go to bed by. The second staircase had been burned out by an evacuated woman trying to curl her hair.

'But didn't you get damages?' Ursula asked.

'Of course I got damages! And as I prefer live wood to dead, I spent them on the timber. If you had eyes in your head, you might have noticed my trees. That's the best lime-tree clump in the county.'

'It must keep out a lot of sun,' said Ursula. 'I don't care for trees so close to a house.'

'I do,' said Horace.

Stopped her mouth, he thought. When, after a night of being kept awake by rats in the wainscot and starlings in the chimney, she went away, he hoped she would not come again. Not that he cared a snap of his fingers for her opinions, but she unsettled him.

Six months later, she reappeared, wondering why he had not thought of getting some active dispossessed couple who would be thankful for a roof to cover them and express their thankfulness by working in the house and helping old Basil in the garden.

Horace said, 'In better days—before you married Julian—it took three housemaids to keep this house in order. Good stout local girls, too. If you think one half-starved Estonian can do it, you're wrong.'

'But you could shut up some of the rooms.'

'Which?' he demanded. 'I can't live like a mouse in a trap.'

'Do you need six bedrooms to feel at liberty?'

'I don't see how I can do with fewer. I use the red room in winter. In summer I can't stand being mewed up in a four-poster, so I move to the Indian room. I have to have a dressing-room, don't I? And as the red room and the Indian

221

room are at opposite ends of the house, that means two dressing-rooms. I keep my boots in the brown room. At my age, a man cannot be forever moving his boots about. That's five. I could do with five. But if you persist in paying me these unexpected visits, I must keep the porch room as my spare room. That's six. No one woman could possibly keep six bedrooms in order.'

'As far as I can see, no woman does,' Ursula said.

A white badge of fury appeared on Horace's nose. She could have impugned his ability to shoot, spell, mix a salad dressing, know the points of a horse, and he would not have shed a feather. Sweeping, polishing, getting dust from the crannics of the stairs, were things in which his self-confidence was less perfectly established.

Ursula felt a womanly compassion and was silly enough to express it. 'I can't bear to think of you toiling and moiling with dustpans, Horace. It's no way for you to live. Besides, when all's said and done, you're only fighting a losing battle. Wouldn't it be wiser to say goodbye to the house before it's turned into nothing but a burden and a misery? Part friends with it, you know.'

'I'll part friends with it when the time comes,' he said. 'And that will be when I come out of it feet foremost. Losing battle, eh? Loss of value, that's what you mean. Nothing to me! I shan't be here when it's put up to auction.'

'Horace, you really are intolerable.'

'In that case, you needn't suffer when you think of me moiling with dustpans. Shall we have lunch?'

Even the turkey figs were soured for her under his inflexible hospitality, and after lunch she drove herself away in such a fury that she forgot her gloves. Returning for them a few minutes later, she saw her pillows being vehemently shaken from the porch room window. Absorbed in purification, Horace did not notice her brief return.

'She upsets me,' he grumbled to himself. 'Damn her, she upsets me! A woman like that would wind an elephant.'

He was indeed horribly breathless. His legs shook under him, and his upper lip felt as though a skin of plaster of Paris had been laid over it. When all traces of Ursula had been removed, he went and sat under the lime trees to cool off. Fatigued, he sat too long, and caught a chill on his liver.

Ursula continued to visit him. Each time, Horace foiled her good intentions. But it was always at cost to himself, for either he would buy something ostentatious in order to flout her, and this would discompose his finances, or, in a fervour of self-sufficiency, he would clean the house from head to foot and become perfectly exhausted. This was the worse; by pinching and scraping one can catch up with a brace of pheasants, but every inroad on his physical resources mortgaged more of his independence to the fear of bodily decay. Privately of the opinion that by dint of hard work and spare living Horace would live to be a nuisance at ninety, Ursula did not immediately understand why Basil, the gardener, should write to her, on a picture postcard, 'Hop you can soon Come Down as it get a Bitt much for me.' The doctor's telegram was more explicit: Horace had pneumonia.

Shaken by illness and further shaken by the up-to-date brutality of the drugs used in curing him (till now, his pharmacopœia had not stretched much beyond calomel and ammoniated quinine), Horace clung to Ursula when he was convalescent, and relapsed every time she spoke of going away. Her presence screened him from his thoughts. She stayed and was kind to him—at first, rather fractiously and as a matter of duty; afterwards, with an amiability which was not like the usual Ursula. The usual Ursula had always blown bracingly on anything like nervous fears. The new Ursula was sympathetic to them, sympathetic and serene. With a cool, autumnal serenity, she spoke of making the best of things, of adapting oneself to old age, of the tapering pleasures that remain when health and strength have gone. And from time to time she told him about friends of hers, friends who were blind, or paralysed, or rigid with arthritis, or careful hosts to a thrombosis, and all of them almost penniless, and quite forsaken except for occasional visits from Ursula, and who yet managed to be wonderfully happy in a quiet way. After a month of this regimen, she took Horace for a little drive, and on the way back she pointed to a small house on the outskirts of the village, a house with a good hedge round its garden, bright windows facing south, and an air of sturdy well-being. 'I always think that's such a dear little house,' she said.

Horace, who had never consciously looked at it before, gave it a glance and remarked, 'Tight little place. Some old woman lives there—a Miss Bulteel, or some such.'

'Not now, I think,' said Ursula. 'She has gone away to live with a niece.'

Horace remarked that there must be some purpose in nieces, and left it at that.

'So now it's for sale,' continued Ursula. 'And I've got the first refusal of it. For you, dear.'

She had timed the drive very well. When they got back, the kitchen fire was out, the rooms were looking their worst in the sallow twilight, and the rising wind was scattering the dead leaves from the lime-tree clump. To its banshee obbligato Ursula spoke of the providential concatenation of Box Cottage for sale at £3500, and a London nerve specialist who had been inquiring from Bond, the house agent, if Bendish Hall would ever become vacant, and who would certainly give five thousand for it. By the end of the evening, she was in a position to disclose that not only had she got a first refusal on Box Cottage but had in fact paid down a deposit to secure it. Victory was in sight. To Horace, bewildered by the ease with which he had fallen, it seemed total victory. To Ursula, visiting the house agent next morning, it was revealed as not quite so total, for the person who had been thinking of Bendish Hall as a possible nursing-home for cases needing seclusion had left off thinking so and had bought a house elsewhere.

'But we shall find a purchaser, of course,' said Mr Bond. 'Purchasers can be found, even for this class of property. The housing situation is so desperate that nothing can be called unsaleable. And "Immediate Possession" are words to conjure with. Of course, a little renovation would help.'

Ursula said that this could not be afforded. Immediate Possession must be left to do the trick.

'Yes, yes! Immediate Possession,' Mr Bond agreed. 'After all, that is the real desideratum in a house—to be able to get into it. Humm! No, I am not unhopeful. By the way, will Mr Winterton stay on until we have found a buyer?'

'Oh no!' said Ursula reassuringly; but Mr Bond's face fell.

'In a way, that is a pity,' he said. 'When a house has been lived in for so long, it makes a better impression if still inhabited. Renovation is best. But if that is out of the question, then one likes to see curtains and carpets about.'

Ursula said that perhaps Mr Winterton might be persuaded to stay on for the present. Mr Bond mewed more hopefully.

'This is intolerable,' said Horace, who during the morning had been teaching himself to look forward to fuel-saving grates. 'Does Bond suppose I am going to act as his unpaid caretaker, sweeping and polishing and opening the door to his revolting customers? Besides, my health won't stand it.'

Having taken so much pains to set him up as a valetudinarian, Ursula controlled the impulse to say 'Fiddlesticks!' and replied, 'That's just it. I don't think your health would stand a move just yet, Horace. Besides, there are those two ceilings at Box Cottage that need replastering. You can't possibly settle in a house until the plaster is perfectly dry. It would be madness.'

'Madness to have a house eating its head off!' Horace said. 'Still, you've paid the deposit on it, not I.'

Having agreed to leave, he was in a fever to go quickly. In the new house, he thought, he would not only be a healthier man, leading a less endangered life, he would be a different man, immune to backslidings and regrets, a man who would not be exposed to blackmail from such things as the shadow of a bough moving across an old wall, the creak of a staircase like the creak of a saddle, a door-knob so familiar that it was almost like a hand in his hand. He wanted to go at once, while going was still like an advance. Later on, it might seem more like a retreat.

But not many people came to see Bendish Hall, and those who did, gave it vague praises and went away. By the end of November, Horace told Bond more or less what he thought of him and put the house into the hands of a London agent. The London agent sent down a young man who took a number of very grand photographs, and followed him up with a flood of possible buyers, who were more articulate and flattering than those supplied by Mr Bond, but equally unbuying. The aconites were in flower and Horace was coming out of his second cold in the head when Mrs Leroy appeared. Neither agent had sent her. She had heard from a man at the local garage, where she had stopped to buy petrol, that Mr Winterton had a house for sale. Her car was large and ornate, so were her shoes, and she talked about knowing her own mind and following her own nose. Her nose, that instrument of destiny, had brought her to Bendish Hall, and she could see at a glance that she was meant to live in it.

'It's not in the least what I want, and it's far too large,' she said. 'But I see myself here.'

As Horace showed her round, more and more insight into futurity was vouchsafed to her. She saw her Boulle mirrors in the Indian room, her seaweed marquetry desk in the library, her Cromwellian chairs in the hall. She saw what could be done about the kitchen. She saw her husband being as happy as a sandboy in the woodshed.

'Mr Leroy loves all the simple, natural things,' she said. 'Sawing logs and polishing silver . . . No, thank you. Do you mind if I smoke one of my own cigars?'

By this time, they were back in the library, and Mrs Leroy was seated as though she had already moved in. 'Of course, for myself, I'm a passionate gardener,' she continued. 'I can't look at as much as a window-box without seeing possibilities in it, and every time I pass a cemetery, I fill it with great herbaceous things—delphiniums and anchusa and hollyhocks and peonies. But out there I see something perfectly simple. Just a mass of lavender and lilies. Of course, those trees would have to go.'

She did not even notice that Horace was silent.

When he rose to his feet, she did not notice that, either. Blind to all but the future, she said between smoke rings that she could see the sun pouring in at every window and that she couldn't exist without sun.

'There won't be much more of it to-day,' said Horace. 'Time we were going.'

'Going?'

'Going to look over the house.'

'But I've seen the house already,' Mrs Leroy said.

'No, you haven't. Not the house that's for sale.'

'Do you mean to say that all this time I've been here for nothing? That this isn't—that you aren't—Then why on earth did you show me all over it?'

'It seemed to interest you,' said Horace. 'I'm sorry there isn't time to show you the garden too. I should have liked your advice—especially about the corner where all the family dogs are buried. But now I really think we should be off.'

Bemused and suspicious, Mrs Leroy entered Box Cottage without a spark of prophetic fire, and at first would only glance and grunt. Lumpishly following him from room to room, she ignored his showmanship of bedroom basins, south aspects, and serving-hatches, and devoted herself to looking censoriously into cupboards or disparagingly at power plugs. She's doing it deliberately, he thought. The spiteful bitch! She means to keep me here kicking my heels while she goes round looking for things to be unpleasant about. I shall certainly catch another cold. Probably I shall die. Bendish will be sold by auction, she'll buy it cheap and cut down all the timber. Pray God I may haunt her!

'And that is all,' he said, 'unless you would like to see the attic.' Mrs Leroy said she might as well.

In the attic, it was even colder, and quite startlingly unfurnished. 'Nice and roomy,' Horace said. Mrs Leroy did not answer. She rushed wolfishly to the cistern and began to claw at the lagging. Horace turned to look out of the window. Basil was working in the garden, raking a newly dug bed, with a seed packet stuck into his hatband. Basil, with no sentiment at all, had transferred all his affection to

229

the easy, friable loam of the new garden, its good concrete paths with no finicking box edgings to harbour slugs. A line of autumn-sown peas was already breaking green and whiskered with twigs, the first row of broad beans stood a couple of inches high. Noticing this, Horace felt a sudden stirring of ownerly warmth toward Box Cottage. Slighted by Mrs Leroy, all its merits became real to him: its trimness, its modest worth, its sound floors and draught-proof windows, its warrant of warmth and comfort and ease with dignity. As though infected by Mrs Leroy, he saw himself there; and what he saw looked very tolerable.

At a sound of scratching, he turned about. A mouse would be positively welcome, a rat inestimable—all women run from rats. But the rodent was Mrs Leroy, who was now on her knees behind the cistern, attempting to dig her purple nails into the floor boards. She's mad, he thought. God help me, I shall have to humour her. For, never before having encountered a serious buyer, he did not recognize the symptoms. When she desisted from what he decided must be a wistful necrophilia, got up, smacked her knees, and advanced on him, saying, 'Well, Mr Winterton, what's your price?' he feigned not to hear her.

'What's your price?' repeated Mrs Leroy. 'Or isn't this house for sale, either?'

'Seven thousand,' Horace said; and, in a frisk of derision, he added, 'guineas.'

Watching her face, where arrogance gradually overcame astonishment and fury, he realized that he was trapped. Or was he saved? Seven thousand guineas was more than double the figure concluded on for Box Cottage, and some two thousand above Mr Bond's most hopeful estimate of what might be got for Bendish Hall. Allowing, and amply, for legal expenses—say three thousand four hundred guineas to call his own, as much his own as the leaves drifting from the lime-tree clump. Noiseless guineas seemed to be falling round him as he followed Mrs Leroy downstairs and looked his last at the fleshpots he had sold for a mess of lime blossom. She did not spend above a couple of minutes re-examining her purchase; in fact, she seemed to be in rather a hurry to get away from it. But purchase it was; the hardening of stubborn arrogance he had watched on her face assured him of that, even before she said, 'Consider it mine, Mr Winterton,' and told him the very expensive address of her lawyer.

The front door closed behind them, and outside it was almost a spring evening—so nearly that Basil's little pretext of mopping his forehead as he turned to scrutinize Mrs Leroy was respectably convincing.

Mrs Leroy got into her car with such speed that Horace had to call after her, 'I say! Do you mind taking me back?'

The word he said was *back,* not *home.* Was he saved, or was he trapped? If it had not been for that one abandoned moment looking down from the attic window, there could not be this doubt in his mind nor this embarrassing sensation that he was returning to live and die in his rightful house as though he were returning to a stern, high-lineaged harridan of a wife after a clandestine amour with a kind middle-aged woman of the middle classes. Calm as a tortoise, Basil had resumed work. Basil would not like this turn of events. But Ursula would like it even less. The massive, unquestionable bulk of Ursula's disapprobation, and her further disapprobation when she met Mrs Leroy (he would see to that), loomed up through Horace's doubts and uncertainties as gratifyingly as the Rock of Gibraltar.

The Reredos

Nowadays, the Church of England is somewhat prim about the extra-rubrical ornaments of its sacred edifices. Memorial windows, altar frontals, new pulpits for old—all must pass a censorship before they can be allowed in; even such trifles as hassocks have to comply with a doctrinal standard. It was otherwise in the days when Queen Victoria was in the last glow of her Indian summer and Florence Larpent in her prime. There was more latitude then. The Church of England was broader and took a broader view, and when Florence's husband, Geoffrey Larpent, D.D., retired from a university professorship to the college living of Woodham Garnish, it did not cross her mind, or anyone else's, that the parish church could be anything but improved by her improvements.

She had not sat through her first Evensong in Advent before she resolved to get the better of those draughts. A fortnight later, the congregation found themselves sheltered, as though in some gigantic pious four-poster, by curtains of the best crimson baize, curtains hanging in abundant folds and lying on the floor in generous, draught-proof rumples. Gratefully sweltering, they looked forward to her next good idea. Their confidence was justified, for it was coconut matting along the aisle. After that came plump hassocks, in place of the old kneeling-boards; hymnbooks in bold type; and an oil heater for christenings. By the time Florence advanced on the chancel, the church council was hers to a man.

While in the nave, Florence had concentrated on the comfort of the congregation. In the chancel, after supplying a nice little Turkey carpet and a suitably Gothic chair for any visiting bishop (it was of oak, richly carved, with the words *'Deus misereatur'* in bold relief where the bishop's shoulders might be expected to seek support), she turned her mind to the glory of God, which, first and foremost, demanded a new reredos. The Ten Commandments, almost illegible in yellow lettering on black-painted deal panels, were not at all her notion of the beauty of holiness. She therefore proposed to supplant them by likenesses of the four Evangelists, which she would paint in oils herself.

'Spider and Pawsey quite agree with me,' she said, looking in on Geoffrey in his study to announce her project and borrow the Iconography. (Spider and Pawsey were the churchwardens, and until Florence's advent they had never been in agreement about anything.) Geoffrey, coming halfway out of Saint Ambrose, murmured something about perhaps consulting the archdeacon, just as a matter of civility. Florence replied that of course she would consult the archdeacon—in any case she wanted him for dinner on the thirteenth.

By the close of dinner, the archdeacon was quite ready to assent to the four Evangelists, and to give his approval to some preliminary sketches, which were served with the coffee. He had no idea Mrs Larpent was such a gifted artist—really, most remarkable.

'I have always painted,' said Florence, with the calm of a fish remarking that it had always swum.

Geoffrey added that in the year '81 Florence had exhibited two pictures in the Royal Academy. The archdeacon's 'Really, really! But it does not surprise me' intervened before Geoffrey could state that both the exhibits had been portraits.

New brushes, oil paints and gold leaf were bought, the canvas was stretched, and Florence began on the left-hand side of the composition with a dash at Saint Matthew. She had devoted some thought to the essentials of her design and had settled that Matthew should be in green and crimson, Mark in brown and gold, Luke in grey with touches of purple, and John in shades of blue; that Matthew should be reading his book, John looking upward for inspiration, Mark and Luke meditating in post-creative calm; and that the evangelical beasts had better be kept small and unobtrusive, since Woodham Garnish was a country parish, where too much interest was taken in animals already. But it was not until she had laid on the first bold swathes of Matthew's drapery that she began to consider the evangelical features. 'Beards,' she muttered. 'How I hate beards! They always remind me of Professor Lothbury.' Four beards, four full, flowing beards; it was really more than she felt equal to. And must all the beards be grey? A grey beard would ruin the effect of Saint Luke's drapery. If Luke had a brown beard and Mark a black beard, then she could give Mark black eyes and a ruddy colouring, and

Luke's eyes could be blue. This would leave hazel eyes for John; and Matthew . . . Could Matthew have green eyes? The thought of a green-eyed Evangelist was rather startling and needed consideration. Perhaps a dark-green eye—and as he would be looking down at his book, not much of it would show.

She was suspended thus when the solution burst upon her. Not for nothing had she two sons and two sons-in-law, and a wonderful talent for catching likenesses. How much more interesting it would be, and how much more in keeping with the great age of religious art, to use her sons, James and Daniel, and her sons-in-law, Pollock and Harold, for the Evangelists. In a second revelation, she knew that Mark must be Pollock, for Mark was the only Evangelist she could imagine with a moustache.

She set to work, and by the next day four portrait sketches enlivened the halos, for which, in order to achieve perfect circularity, she had used a basin.

'Dear me,' said Geoffrey, peering in. 'Dear me! I hope they won't mind.'

'Mind? Why, who should mind what? They'll infinitely prefer it to those battered old Commandments.'

'I was only wondering how Pollock would take it. Army men are sensitive. I don't suppose Harold will object— you've made him extremely handsome, my dear—and, of course, James and Daniel will think nothing of it. I mean, it won't surprise them in the least. They'll be delighted, I'm sure. But Pollock . . . I admit to feeling a little dubious about Pollock.'

'I think he's the best of the lot,' said Florence.

'Oh, yes, he is. Undoubtedly he is. And, of course, he'll have a lion. That will please him. He's shot several. I could never willingly shoot a lion myself.'

Saint Mark might be the best likeness, but Saint Luke was by far the most admired when the finished reredos was set in its place and burst on the congregation for Whitsunday. Such a handsome Evangelist had never been suspected in Woodham Garnish—such flashing eyes, such regular features, and looking, so to speak, such a real gentleman. For, at the time of painting, Harold was very much Florence's favoured son-in-law. The cult spread. During the next twelvemonth, several children were christened Luke on the strength of him. The mother triumphing over the artist, Florence touched up Matthew and John a little and, while she was about it, added some ten years to Mark's age, for Pollock was being rather trying just then, always catching colds and backing the wrong horses, till Cecily was quite fagged out with nursing and economizing. Not that Cecily complained. It was the younger daughter, Rosalind, who complained. Like other wives of very handsome husbands, Rosalind was apt to feel herself neglected, and she had enough of Florence in her to resent being Harold's third leg. Rosalind had even gone so far as to say, her tone of acrimony only slightly disguised by her mouth being full of moss (for, having come down with the children for Easter, she was helping to decorate the church), 'If you knew Harold as well as I do, Mother, I don't think you'd put him in an altarpiece.'

Evading the main issue, Florence replied, 'How disobliging daffodils are! It would be quite easy to alter him, if you don't like him as he is. I've made several changes in Saint Mark, and your father thinks they've been the making of him.'

Rosalind snatched up a bucket and put it down again rather violently, but said no more. It will soon blow over, thought Florence.

It blew over. Saint Luke remained in his prime beauty, and the cult continued, though now, identifications having been established, the votive infants were christened Harold. Except for some dutiful aspirations that Geoffrey might now and then be called on to sprinkle a James, a Daniel, or even a Geoffrey, Florence had not a care in the world. As Edward VII succeeded Victoria, and the harmonium gave place to an organ, and the crimson curtains mellowed, Harold's mellowing career in the Civil Service took him and his family to Cairo. It was from Cairo that the telegram came: THIS TIME HAROLD HAS GONE TOO FAR AM RETURNING WITH CHILDREN ROSALIND.

Florence, having read it through, exclaimed, 'Goodness! Geoffrey, do attend. This is from Rosalind, and she says Harold has gone too far and she's coming here with the children. What on earth can she mean?'

'A woman,' said Geoffrey, coming up from Saint Jerome.

Florence said she couldn't believe it; Harold was attractive, but not that kind of man. A letter from Daniel, in the course of which he remarked that there were some odd rumours about Harold going the rounds and that he was afraid poor Rosie would have to open her eyes at last, shook her disbelief, and when it was followed by thirteen closely written pages from Rosalind, with exclamatory postscripts squeezed into all their corners, the last hope of incredulity vanished.

And with an acrobat, too!

The letter with the story of Mlle Zizi came on a Saturday. By the following Wednesday, Rosalind and her children would be arriving at Woodham Garnish. 'I must change everything as much as possible!' cried Florence. 'We can't have the house looking just the same as it did when they were here together. I have decided to turn the spare room into the nursery, and put Rosalind into——' She was about to say '——your dressing-room,' when the thought of a more essential change stopped her breath. Harold could not possibly be left flaunting in the character of St Luke. Too full of purpose to explain her intentions, she hurried off to the church with her paints, brushes and palette, seated herself on the altar, and set to work.

But now something went wrong. Try as she might to expurgate him, Harold continued to exercise a demoniacal possession of Saint Luke. Twice and thrice it seemed to her that she had got him down under quite a new countenance, and each time some final improvement——the arching of an eyebrow, the flaring of a nostril——conjured him back. Realizing that she was at the mercy of her talent for catching likenesses, she resolved to base a Saint Luke on Mr Pawsey. This came better. As a basic Saint Luke, Mr Pawsey was everything that a rector's warden should be, helpful yet unobtrusive. Satisfied at last, Florence scrambled off the altar and took the artist's few paces back to view the completed work. It was no use. Draped in Mr Pawsey's cheeks, and leering through Mr Pawsey's mild blue eyes, Harold surveyed her with a sardonic bo-peep.

'Very well!' she exclaimed, addressing only Harold. 'Very well! Have it your own way. Since you insist on being Harold, I'll Harold you!'

Dusk had fallen before she laid on the last strokes. As she gave the renewed Harold a parting inspection, it seemed to her that she had shown him in his true colours.

The pure light of a Third Sunday in Lent revealed an interpretation of Saint Luke that came as a surprise even to the artist, and perfectly outraged the congregation. What had happened to their Beloved Physician? Whatever had come over Mrs Reverend? It seemed to the more imaginative of them that the Devil had got into the church overnight, leaving a strong smell of oil paints and a self-portrait.

'I am very sorry, Florence,' Geoffrey said at luncheon, 'but I cannot possibly conduct divine service under the supervision of that malevolent cardsharper. I quite understand your feelings. As far as they are feelings of a parent, I share them, and as the feelings of an artist, I respect them. All the same, my dear, you must repaint Saint Luke before next Sunday. And before Evensong it would be as well to fill the altar vases with laurel, or some vigorous shrub of that kind.'

Florence readily admitted that Saint Luke had gone beyond the bounds of sacred art. 'The trouble is,' she pleaded, 'I can't paint a face unless it's a likeness. And if it's not to be Harold, who is it to be? I tried Pawsey, but Harold got the better of him—and even if he hadn't, the village might have thought it not quite reverent, and Spider would have had every reason to be jealous and talk about favouritism.'

'It would not be irreverent to paint me,' said Geoffrey. 'I shall sit to you to-morrow afternoon.' On the Fourth Sunday in Lent, the congregation observed that Saint Luke was now the Reverend.

Rosalind had not gone to church. She was not equal to it. The energetic wrath that had whirled her across Europe evaporated in the climate of home. She lay in bed, weeping copiously, refusing all nourishment except cups of strong tea and anchovy toast, and incessantly talking of Harold. Not even the fact that she was bedded in her father's dressing-room was able to distract her from what seemed an inveterate determination to be reminded of Harold by everything she saw or heard, including her father's confident approaches to her door and his sighs of frustration as he went on toward the bathroom. She wept, and talked of Harold's cynicism and her ruined life; and Geoffrey said, 'My poor child, what you need is rest. Try to sleep a little,' and went away; and Florence persisted in expatiating on all the other delightful, stirring things there are in the world besides husbands; and the children, that natural solace for the feelings of an injured wife, were no solace at all, for they had made friends with a pig farmer and talked of nothing but boars and farrowings.

After a week of this, with no letters except letters of sympathy and approval from her sisters-in-law, Rosalind turned to religion, put on a hat, and crept out to sit quietly in the church by herself. Being shortsighted, she was half-way up the aisle before she noticed that a change had taken place in the third Evangelist. She hurried into the chancel for a closer examination. After a minute, she leaned forward and planted her finger on Saint Luke's nose. The rich impasto was still moist.

From the drawing-room window, Florence saw Rosalind crossing the churchyard with a springy, purposeful gait, and rejoiced to think that at last the poor little soul had taken a mother's insinuations to heart and found something better to do than brood on Harold. If by any chance it were the unfolding beauties of nature, and she could be persuaded to take the children for some good, long walks . . . The springy and purposeful gait now entered the house, the door flew open, and Rosalind came to a violent halt in the middle of the room.

'Mother! This is too much! I have borne a great deal, but there are some things I ought not to be expected to put up with, and will not put up with, and one of them is to be held up to derision in Woodham Garnish. I should have thought you might feel that I had enough to endure already, what with Harold breaking my heart, and that appalling journey, and the children getting so spoiled that they are completely beyond my control, and my health ruined by all these worries, and never able to snatch a wink of sleep because of that odious dovecot below the dressing-room.

I must say I didn't expect this. I didn't expect my own mother to turn against me. But now I see that I was wrong.'

'My dear,' Florence said, 'if it's the doves that are troubling you—'

'Doves! Doves! I'm not talking about doves. I never mentioned doves. Poke me away anywhere you like—why not the box room? That's nothing to do with it, I'm quite accustomed to that sort of treatment. But I am still a married woman, and entitled to some respect and consideration, and now to be insulted in this way, held up to ridicule, and published in church like banns—it's outrageous, outrageous, outrageous!'

'Rosalind!'

'Outrageous, I say. To come home, as I did, after all I'd gone through, and then to find my husband obliterated from a reredos! The paint still wet! And not a touch on any of the others, so you can't pretend it's one of your old fiddle-faddle improvements. Quite apart from anything else, I'm positive it's libellous, and if Harold were to sue you, he would be more than justified. What do you suppose people will think? Everyone knew Saint Luke was Harold, and now you go and plaster Father on top of him, and what other conclusions can they come to? I've never been so insulted in my life. And you always pretended to be so fond of him, too. You might have remembered that, even if you've got no consideration for what it all means to me.'

'Don't rant, Rosalind. Your father and I both agreed that in order to spare your feelings—'

'Pooh! I don't for a moment suppose you said a word to him. Father would never want to rob me of my one little crumb of comfort, my only chance of catching a glimpse of Harold's old self.'

'Really, Rosalind, if you can find no better consolation in a visit to church than——'

'What else do you suppose I went for? To glut my eyes on Pollock?'

'I had not expected that Canon Burroughs would be so late,' said Geoffrey, coming in with his watch in his hand and an appearance of not having heard anything out of the usual. 'Well, my dear, I see that you have been for a little turn in the fresh air. It has done you good. You have quite a colour.'

'I'm going out again,' Rosalind said. 'Now. To the post office.'

The front door slammed. Geoffrey said, 'She has gone to send a telegram to Harold, to tell him she's coming back.'

'Poor Rosalind!' said Florence. 'Do you suppose he will want her?'

'I'm sure he will. Men like Harold are always pleased to see a wife come back. My dear, do you suppose she will take the children?'

She did. Thanks to their artless farewells, it was a touching and seemly departure, and after the last wave to the wagonette, Geoffrey and Florence finished the breakfast coffee and turned their minds to the arrangements for Holy Week. As for the reredos, its fangs seemed to have been drawn, until just before Trinity Sunday, when Geoffrey said that Florence must buy a length of some handsome brocade of the correct liturgical green, and make curtains that could be drawn in front of it, after the style of a dossal. For while cutting a bunch of asparagus he had overheard two little girls disputing in the lane, and one of them had said that Saint Luke didn't half look queer now he was the Reverend, and the other had said, correctingly, that when he was Mr Harold, it was Saint Luke, but that now he was the Reverend, it was God the Father.

A Second Visit

A wilderness of war and peace divided Roger Tilney from his first sight of Batshanger. He had come to it in August 1940, when the threat of invasion made every house along the coast of southeast England a potential redoubt. While it was still only a name on the list of houses he had been told to inspect, it had crept into his imagination, partly because Batshanger was one of those poetically ridiculous English names, and endeared itself to the romantic imperilled nationalism of the hour, and partly because the Adjutant did not know how to pronounce it, and referred to it as Bat-shanger—an error which intensified Roger's personal variety of nationalism.

It had not been easy to find, for it stood amidst a tangle of lanes, and all the signposts had already been removed as a measure of defence. Finding it, he realized with an agonizing cleavage of mind that it was the house of all houses that he wanted to live in for the rest of his days, and that it was a house he must certainly recommend for requisitioning. Embarrassed by the noise of his boots, the creaking of his belt, the flashes of light darting from his buttons, he inspected it under the guidance of an intimidating Miss Parminter, noting simultaneously that the drawing-room had a coffered ceiling and would sleep a dozen men, that the fig-trees were as fruitful as the patriarchs, and grew where the latrines could most conveniently be sited, and hearing between his inquiries and the fatally satisfactory replies, the quiet thunder of the sea. If there had been even the smallest loophole for evading a plain duty, the presence of Miss Parminter would have closed it. Thoughts of trickery could no more be entertained in this presence than azaleas could take root in a limestone soil. She had been the family governess, she informed him, and was now Mrs Gauntlett's secretary. As for Mrs Gauntlett, who did not appear, he gathered that she was widowed, and that the war had already made her childless.

Now, seven years later, he saw Batshanger again. This time, it was not so hard to find. He drove along a widened road. Under the oak trees groups of Nissen huts brooded, melancholy as yaks, exuding a false sentiment of domesticity. All the seclusion and free wildness through which he had driven before seemed to have gone for shelter behind the iron gates of Batshanger. The gates were locked. Looking through the ironwork he saw, where there had been a winding drive, nothing but tall feathery grasses and pale feverfew; it was not till he looked more attentively that he saw the barbed-wire tangles through which this vegetation had grown up. Remembering that there had been a back-drive, he presently walked round to it. Its gates were off their hinges, and the rutted gravel had recent footmarks on it. He walked up, wondering who came here now—birds-nesting children, perhaps, tramps, or courting couples, with their freehold tenacy of what's disinhabited. Drifts of nettles had sprung up among the laurels, the moss-hut had fallen to bits, and he saw swallows flying in and out of the pillboxes. Then he caught sight of the house. In a quieter, more fatal, way it was as much a ruin as any dwelling he had seen in Europe. It had kept most of its roof, and some of the windows were unbroken. But the walls were cracked, and slabs of their plaster had fallen away. The paint was shrivelled, and the exposed woodwork had rotted. The steps and the balustrading were broken, the vine, its stem hacked through, hung on the porch like a black cobweb, and mounds of rusty tins and mounds of clinkers were heaped in a methodical alternation against the fruit-wall.

Some houses die a violent death in war, and some a slow death. Batshanger had died a slow death, dying of maltreatment like a labour-slave.

He seemed to have been standing there for a lifetime, feeling the sun on his back, hearing the distant sighing explosions of the waves. But because one is never satisfied with a sorrow, he thought he would walk round and examine Batshanger from the garden side.

In 1940 there had been, he remembered, a grumpy gardener, so grumpy that he had not deigned to be pleased when Roger promised to arrange that the kitchen garden should be made out of bounds for the men. And some sort of cultivation must have been kept up, for the fruit and vegetable plots were still in a discouraged sort of order. Roger stood thinking of the grumpy gardener and rubbing a sprig of southernwood between his fingers when a woman's voice floated into the garden, calling, 'Ethel!'; and immediately Miss Parminter rose up from among the gooseberry bushes.

She gave him a little nod, and said, 'Stay where you are. I'll be back in a moment.' Then she went up the path between the apple-cordons. Nothing would have been simpler than to go away, and there was nothing he more impetuously wished to do. But he was in a false position, a trespasser, so there was nothing for it but to remain. Presently Miss Parminter returned, looking exactly as he now remembered her to have looked seven years earlier—tall and large-boned, with the sun shining on her unadorned face and sandy-grey hair. Standing perfectly still, her hands reposefully folded, she listened while he went through with his apologies and his explanations.

'I remember you perfectly well,' she said (along with the Kings of England, the rules governing the dative, the collects for the Sundays after Trinity, no doubt). 'Your name is Tilney, and you came here on the twentieth of August 1940, about requisitioning.'

He muttered, 'I feel like a murderer.'

'Nonsense!' said Miss Parminter briskly. 'The place was bound to be requisitioned, and somebody had to come here and say so. That somebody happened to be you.'

'I can't see it quite so straightforwardly.'

'Then you are sinning your mercies. Surely, it is one of the compensations of war that doing one's duty is made elementary and straightforward.'

He looked towards the house and then towards the neat construction in concrete which had replaced the gazebo.

'What happened afterwards was no fault of yours. Shut up a lot of young men in an old house, give them far too much food badly cooked, train them for war and give them no opportunity to fight . . . What else can you expect? You don't look in the least like a murderer. Are you still in the Army?'

'No!' he replied, and left it at that.

'Do you like gooseberries?' She picked up a half-filled basket, and moved towards the place whence she had arisen at the cry of 'Ethel!' 'You'll find the best ones on that bush. Personally, I wouldn't give a thank-you for a gooseberry that I didn't eat off the bush. They lose their flavour from the moment they are gathered. So do potatoes from the moment they are dug. But people are either too rich or too poor to have palates.' She seated herself on the ground and began to pick.

'May I help you?'

The words were out of his mouth before he could examine them.

'Thank you. That will be very kind. You'd better sit down to it, and you won't get so scratched. Not there. You're on an ants' nest.'

When he was seated to Miss Parminter's satisfaction, they had the bush between them. It was large and branchy and very old, the sleek berries dangled from grey-mossed twigs. Miss Parminter's hands, square-fingered and the colour of brown holland, moved through the bush with amazing rapidity and never got scratched.

'All these will be jammed by the Women's Institute,' she presently remarked. 'And this year, I rejoice to say, we have plenty of jam pots.'

'Is that thanks to the Ministry of Supply?'

'Good gracious, no! I secured them after old Mrs Cutler died. She had nine dozen stored away under her bed.'

He had a vision of an old Mrs Cutler, narrowed by death, lying in a wide bed with brass knobs while Miss Parminter competently explored beneath it. Meanwhile Miss Parminter was explaining where, in her opinion, the dividing-line between foresight and hoarding should be drawn. Her hand, sweeping unscratched among the branches, came into contact with his. It was a cool, strong hand, and he felt an incomprehensible impulse to cling to it.

'What became of that rather severe gardener?'

'Gulliver? He went into the Observer Corps and saw the first rocket. Now he's hoping to find a Colorado Beetle. Invasions have gone to his head, poor fellow! But he still gardens very well. I think we have finished this bush. It's really very kind of you to help me.'

She might be dismissing him, at any rate she was affording him an opportunity to go. But they wriggled themselves along to the next bush.

'It has steadied Gulliver to have us back. We have been living here since the fifth of April, Mrs Gauntlett and I.'

'Living? I did not think the house was lived in.'

'Of course you didn't. I saw that when I noticed you standing there. You looked so pale that I wondered if I should bring you out a cup of tea. But I decided it is always better to be left alone with a shock. So I left you with yours and came to pick gooseberries.'

'I can't imagine how you live in it.'

'There are four quite habitable rooms. And the War Office has given us twelve shower-baths—though it only troubled to fix seven of them. We manage.'

. . . The plaster-work falling from the coffered ceiling, the silence of the windless days and the long lament of the wind, the leaves blown in through the broken windows and whispering in corners, the sunlight traversing the empty rooms, the muteness, past reproach, of the done-to-death . . .

'And now tell me about yourself, Mr Tilney.'

He realized with the tranquillity of the lost, that he was going to take her at her word. Everything rose up in order, unfussed and unfalsified: the childhood smothered in sweetness and whimsicality *(Roger says there is a dear little blue-eyed bogey under the stairs)*, the careworn pilgrimaging adolescence *(Well, Tilney, and what is engaging your attention this term? Cricket, or the Byzantines?)*, the aficionada who was sick at a bullfight, the disdainful warrior decorated for an outburst of schoolboy exhibitionism, the cultivated snob who had supposed he could live at Batshanger. He could tell all this to Miss Parminter, and not be thought pathetic, or charming, or a perfectly simple case of schizophrenia. He had only to dive into her silence, and he would find that he could swim.

But the voice which had cried 'Ethel!' now cried 'Ethel!' again. This time it was nearer.

'Here is Mrs Gauntlett.'

An old woman was drifting down the path towards them. Her dark glasses and the inconsequential way she moved gave her a resemblance to a moth. Miss Parminter said, 'I will introduce you, I think.' As they had both risen and must be plainly visible, this remark struck him as so nearly an ineptitude that he felt a piercing disillusionment. Answering his thought, she continued, 'She won't have seen you. She is blind.'

He was introduced. Turning her face towards the sound of his voice, Mrs Gauntlett said that it was very kind of Mr Tilney to help Ethel with the gooseberries, and she hoped he would come in and drink some sherry. Just as under happier circumstances Miss Parminter would have seen to it that his nails were clean enough, his hair sufficiently combed, for tea in the drawing-room, she now substantiated his regrets, his obligation to keep an engagement elsewhere. Serenely hospitable and quite unconcerned, Mrs Gauntlett said that he must come in August, when her grandchildren would be there. He replied that he would certainly come if he could, knowing full well that he could never come again.

It was farewell to Batshanger—in every way, farewell; for even the squirming residual hope that one day he might buy it and somehow put it together again had been knocked on the head by the mention of the grandchildren. Yet, as he drove away, he realized that though he yearned for Batshanger he yearned even more for Miss Parminter. He thought of the two children who had grown up at Batshanger with Miss Parminter's cool, strong hand to cling to, and now were safe dead, and wondered how even the gods could pour such felicity on those they elected to love.

Acknowledgments

With the exception of *At the Trafalgar Bakery, Under New Management, At a Monkey's Breast, Absolom, My Son,* and *A Funeral at Clovie,* all these stories were first published in the *New Yorker* to whom my thanks are due.